FROM THE BOOKS OF

Maria Helena Salazar

LAST MOVEMENT

Books by Joan Aiken

LAST MOVEMENT
VOICES IN AN EMPTY HOUSE
A CLUSTER OF SEPARATE SPARKS
THE EMBROIDERED SUNSET
THE CRYSTAL CROW

DARK INTERVAL
BEWARE OF THE BOUQUET
THE FORTUNE HUNTERS
THE SILENCE OF HERONDALE

Juveniles

NOT WHAT YOU EXPECTED
ARABEL'S RAVEN
THE MOONCUSSER'S DAUGHTER:
A PLAY FOR CHILDREN
THE GREEN FLASH AND OTHER
TALES
WINTERTHING: A CHILDREN'S
PLAY
THE CUCKOO TREE
DIED ON A RAINY SUNDAY
NIGHT FALL

MIDNIGHT IS A PLACE
SMOKE FROM CROMWELL'S TIME
AND OTHER STORIES
THE WHISPERING MOUNTAIN
A NECKLACE OF RAINDROPS
ARMITAGE, ARMITAGE FLY AWAY
HOME
NIGHTBIRDS ON NANTUCKET
BLACK HEARTS IN BATTERSEA
THE WOLVES OF WILLOUGHBY
CHASE

Poetry

THE SKIN SPINNERS

Joan Aiken

LAST MOVEMENT

Doubleday & Company, Inc.
Garden City, New York   1977

All the characters in this book are fictitious,
and any resemblance to actual persons, living or dead,
is purely coincidental.

Designed by Laurence Alexander

ISBN: 0-385-12620-4
Library of Congress Catalog Card Number 76–42055
Copyright © 1977 by Joan Aiken

{ 1 }

PRELUDE

The soft, hollow clunk and thomp of tennis balls, and voices calling scores, came echoing faintly across Crowbridge Park as I walked back to my flat. Evening sun sat comfortably on my shoulders. The birds were all singing like crazy creatures, because it was April and the apple trees were in bud and everything out of doors smelled new, cool, sharp, tingling with promise. I felt the same as the birds, could have sung like a crazy creature myself. I was going home for a bath and a cat nap—having been up since five that morning; then back to the Crowbridge Theatre Royal for a last couple of hours' work on the sets and costumes of *The Cherry Orchard* before the curtain rose on the first-night performance. It was going to be a terrific evening, I felt in my bones. For once, the parts had all fitted like gloves over the mixed members of the Crowbridge Repertory Company; everybody, inspired with enthusiasm, had shelved feuds, forgotten differences, and worked in harmony, and the result was tight, coherent, animated, and heartbreaking. Further, it was the first time I'd been in sole charge of the scenery and costumes; fired by pride, I had worked till I was half dead. My sleep average during the past month had been about three hours per night, in spite of which I felt marvelous. For the first time in my life, I was completely fulfilled—happy—truly part of the professional group I belonged to, and, what was more, almost satisfied with the work I had done. Not *quite*, of course; the resources of the Crowbridge Rep were limited; but still, considering the costumes were made from all the cheapest materials we could get, polythene to hessian, and the scenery was painted on offcuts from the local do-it-yourself-furniture-kit factory, I considered the result a triumph. And so, in fact, did the rest of the company. At intervals during my three-hours-nightly sleeps, I couldn't help waking to think adoringly of my painted cherry orchard, with its greens, grays, and whites, which exquisitely offset the black, dove-colored, and mahogany tones of the costumes (luckily, there was also a dye factory in Crowbridge, and Rose Drew, the manager's daughter, was our Varya). I feared that after the play had ended I would never be able to bring myself to throw out those beautiful sets, and I foresaw they'd be furnishing my flat for the next five years.

The flat was another happiness. One room, semibasement—true; but it faced out across the park toward the golden, peeling dome of the Theatre Royal, and I had been able to afford it only since my elevation to the status of Stage-Manager-plus-props (with concomitant raise of four pounds a week); one month, to be precise. Before that, I'd shared a room and use of kitchen with Rose Drew. Now I possessed a kitchen of my own, and even a bathroom with a brass geyser and mildew on the walls. No matter; it was mine; in time I'd cover or replace the landlord's hideous furniture with items chosen from junk shops and painted to suit my own taste. All that pleasure lay ahead! And meanwhile I could enjoy the evening sun sliding through my front window, my view of the park, and the privacy of my own dank bathroom.

I crossed the little front garden full of languidly sprouting hydrangeas (my landlord's; chosen presumably because they gave the least trouble, that being his line in all other departments), walked down the narrow, concreted alley at the side of the house, which led to my own front door, found my key, unlocked the door, and went in.

On the red tiles of the small entrance hall a telegram was lying.

I can remember exactly the way its rough yellow envelope picked up a touch of reflected light from the open, glass-paned door which led through into the living room.

It was addressed to Priscilla Graffin, which is my name, but which startled me a good deal because, when my father died, thirteen years before, and Mother went back to using her maiden name of Meiklejohn, changing by deed poll, I had followed suit. And nobody, either at my school or in the Crowbridge Rep, had ever used my first name, which is suitable only for tombstones. Everybody called me Mike. So it brought me up sharp just to see the words, formal and frightening, on the envelope, and I picked it up with hands grown suddenly cold and sweaty, aware, too, at the same time, that the evening's sunshine was only a trailer for spring and that my flat felt as arctic as the inside of a Deepfreeze.

PLEASE COME TO STRETFORD HOSPITAL AT ONCE YOUR MOTHER SERIOUSLY INJURED said the impersonal, computerized letters on the rough buff paper they use for telegrams.

It was the kind of message that, deep down, we all know that we are going to get someday—because, however much we play about with lights and furnishing materials and words of powerful dramatic significance, the world is, in fact, a nasty and ruthless place, not intended for the welfare of humans.

I laid the telegram down on the ugly, unfunctional, varnished sideboard and began wandering about, mechanically putting things into a small overnight bag—slippers, toothbrush, money, sweater. If only I had a telephone. Engineers were coming to install one—but, knowing the G.P.O., another sixteen weeks would elapse before they arrived.

Sixteen weeks—what would have happened by then?

Luckily at that point it occurred to me that I might phone from my landlord's flat upstairs. His wife was not normally accommodating, but this was an emergency, after all. So I walked out, around, and up the steps to her front door. Besides, I ought to tell her that I was going away, and leave messages about laundry, the gas-meter man, the window cleaner. . . . As my brain clicked automatically through these patterns I saw the tall, coffin-shaped figure of Mrs. Charm appear behind the reeded-glass door.

Charm: never was such an inappropriate name applied to anyone so signally lacking in it. Her pale mauve face was like an unsuccessful cake camouflaged with icing. Her damp eyes wept all the time behind gold-rimmed glasses, and her straw hair was nagged up into an inefficient, hassock-shaped pile.

"Eh, Miss Meeklejohn?" she said in a Belfast accent you could have bent into a coat hanger. "Was it abewt the telegram, then? The boy came heerr furrst, but I tawld him ye werr the grround-floor—"

"Yes, that's it," I cut in quickly—she was capable of going on for a long time yet—"It said that my mother's been injured in an accident, and I have to go to Stretford Hospital—I was wondering if I could use your phone?"

"Oh, how tairrible!" she was all fussy solicitude at once, very self-important with it. She ushered me to the phone, which perched precariously on a gruesome little glass occasional table among their tight-packed furniture. "Was it a car crash, then?"

I hadn't got as far as wondering about this. "Do you know where Stretford is?" I asked while waiting for Directory Inquiries to answer. Mrs. Charm had never even heard of Stretford. "I dew hope it's not tew far," she said unctuously.

As my mother was headmistress of a large comprehensive school in the Midlands, where the accident had presumably taken place, and as Crowbridge is on the south coast, I thought her hope was probably vain.

Directory Inquiries answered at last and found me the number of the hospital. I got through to them after the usual inter-

minable delays filled with clicks and warblings and long periods of total silence.

"Is that Stretford Hospital? May I have the casualty ward,
please?"

Connected with Casualties after another lengthy wait, I was
lucky enough to get an intelligent-sounding, clear-spoken
voice.

"Sister Crouch here, Casualty? What do you wish to
know?"

I said, "M-my name is Meiklejohn. I had a telegram about
my mother, Mrs. Barbara Meiklejohn—"

"Meiklejohn? Thought your name was Graffin. Sorry about
the slip-up. I'm very glad you rang." The voice became
slightly reproachful. "We tried to contact you but you don't
seem to be on the phone."

"No, I'm not. Is she—what did—how is my mother?"

"It's too early to say yet. They operated this afternoon at
half past four."

"*Operated?* What *happened* to her?"

"A roof fell on her."

"?"

"The school gymnasium roof, I understand. She suffered
from a head injury. . . . Where are you phoning from, Miss
Meiklejohn?"

"I'm in Kent. I've only just got home and found your telegram."

"I think you should come here as soon as possible," Sister
Crouch said.

Her voice was kind, human, sympathetic, but it frightened
me to my roots. The relationship between Mother and myself
was not a warm one, but we were each other's only relative;
the prospect of a world without her seemed bleak indeed.

I dared not ask for any further details. My voice was only
just under control—and I could feel the silent presence of
Mrs. Charm, ghoulishly attentive, just behind my shoulder.

I said, "Wh-where is Stretford Hospital? How do I get to
you?"

The sister seemed surprised at my ignorance but said, "You take a train from King's Cross. The fast trains take two hours."

"Thank you. I have to get up to London first, so I'm afraid I shan't be able to make it under four or five hours. Can you tell—is m-my mother conscious?"

"Not at present. If she does become conscious, I will tell her that you are on your way."

"Thank you, Sister," I said humbly, but she had rung off already.

"Eh, ye have tew go all the way up thrrough London, that's tairrible," said Mrs. Charm. "Why don't ye rring for a taxi to take ye tew the station while ye're heerr?"

That struck me as a good suggestion and an unusually kind thought. I did so.

But then Mrs. Charm rather spoiled the effect by saying, "Don't trrouble to pay me for the calls now, Miss Meeklejohn —I'll pewt them on yer rent bewk. Was it a car crash, then?" she asked hopefully.

"No—a roof fell on her," I said, and escaped, leaving her popeyed.

The taxi had said it would take twelve minutes to reach Parkside Villas, so I had time to finish my packing. Then, coming over faint and queer, I drank a cup of water and collapsed into one of my two repulsive armchairs. They were from the art-deco period in the thirties—dirty-gray-uphol-stered semirockers of a curved shape, which tilted and slid back disconcertingly when one sat down in them; the sensa-tion of the chair doing this under me added to my sick, terrified feeling that the whole *world* was about to cave in under me. I gazed around the ugly, dim room, with its orange dado, vomit-colored curtains, mustard wallpaper, and won-dered if I would ever feel about it again as I had before the telegram came; my capacity to hope and plan for its regener-ation seemed to have deserted me. The evening light had left the windows, and the room looked indescribably dismal.

I heard the crunch of a taxi's brakes in the road outside,

jumped up, and hastily pushed a few last oddments into my bag, then left without a backward look. Mrs. Charm had a key to the place; let her come in after I had gone and find it untidy, as no doubt she would.

"Will you stop at the Theatre Royal first, please?" I asked the taxi driver.

Rickie would be there, for he lived an hour's motorbike ride outside Crowbridge and had said that he was going to stay in the theater and take a nap in the greenroom; I could give him a message for the rest of the cast.

I hated to wake him. He was fast asleep, curled up on a pile of leftover sacking, looking defenseless. When I shook him he sat up, tousled, rubbing his eyes; he could have been about fourteen years old. In fact he was twenty-two, six months younger than I, and highly experienced; he had been in various repertory companies since the age of sixteen.

"What's the row?" he said, yawning. "Anything wrong?"

"Rickie, I can't stay; I have to go. My mother's been badly hurt in an accident, and I have to get halfway across England. Will you please tell the others, and say how sorry I am?"

"Oh, my *god*." He gaped at me, slowly taking this in. "Oh, how terrible, Mike!" The same words that Mrs. Charm had used, but what a difference! "You couldn't just wait till after the—No, of course you can't. You'd be worrying all the time. But how ever shall we manage without you?"

"You'll manage perfectly well." Rickie was my assistant. In most ways he was my equal, in some my superior. But I was touched by his look of devotion as he said, "Oh, but it won't be the *same* without you, Mike. It seems so unfair—Still, I can see that you've got to go." He gave me a hug and said, "Poor darling. How frightful for you! Where do you have to get to?"

"Stretford; I don't even know where it is."

"Oh, I know. My grandmother lived there. It's near Northampton. Are you on your way now?"

"Yes, I must go. I've got a taxi waiting."

"I can't *bear* that you have to miss this evening," he said miserably.

I couldn't bear it much myself, so I said again, "I must go."

"Wait—have you eaten anything?"

"No, but I'll get something at King's Cross. Tell the others how sorry I am. Say to Eve—"

"Here, take this—" He was thrusting a greasy package into my hands. "And a paperback—I bet you haven't got one, and the journey to Stretford takes forever—I should know—"

I tried to decline, but he overpowered my unspirited resistance and escorted me out to the taxi. "Are you all right for cash?" he said. "How about five pounds?"

"No, I've got plenty." I'd just been paid, luckily.

Rickie was an unimpressive figure—short, frail, and consumptive-looking, his eyes myopic behind thick pebble glasses —I've never met anyone kinder or more reliable. I suddenly wished he could come all the way, longed to have his considerate company on the journey. "I do *hope* you'll have good news when you get there," he said earnestly, shutting the taxi door on me.

I nodded, bit my lip, swallowed, and said, "I'll phone tomorrow."

"Yes, *do*."

Then he went back inside—I hoped, to finish his interrupted nap.

The journey was quite as long and horrible as I'd expected. Trains from Crowbridge to Charing Cross are mostly slow, and this one was. London was crowded and disgusting, as usual. I battled across from one main-line station to the other as fast as I could, but it was now half past nine, and the tube trains were dismally infrequent. At King's Cross I found that a train was due to start for Stretford in five minutes, which seemed at first like a piece of good fortune. I hurled myself into its corridor—of course it was full and there was no seat to be had—only to have it then spend half an hour sitting two hundred yards outside King's Cross before it hauled itself jerkily off northward. It proved to be another slow train, stopping at unheard-of, terrible little home-county stations with names like Scroop and Priddy's End and Moleham and Gazeby-on-the-Wold—places that nobody has ever heard of and where nobody could possibly want to live.

I was immeasurably grateful for Rickie's large, greasy slice of bacon between two chunks of stale brown bread, as the hours went by, and I stood lurching between two strangers in the narrow, dusty corridor flavored with cigarette butts and Coke trickles. The paperback Rickie had given me turned out to be *Candide*, which I knew too well and found too depressing, so I fell back on thoughts instead.

There were plenty of *them*.

I thought about how I'd feel if Mother died.

My relationship with her had been an arm's-length one for years; it filled me at all times with guilt, often with sorrow. Now that I was grown up and earning my own living, we saw each other rarely; I had invited her several times to productions at the Theatre Royal, but her life as headmistress of the huge Market Broughton Comprehensive School was packed tight; any space left over from her school duties seemed to be spent at educational conferences, and she had never found time to come. And I on my part went to see her for two or three dutiful weekends each year; they were strained and uncomfortable, because our interests were so different that we had practically nothing to exchange. Even her house was not the one I had grown up in. When, after Father's death, she went back to teaching, her climb up the educational ladder, arduous, tough, but ultimately successful, had necessitated frequent moves from one school to another all over England. And I, in the meantime, had been sent off to boarding school (because she thought it would be bad for me to be in the same school where she taught). Then, later, of my own choice, I had gone to a drama school in France. Holidays, which might have been spent together, had more often than not been separate; Mother had found seminars and courses for me to attend, or she had been away on courses herself. And all these arrangements, I felt with unhappy certainty, had been made only to disguise an inner failure, the fact that Mother had no particular feeling for me, and, indeed, found me simply boring. The only real feeling she had, I was convinced, lay buried with my father and elder sister, who had died in the same year, though not together, when I was nine, long ago.

The fact that Mother had been obliged to go through the ordeal of their deaths on her own, for I was in Greece at the time, on a visit, had increased the distance between us. If only I had been with her at that time, I often thought, our relations would be different now.

Before Father's unexpected death I had been sent to stay with a Greek family on the island of Dendros. This had been Father's idea, in fact; he had spent time on Dendros during World War II, fell in love with the place, made friends, and wanted his children to share the experience. My sister, Drusilla, had gone some years earlier, but her visit had not been a success; she was delicate, hated heat, and wrote miserably, begging to come home. I, however, loved it there; I adored Father's friends, the Aghnides family; Calliope Aghnides, who was my age, became my special friend. When Father died, Mother found herself obliged to sell our house and move to a smaller one. (Father had been a singer, and taught singing and voice production, from which he had made a good though not lavish living.) Mother wrote to the Aghnides, explaining that the move would be even more distressing if I were there, getting in the way; Drusilla could give her all the help she needed; she asked if my visit could be extended a few months longer. Of course the Aghnides, in their kind and hospitable way, invited me to remain for as long as Mother wished.

And so the transfer from the house where I had been born and lived all my life took place when I was not there. I never entered it again. It was a big, pleasant farmhouse on the outskirts of Oxford. The loss of my father, who was kind, gay, gentle, fond of gardens, birds, and Victorian music-hall songs, together with all the familiar surroundings of my childhood—even my cat, Othello, had somehow got lost in the move—was a strangely numbing shock. I used to dream wretchedly at night of my bedroom, with the irregular beams in the ceiling and the view of the orchard; it seemed impossible to believe that I would never go to sleep in it again. (Years later, I went past the house and wondered if I dared knock at the door and ask to see inside, but courage failed me; it would have been too painful.) Strangely enough, I never dreamed about Father; it seemed as if he had sunk out of reach, down to the very bottom of my mind.

The Aghnides were as kind as they could possibly be during this time, and I was happy in Dendros; I loved the Aghnides home, which was old and cool, with orange trees growing round its pebbled courtyard; I loved Calliope and enjoyed going to the Greek school with her; in time the pain grew less painful. But then came another pain; my sister, Drusilla, died in an accident at school on her seventeenth birthday. Mother wrote this appalling news to the Aghnides and asked again if my stay could be extended; to me she did not write at that time. I was not told then, and had never, at any later juncture, found myself able to ask Mother what kind of accident had killed Dru.

This inability was, I suppose, a measure of the distance between Mother and myself. I knew she had preferred Dru to me. Dru was kind, reserved, serious, hard-working, wanted to become a geologist; Dru took after Mother, in fact; she had intended to go to Cambridge; whereas I, if I stayed in educational establishments for twenty years, would never have turned into an academic; I was not intelligent in that way. Also, I was sure, Dru had been a planned child, whereas I was an unexpected, inconvenient afterthought. At the age of ten I had grieved sadly for Dru, who had always been kind and loving to me, more like a third parent than a sister, because of the seven-year age gap between us; but I did not, as I had after the news of Father's death, wish that I could go home. The prospect, the thought, of all the changes that had taken place, the idea of being alone with Mother, was too frightening.

I acquiesced readily enough in the plan that I should stay on with the Aghnides at least until the following year. In the end,

I remained in Dendros for nearly three years, and only returned to England because the Aghnides were planning a mass
family visit to relatives in the U.S.A. They kindly suggested
that I should go along with them, but Mother could not afford
my fare, and although they offered to pay it, she could not
allow herself to be beholden to them to such an extent. One of
her primary qualities was a streak of granite independence. So,
at last, when I was going on twelve, I returned to England. By
that time the Aghnides felt like my own family; I hated to
part from them, hated to leave the hot, happy island.

It was a strange, sad return. Mother at that time was teaching history in a big school in Birmingham and had a flat near
the school, so that was where I went. The flat had come
furnished, so she had put all our furniture in storage and there
was practically nothing in any of the three rooms to remind
me of our home, save a box of my outgrown toys and books,
which Mother had scrupulously saved for me. The worst part
was that she and I seemed to be strangers to one another and
remained so. She had arranged for me to begin the following
week at a boarding school in the country, for, as she said, a flat
in Birmingham was no place for a child; so, in a week, off I
went, before we had had a chance to rediscover one another.

And, during the course of the following eleven years, the
chance never did seem to come up. Mother did her duty by
me, but her heart was now in her career, which she pursued
with stoic tenacity and resolution. I looked up to her for this, I
admired her, but I found it hard to love her, except in a
remote and cautious and non-reciprocal way. She was so very
unresponsive. I knew that she found it hard to get on close,
relaxed, affectionate terms with anybody—she was a thorough
Scot, and the double tragedy had the effect of accentuating
her Scottishness and turning her inward even more. I felt it
must devolve on me to bridge the gap between us, for I found
contacts easier to make than she did, particularly after I was
out in the world and mixing with congenial colleagues. But
making contact with Mother still and always defeated me. I
felt myself frozen by her reserve as soon as I ventured near.

Consequently I kept deferring the effort until a time when I should have gained the required age and experience.

I hoped that I had not left it too late.

At last the train reached Stretford—a dark, flat, greasy industrial town that smelled, in the cool night, of breweries and tanneries and hot metal; the glow from its various factories splashed the sky with murky orange. It seemed a wealthy place—at least, there were taxis, quite a few of them, still waiting after midnight in the cobbled station yard; I asked one to take me to the hospital and was glad I had, for it proved to be a fifteen-minute ride to the outskirts of the town. Stretford, apparently, sat cheek-by-jowl on the Midland plain with Market Broughton, where Mother's school was. I could have caught a train to Market Broughton just as easily, and it would have been faster.

Sister Crouch was still on duty in the casualty ward. She turned out to be a small, sharp-faced, sandy-haired, freckled woman, who took one look at me and said, "Eh, ye poor child, have ye been traveling ever since ye phoned me? Ye'd better come in my office and have a cup of tea and a warm-up. Yer mother's still unconscious, so there's no point in rushing in right away. I'm glad to have ye here, though. The time we'll want ye is when she comes round."

"What happened to her?" I asked again, sipping the scalding, tasteless hospital tea.

"It was a head injury. A beam fell on her. They had to mend a fracture in her skull and remove a clot."

"Was it—will she—" I gulped and began again. "What are her chances?"

Sister Crouch gave me a hard, measuring look. "Does your mother have no other relatives—no brothers, sisters, other children at all? No parents—grandparents? Just you?"

I nodded, terrified.

"You're very young," she said. "But you look sensible, I must say. Well, I'll tell you: the surgeon who operated thinks her chances are only about one in ten."

"Of surviving?"

"Of surviving—*or* of getting back to normal life. *But—*" she raised a hand, though I had not spoken; I was staring at her numbly—"*but*—I don't agree with him. Being a woman myself, I can understand better what kind of a person your mother is: I think she's tough, she has a very strong natural resistance. I think her chance is better than that. But it may be a long, slow job. And I may be wrong. Don't get your hopes too high. Mr. Wintersmain has a lot of experience. It all depends how she comes through the next thirty-six hours."

"Yes, I see." I didn't see much, really.

Sister Crouch gave me a kind look and said, "You can come and see her now; then you might as well go home and get some rest."

Home? I thought bemusedly, following along the wide, glittering passage that smelled of warm drugs; where is home?

Thanks, no doubt, to her status as headmistress of M. B. Comprehensive, Mother had been placed in a private room, and there she lay, flat under a white cover, her head swathed in bandages, and various tubes connecting her to bottles clamped on tripod stands beside the bed. Her face, which, I was relieved to find, had not been injured (I had been nurturing some awful fears about that), was exactly as I had often seen it: pale, rather severe, the lips pressed tightly into a firm line; a slight frown creased her forehead as if, even in the depths of her unconsciousness, she had many anxious preoccupations. Her brow looked very high, under the bandage; then it came to me that, of course, they would have had to shave her head for the operation. Poor Mother—not that she attached any importance to physical appearances; but her hair had been pretty, a pale, Scottish straw-gold which, even in her early fifties, had not shown a single strand of gray. And she always had a look of great dignity; it was sad if that had been taken from her with her hair. Oh, well; there she lay—remote, forbidding, like a helmeted crusader on his tomb, her face the color of gray marble. I suddenly had a woeful childish longing to kneel down, bury my face in the side of the bed, and cry out, "Mother, Mother, *say* something to me! Tell me you love me! Tell me you're going to be all right!"

Instead I leaned over and gently kissed her unconscious cheek.

Sister Crouch, looking as if she found such behavior irrational but humanly understandable, said, "Now ye'd best go home and get some sleep."

Where is home? I thought again, but she went on, "I'd call a hospital car to take ye, but it's only ten minutes from here to yer mother's house and a walk will help ye to sleep."

"I—I haven't a key to her house," I muttered confusedly, but Sister Crouch said, "We have her bag here; it was brought in with her; I daresay there's a key in it. When ye come in the morning, bring a little case, will ye, to take her clothes away; and I'll give ye a list of other things that she'll be needing. Of course we'll phone you directly there's any change if we think ye should come back. We have the number. It's very lucky ye're so near. And you call us any time, of course, if ye want to."

Very kind, Sister Crouch; she really wanted to do her best for me.

She gave me Mother's severe, executive-type, black handbag; and of course the keys were in it, along with a lot of other orderly belongings: diary, driver's license, and various professional cards.

Mother lived in the headmistress' house, on the edge of the huge school complex, which, as it happened, abutted on the hospital grounds. Not an ideal arrangement from the point of view of the patients, but nineteenth-century manufacturing towns had to grow where they could.

So I walked off through the solid Victorian suburbs with their wide streets and manufacturers' villas, gothic-turreted and set about with cedars, araucarias, and rhododendrons, thinking how strange it was that I should be entering Mother's house like a burglar at three in the morning; I had been there only once before, six months previously, driven over by some friends in the Birmingham Rep. Mother had not held the appointment long; less than a year.

The house, like the rest of the school buildings, was post-

World War II, a small, square, plain block not much better than a glorified Council house. At least it was functional.

I let myself into the narrow hall and removed a large pile of business mail from the doormat to a side table. Sitting room on the right; behind it, dining room, which my mother used as an office; and kitchen straight ahead. The house smelled of nothing; it was strictly tidy and scrupulously clean. I went into the kitchen and poured myself a glass of milk; thought about making a cheese sandwich and abandoned the idea; turned the kitchen light off and went upstairs.

On the second floor the layout was identical: Mother's room, spare room over the office, bathroom over the kitchen. I left Mother's handbag in her bedroom, which, like the rest of the place, was ascetically bare and tidy, furnished with what I suppose must have been fashionable modernity in Mother's youth: blond, curved Swedish wood, rugs and curtains in pale buffs and grays. No ornaments, no treasures, souvenirs, or bits of nonsense. No photographs, either. Nothing to say the person who lives here once had a husband and children. Discouraged, I laid the bag on her tidily made bed, found the linen cupboard, took out sheets, and made up a bed in the spare room for myself. It would have been more practical to sleep in Mother's room, where there was a phone extension, but I couldn't fancy the idea.

It was so quiet and lonely in that house that I found it almost impossible to get to sleep; I seemed to be the only person in the world. Night sounds from the town kept me awake, but they were disembodied, mechanical noises: trains shunting, factories grinding and wailing; they did nothing to allay my solitude.

Finally, at about ten to six, I fell into a heavy sleep, and was roused, almost at once, it seemed, by the phone ringing. Startled, confused, I stumbled into Mother's room and grabbed the receiver, expecting Sister Crouch to say, "Come at once," but the voice was unfamiliar.

"Gina Signorelli here," it announced without preliminaries. "I've just called the hospital and they say there's no change."

"What—who—?"

"That *is* Miss Meiklejohn, isn't it? They told me at the hospital that you were staying in your mother's house."

"Yes—yes, I am. I'm sorry, I've only just woken up." I looked at my watch. It was half past seven. "Who did you say you were?"

"Gina Signorelli. I'd like to call around in half an hour and collect Mrs. Meiklejohn's mail if you don't mind. There will be a lot of things that need answering. Is that all right?"

"Yes, of course," I said, vaguely remembering from the previous visit that Gina Signorelli was my mother's secretary and personal assistant.

"Can I bring you anything when I come?" she said, sounding less staccato, more human and friendly. "Eggs? Bacon? It's a long way from you to the shops. Or are you a vegetarian, like your mother?"

"No, I'm not, but please don't bother, thanks; I'll go out and get something later."

"Sure? Good-by, then," she said and rang off briskly.

Still dazed from my short, broken sleep, I wandered shivering to the window and looked out. Here, more than half way up England, winter still had a firm grip on the landscape; icy, gray fog mostly concealed the town, but I could hear its industry revving up for the day: buses and trains rumbling along, factory hooters screeching, traffic snarling. I had a bath —cold, because I had failed to find the heating switch the night before, but at least it roused me; dressed, and was making a pot of coffee when Miss Signorelli arrived, announcing herself by a long peal at the front-door bell.

"I decided not to take you at your word," she said, dumping a carton of groceries on the kitchen table. "I daresay you're like your mother—hate to put people to trouble. But there's only food for rabbits in this house. And you need to eat to keep your strength up. Cheese and fruit may be all very well for *her*—goodness knows how she manages all she does on it— but I'm sure it won't do for you. It'll be a long day for you, I daresay.

She looked at me severely. She was a short, brisk person about my mother's age, high-colored, with snapping black eyes and dyed black curls. I remembered her now; she had taught shorthand and business methods at a school in Bath where Mother had been senior housemistress. Greatly impressed by Miss Signorelli's formidable efficiency, and liking her robust good temper, Mother, when she achieved her headship, had written and asked if Gina would be interested in the job of school secretary. Gina had accepted and moved to Market Broughton with her invalid father. I vaguely supposed that in Mother's rather lonely and nomadic existence, Gina Signorelli was one of her few semifriends, a small remaining link with an earlier epoch, about the closest thing to a confidante that she allowed herself. They even, I remembered, called each other by their Christian names.

Miss Signorelli seemed disposed to be friendly to me, and since she was evidently familiar with the house I was able to ask her where the various things were that I had been unable to find.

While I poured cups of coffee for us both, she went into the front office and collected a daunting stack of work for herself.

"There'll be three times as much to do, with your mother not there," she said. "I'll be over at the school all day, so give me a call if there's anything you want. And try not to worry too much about her," she added unconvincingly. "I'm sure she's putting up a terrific fight."

But I could see that she was sad and worried herself. "Can you tell me exactly what happened?" I asked. "The hospital didn't give me any details."

"It was the new gym roof." Miss Signorelli sat silent with her lips pressed together for a moment, then burst out, "Your mother told them and *told* them that the design was bad. But the board of governors insisted on accepting the lowest tender. Trust *them*. The cheapskates! Your mother was watching the end-of-term gym display yesterday afternoon, and suddenly there was an awful cracking from the roof and it started to sag in the middle. I wasn't there myself, but Emily Johns is a pal of mine—she's the gym mistress—and she told me what happened. There were about sixty people in the place—mostly children, a few parents—and four exits; Emily and your mother shouted to them to keep calm and make for the nearest door in an orderly way, but the roof collapsed before they were all out, and of course your mother had stayed till the last —very properly, she'll get a Royal Humane Society medal or some such thing, damn those penny-pinching misers—one of the concrete girders broke in half and came down on her. I will say for the ambulance service here, they're efficient: they were round in ten minutes and she was in the hospital on the operating table in half an hour; all that *could* be done *was* done, but it shouldn't ever have happened in the first place. Hers was the only serious injury; otherwise it was nothing but cuts and bruises."

She paused with trembling lips and blinked at me furiously. "Well—I won't fuss you with all that. You've enough to bother you without going into whether it should have happened. Oh, when you go round to the hospital—I assume you'll be going fairly soon?—could you take your mother's Teachers' Provident Association card—they need the code number for their records, because she's in a private room; you'll find it in her desk, pigeonhole at the extreme right-hand end, the one marked PERSONAL. Right?"

"Yes, of course."

"Make yourself a decent breakfast first, though. And I hope they have better news for you by the time you get there," she said gruffly, and stumped away, clutching her bundle of papers.

I did not feel in the least hungry, but Miss Signorelli was right: it would be a long day; so I made myself scrambled eggs and ate them fast. Hurriedly washing the dishes, I found in myself a neurotic urge to leave the kitchen as specklessly tidy as if Mother herself might walk in at any moment.

I left the kitchen immaculate and then did a quick check through the list that Sister Crouch had given me—nightwear, handkerchiefs, talcum, eau de cologne, slippers, dressing-gown, bed-jacket (not that she would be needing most of those for a while, I feared). Then I remembered the TPA card Miss Signorelli had mentioned. Carrying the little overnight case, I went into Mother's shadowy, unheated study and opened the desk, which was of the sloping-lid bureau type.

The contents were characteristically tidy and ordered—clean stationery neatly stacked underneath, tray full of pens, pigeonholes individually labeled: ACCOUNTS, TAX, BANK, HOUSE, UNPAID BILLS, TPA, SCHOOL, and the one on the far right indicated by Gina Signorelli, PERSONAL. I pulled out the bundle of papers it held, which were secured by an elastic band. There was a brown envelope marked Birth & Marriage Certificates, a passport (up to date and quite well used, due to Mother's frequent attendance at educational conferences), some National Insurance papers, and a plastic folder containing a few photographs.

So this was where she kept them. Filled with curiosity, I opened the folder and pulled out the half-dozen prints it contained. Here they were: two or three each of my father and sister, one of me, taken at the age of seven, holding Othello; my father had taken the picture, I remembered. Now I came to consider the matter, I was not even sure that Mother owned a camera; she certainly was not given to taking snapshots. That picture at age seven was the last I could remember having taken, apart from school and passport photographs.

I looked at the pictures of my father and sister. He was a thin-faced, smiling man with black hair, like mine, and a heavy mustache. The pictures of him were blurred and not very good—one had an impression of a young, gay, rather reckless character; that was about all. In one shot he was leaning back and laughing; in one he held a tennis racket, squinting at the sun; the third showed him in swimming trunks, a towel around his neck. He looked youthful, happy, carefree—not a strong personality, perhaps; yet not, surely, a man looking at whose picture you would say, "He will die at forty-one?"

And Drusilla? A serious girl—straight features, direct gaze; mouth set in a firm line, like Mother's, page-boy-style hair;

rather a broad nose; wide-apart eyes, defenseless and concerned; I struggled to remember their color—gray, like
Mother's? blue, like mine? This was a passport photo, taken, I
thought, when she was sixteen, about the age when I remembered her last; all three prints were the same. My sister,
Drusilla: why did she have to die before she had explored even
the edge of her experience? What tide swept her away? Why
were she and my father so lacking in stamina? Compared with
them I felt vulgarly tenacious of life, full of obstinate health
and vitality. I wondered if Mother shared this attribute? Or
would she let go, as they had done? Shivering a little in the
cold, gray room, I slipped the pictures back into their case and
snapped the elastic band around the bundle again. A last envelope fell out from among the rest, one I had overlooked. I
turned it over. On the front it bore a typed message:

TO BE GIVEN TO MY DAUGHTER PRISCILLA
MEIKLEJOHN IN THE EVENT OF MY DEATH.

I stared at this in a numb, stupid way for a long time. To
come across my formal name never fails—as I have indicated
—to throw me off balance. And to have such an experience
coupled with that freezing conclusion, that irrevocable period
—"in the event of my death"—that is enough to loosen the
roots of one's being at *any* time.

Suddenly I couldn't bear the sight of the envelope or its in-
scription. I bundled it back under the elastic with the other
papers, removed the TPA card, which I put in the case with
Mother's toilet things, and rapped the desk lid down. Then I
hastily left the house, locking up behind me, and hurried off to
the hospital as if the devil were on my heels.

Sister Crouch had gone off duty, of course. She had been
replaced by the day sister, a lugubrious, cowlike woman called
McCloy. Sister McCloy was kind in her way, and doubtless an
excellent nurse, but I missed Sister Crouch's astringent common sense. Sister McCloy seemed to be irresistibly attracted
by doom, to assume the worst as a foregone conclusion.

"Ach, not one in a hundred of those cases recover," she
sighed, escorting me to Mother's bedside, where the scene was

unchanged. She fetched me an armchair and left me alone in the melancholy little cube of a room, whose features I came to know acutely well during the next few days. Every hour or so, a nurse would come in to check that the drip feed was working and that Mother's temperature and pulse were unchanged. Otherwise Mother and I had the room to ourselves and I sat looking at her marble profile, wondering what was in that sealed envelope, what crucial piece of information, what terrifying fact, was so important to us both that it *must* be withheld from me throughout Mother's lifetime, and *must* be imparted to me after her death.

At half past eleven the surgeon who had operated on her, Mr. Wintersmain, came to look at her. He was a big, smooth man, like a gray seal, beautifully turned out, full of kindness and consideration, and I didn't like him. Everyone had assured me that he was a first-class surgeon, one of the best in the country, that Mother was uncommonly lucky he had been at hand after her accident—but I couldn't stand the way he called me "young lady" and assured me that everything possible was being done. It was all bedside manner, poured out as easily as cream from a silver jug; I couldn't believe a word he said. He, like Sister McCloy, had already prejudged my mother and dispatched her, in his mind, to the undertaker's parlor; to him, she was just an interesting case, and his only concern was to extract the maximum information from her state which he might use on some future occasion.

He discouraged me from remaining at Mother's bedside, making it plain he did not think she would come out of her coma. "It's not good for you to stay indoors all day," he said indulgently, as if I were about sixteen. "Why don't you go out and take a walk in the park, have lunch at a café, go to a movie? You could come back here at about teatime, but I really don't expect any change at present."

I said very well, without the least intention of following his advice, and stayed put. At noon I went down to the hospital canteen and ate a horrible sausage roll and a tasteless orange; then I returned to my vigil.

I imagined living in a bed-sitter in Crowbridge, pushing Mother along the promenade in her wheelchair once a day, paying Mrs. Charm to keep an eye on her. . . .

In the afternoon there came a message from the board of governors of Market Broughton School to say how terribly sorry for me they were and offering help of every kind; if there was anything at all that either Mother or I myself needed I was to let Miss Signorelli know . . . and of course all the medical bills would be taken care of by the school, I was not to have the least anxiety on that score.

"That's because they're scared your mother will sue—or you will," said Gina Signorelli, who had brought the message. She looked thin, feverish, and belligerent, in a bright-red plastic raincoat and hood trickling with drops, for a violent rainstorm had set in outside. "I'm quite surprised they offer to pay the bills; that's practically an admission of liability." She pinched her lips together. "How is she now?"

"No change."

She scowled at me and said, "You look terrible. How much did you sleep last night? I suggest that I drive you home this minute, otherwise you're going to get soaked. Come on. They'll call you fast enough if they want you."

"I don't like to trouble you."

"Bosh. I'll be glad to get away from my father for once. And I picked up your mother's car, which was having its M.O.T. test—you might as well have the use of it."

So she drove me home in Mother's little Renault and then came in and cooked spaghetti Bolognese for us both, with the maximum speed, efficiency, mess, and clatter, banging saucepans about, frying onions till the kitchen reeked with blue smoke, leaving a trail of greasy dishes and tomatoey spoons behind her, smoking all the while, dropping cigarette ash on the floor, and onion peels and crumpled paper, meanwhile telling me tales of the parsimony and stupidity of the school governors; my mother, a very fastidious, tidy, silent worker, would have been thunderstruck at the chaos created all over her kitchen during the space of half an hour.

While we ate, still in the kitchen, which by now felt quite warm and friendly, as if it were in some other house, Gina Signorelli put questions to me about my job, displaying considerable knowledge of the theater. She had brought along a bottle of fierce red wine, which, together with the food and the cheerful conversation, helped me to forget, for half minutes at a time, the cause of my being there, the waiting that seemed to press on my shoulders and temples like a whole universe weighted with rocks of silence.

We drank all the wine between us and Gina became fierily lachrymose.

"I'm just so *angry* that such a thing should have happened to your mother, after all her battles and her struggles," she said several times over. "She is such a wonderful person. People often don't realize about her—they think she's tough."

"The thing is that Barbara's so bottled up inside herself," Gina continued, flushed and voluble, pulling grapes off a bunch she had brought and spitting out the pips. "Ever since your sister's suicide, she's been scared to invest affection in anything with more life in it than a cactus—except in the most cautious, distant way—"

I could hear her sharp voice talking on, but what it said made no sense; the room had gone black and scarlet around me; I had to clutch the edge of the enamel table hard to prevent myself from toppling right off my chair. Gina, fortunately, noticed nothing; she was away into a dissertation about my mother's character: her sagacity, her pride, her judgment, her keen intelligence.

"Excuse me," I said, when I had somewhat recovered, seizing on a gap in this eulogy. "I'd forgotten you knew my sister."

Drusilla had been at the school in Bath.

"Well, I never actually taught her, dear, because she was in the science stream and I was tutoring in business methods at the Pulteney school, but of course I knew her to say hello to."

"I've never been told," I began, slowly, very cautiously, "what—what happened to her. What she actually—did. You remember, I was in Greece then. And Mother's never talked about it."

"I'm not at all surprised. It was dreadful for your poor mother. Dreadful! And so soon after she lost your father. . . . It was assumed that was why your sister did it. Poor girl. I suppose she just couldn't get over his death."

"What *did* she do?" I asked, swallowing. The taste of tomato and onion and wine burned in my throat.

"It was on her seventeenth birthday. That's a nervous age. And I suppose the anniversary upset her."

"She—?"

"She went to school as usual and locked herself in the chemistry lab and swallowed a bottle of sulphuric acid."

"*Oh—*"

The next thing I knew, I was lying on the floor among the onion skins and Gina Signorelli was worriedly wiping my face with a damp teacloth.

"Stupid ass I am," she said, wielding the cloth, angry and remorseful. "Shouldn't have told you that. Got carried away, thinking about it all. Obviously Barbara felt it best to keep it from you, and quite right too. Here, drink this." She handed me a mug of hot, black coffee.

I said, "I'm glad you told me." I gulped the bitter, burning stuff, and added, "I'd have had to know some time. Mother couldn't have kept me insulated forever. I'm grown up now. Besides—" Besides, suppose Mother died, leaving me in ignorance? But perhaps she meant to? Or was that the message in the envelope? I stopped short, wondering this.

Gina said, "Yes, you're grown up—but you've enough to do with fighting your own battles, no need to be burdened by what's past and gone. That's why your mother's always kept you at a distance, you see; she wanted you to stay clear of it all." What all? I thought. "She was teaching at the Pulteney, remember, when Drusilla ki—died; they were together too much, Barbara thought, after it happened—they'd kept upsetting each other all over again, hadn't given the grief a chance to heal. And girls of seventeen are emotionally unbalanced, it's a tricky time—so Barbara was determined the same thing mustn't happen to you."

Well, she succeeded, I thought. Here I am, alive to tell the tale.

We washed up, sober and silent now, and Gina said she'd better be getting along. "*Don't* sit around brooding, now, dear; have a bath and get to bed."

Yes, I said, and thanked her; the same advice in one form or another had been given me a wearisome number of times in the past twenty-four hours. Why shouldn't I wear myself out if I wanted to?

But of course she was right.

It was still pouring, so when Gina had put herself back into her red plastic rainwear I drove her home—she lived with her aged father about a mile away in a different bit of suburb—and then came back via the hospital, stopping to inquire.

Still no change. Call again later if you like. Or tomorrow.

I re-entered Mother's house; the smell of onion and tomato and bayleaf had almost dispersed already, as if the secretive aura of the place were so dense that it expelled all common domestic vapors.

Then it occurred to me for the first time that day that, in my single-minded preoccupation over Mother's condition, I had completely forgotten my friends at the Crowbridge Theater Royal. It would not be too late to phone them now.

I put a call through and asked to speak to Eve Kransky, who was our manager.

". . . Eve? This is Mike. I just rang to ask how it had all gone?"

"Mike! My *dear!* How are *you?* How's your mother?"

"No news yet; she's still in a coma. I'm just waiting about."

"Oh, how awful for you! We've all been thinking of you *so much*. We're so sorry for you."

"How did the play go?" I said quickly.

"My dear, a triumph! Really—all we'd hoped. Oh, well, Sam fluffed his lines, of course, and Mary came in too soon and was watery but—all in all—wonderful! And wonderful reviews—not only in the Crowbridge *Advertiser*—the Kent *Messenger* and the East Sussex *News* as well!"

"Really?" I was impressed. "That's marvelous."

"Special mention of your sets and costumes, too, dearie— we're really on the map. I'll send you stats of all the notices— or will you be coming back in the next couple of days, do you think—?"

She stopped awkwardly, and I said, "No, I don't see how I can get back at the moment; I'm terribly sorry to leave you all in the lurch like this—"

"Don't be absurd; we miss you, but we're managing. Hope the cuttings cheer you—they ought to. Keep your courage up, Mike, love; we're all thinking of you."

I thanked her, gulping, and rang off.

Then I started upstairs, walking very slowly.

I was thinking about my sister, Drusilla.

Drusilla was a *brave* girl, as I remembered her from thirteen years back. She had turned to face a charging bull, as I scrambled through a fence to safety. She had flown at a man who was hitting his small child in the Oxford High Street, and told him to stop or she would fetch the police. She had lanced her own boil when it was swelled up as big as a plum. What situation could have been so terrible that she was afraid to face it?

I am entitled to know about this, I thought, standing with my hand on the square-carved newel post at the head of the stairs.

Drusilla was my sister. I loved her too, even if she was seven years older. She used to bathe my knees when I fell down and grazed them, she dug splinters out of my fingers with a needle, she read to me when I was in bed with measles, she made a set of Greek dresses for Katina, the doll she brought me.

Ever since I was nine, I have been cut off from my family. If it were not for the Aghnides—whom I had contrived to go on seeing occasionally after I left Dendros—my life would have been completely destitute of affection, dry as a bone. Nobody could help that; it was just misfortune; but the truth, at least, I am entitled to; and if the truth is in that envelope downstairs, I am going to have it now.

So I walked back downstairs, entered Mother's study, took the packet from the PERSONAL pigeonhole, found the envelope, and opened it.

For a mean second, I was tempted to slide a pencil under the flap, or steam it open, so that, at a pinch, I could reseal the flap and pretend I had not tampered with it; then I thought: "Hell! If I can't be honest about a thing like this, there is no hope for me."

So I boldly tore the flap across and threw the crumpled envelope into the wastepaper basket.

Inside, there was a single sheet of typed paper. No date.

It said:

"My dear Priscilla,

I hope you will understand why I was never able to bring myself to talk to you about this.

The fact is that it was just too painful for me. And if you can't understand that—well, there is nothing to be done about it now.

You will be an adult by the time you read this letter, able, I hope, to stand distress and pain—because I have done my best to ensure that you had a peaceful, untroubled childhood in which to grow up without these troubles impinging on you.

You have a right to this information now, though.

Your father is not dead, as you have always understood. James Graffin is still alive, although he has changed his name. He is alive, but I must warn you: the *way* in which he is alive may be such a terrible shock to you that even the cushion of thirteen years'—or however much more it is—separation from him is not sufficient to prevent knowledge about him doing you profound psychological harm. Nor can I see that you could derive any benefit from knowing about him. So I do urge you, most earnestly—I *beg* you—to think very, very carefully before taking any step towards getting in touch with your ex-father.

If, however, you feel you must take this step—then you can write to Hazeler, Malling, and Tyrwhitt, Solicitors, at 87,

Turl Street, Oxford, who are instructed to give you further information.

Believe that I did what I thought was best for you."

It was signed, *Mother*.

I was still reading the final paragraph when the telephone rang. The downstairs extension was on the wall by Mother's desk—about a foot from where I stood. Automatically I put a hand out to the receiver.

"Hullo?"

"Hullo, this is Sister Crouch. I think you should come round to the hospital, Miss Meiklejohn; your mother has begun moving a little, which might be the prelude to a return to consciousness."

"I'll be there in five minutes," I said.

It wasn't much more. Sister Crouch and a young house doctor I didn't know were by her bedside when I slid into the room. Mother was stirring a little, restlessly; her fingers clenched and unclenched. Sister Crouch gave me a brief, approving nod, which both commended my speedy arrival and indicated that I had better sit down by the bed.

"It may be a while yet," she murmured. "And even if she does come round, she may not be very clear, of course; ye realise that? Ye've got to be prepared for *anything*. Ye've got to be tough."

I nodded, with a dry mouth, feeling about as tough as a mashed potato, and fixed my gaze on Mother's gray-marble profile, which was now, from time to time, disturbed by flickering frowns, brief contractions of the brow, as if she anticipated all the problems that awaited her just over the frontiers of consciousness.

In fact it was about fifteen minutes before she opened her eyes. When she did, she fixed them on me immediately, and a look of perplexity came over her face.

"Why, Prissy!" She hadn't called me that since I was about four. "What ever are *you* doing here?"

" 'Lo, Ma," I said. "I just thought I'd come and see how you were getting on."

I tucked my fingers around hers, which, for once, clasped

mine quite firmly, but she said, "Oh, there was no need for that. That was very naughty of them—very naughty. Did they send for you? They shouldn't have made you come all this way—what about your first night?"

She was half whispering; her voice almost faded away at this moment; she was plainly a good deal puzzled, trying to comprehend these unusual circumstances. Her eyes roamed about the room and she slightly moved a hand, as if to try to feel her head.

"It's all right, Mrs. Meiklejohn," Sister Crouch said firmly. "We want ye to lie quite still, if ye please. Ye're in hospital, and ye're going to be perfectly okay"—over Mother's recumbent form she gave me her short, brisk nod—"but in the meantime we want ye to co-operate, and not try to move about, just lie absolutely still. Will ye do that?"

"Yes, if I must," whispered Mother, with a touch of her usual dry manner. "But why did you fetch my daughter? There was no need for that."

"Naturally your daughter wished to see how ye were getting on," Sister Crouch said reprovingly. "Now we want ye to rest all ye can, Mrs. Meiklejohn."

"Oh, very well."

Mother's eyes moved back to mine. I did my best to give her a big, wide, cheerful smile, though I was feeling pretty beaten up, one way and another.

However, Mother seemed to accept my grin at face value and her own cheek muscles faintly crinkled in response. Her eyes were closing again, but she opened them momentarily to say, "What about your opening, though? Wasn't that tonight?"

"No, it was last night."

"Good gracious," she muttered in a perplexed tone. And then, "Did it go well?"

"Big success. I'll show you our press notices by and by."

"Good," she said, and then she floated off into what seemed to be an ordinary peaceful sleep.

"She'll be all right now," said Sister Crouch.

⁅2⁆

FUGUE

Julia Saint was moving slowly, idly, along Winston Churchill Street, enjoying the delicious warmth of the sun, and the smell, so strong that it was almost a taste, of orange blossoms mixed with souvlaki. The orange scent came from the municipal gardens, to her right, where, between the formally spaced and trained trees, bright scarlet hibiscus clashed madly with bougainvillaea, which was the hideous color of black-currant purée mixed with milk. Chinaberry trees dangled clusters of lilac blossoms, which added their faint fragrance to that of the orange blossoms. Big, fat cacti writhed octopus tentacles, and the sandy ground, already bare and dusty, seemed to exude a light, salt sweat.

The smell of souvlaki drifted from the harborside cafés ahead of Julia, where prelunch customers were already settled at the gaudily colored tables, sustaining themselves with coffee, ouzo, and Fix.

Julia surveyed the tables with leisurely satisfaction. Presently, when she had done all her shopping, she would return to the hotel and pick up Dikran, they would stroll back here and have a long, unhurried, enjoyable lunch at one of the harbor cafés—finding a sheltered spot, however, because, although the sun was powerful, the wind, as so often on Dendros in April, still blew keenly; waiters were darting among the little tables clamping down flapping tablecloths with metal clips. When, presently, Julia sat on one of the waterside benches to write some postcards, she found it necessary to tuck each card into her bag as soon as written, or they would have blown into the slapping, turquoise water, which bounced all the little red and blue and green boats up and down, and caused the masts of larger ships—cruise liners and yachts—moored farther out, to crisscross in a perpetually changing pattern of X's and Y's.

"Dendros is delicious," wrote Julia on a postcard to her brother. "We are having a charming time. Dikran is looking after me hand and foot. What a contrast! I feel I've never been pampered in my life before; am thoroughly appreciating it."

"Dendros is the most heavenly island in the world," she wrote to her daughter. "There are piles of oranges everywhere and a dusty camel sits perpetually outside the town gate for local color. I hope your finals aren't weighing on you too much. Give my love to Pa if you see him." Then she crossed out that line, x-ing it vigorously to ensure its illegibility. Though, no doubt, shrewd little Tansy would decipher it just the same.

To her son Julia wrote, "Darling Paul, Dendros is terrific. You would love the swimming. The interior is like trying to drive over Ryvitas turned edgeways on. I have collected some roots of plants for you. . . ."

Then she wrote to her best friend. "Dearest Dee, a second honeymoon is really a rejuvenating experience. I would never have believed that I could feel eighteen again. Dendros is the most wonderful island in the whole Mediterranean. Believe it or not!"

Having stuck stamps on all her cards, she carried them to

the stately stone post office, which looked like the head-
quarters of the League of Nations, adorned with carved stone
lions and blue-and-white flag fluttering overhead. There she
posted them, bought more stamps, and walked on, at a slow,
enjoyable pace, beside the harbor, under the crumbling,
honey-colored stone arch, and so into Dendros Old Town,
where the streets, become suddenly narrow and cobbled, ran
steeply uphill or downhill, with distant views of the sea under
Turkish arches, and were lined with dark, aromatic shops
displaying, near the harbor front, everything the tourist heart
could desire, and, farther away from the water, more com-
monplace household requisites for the natives themselves.
There Julia bought muslin shirts for her daughter and nieces,
silver jewelry for her friends, Turkish delight—only, of
course, it was different here and called by a local, unpro-
nounceable name—for her brother, who had a sweet tooth; records of Greek music for her son, and a scarf for herself. She
wished to buy something for Dikran but could not fix on anything suitable; what can you give somebody who is rich enough
to buy up the whole island if so minded? His wealth was delightful, but it did give rise to such problems from time to
time. In the end she bought him a simple set of blue worry
beads on a leather thong; very plain, but a beautiful blue.

By now she had reached the oldest part of the Old Town,
where there were few shops but the houses had blossomed into
the most exuberant colors possible; they were painted in siz-
zling lime greens, luminous powder blue with a touch of lilac,
fondant pink, french-mustard ochre, lavender, and pea green.
Roses, red lilies, sweet williams, and geraniums blazed and bur-
geoned in the tiny courtyards behind the secretive façades.
Cascades of feathery green hung over the walls into the narrow alleys, and cats lay drowsing on stone doorsteps. Old ladies, dressed in black from head to toe, with faces brown,
wrinkled, yet clear-cut as the lines of the ships in the harbor,
plodded past in their canvas shoes and gave Julia brilliant
smiles in return for her murmured greetings. I hope I look exactly like that when I am old, thought Julia, and also: What a

pleasure not to be recognized anywhere, to be completely anonymous wherever I walk! What a comfort to slip through these narrow streets as unremarked as the old ladies in their black shawls! Probably not a soul in this island has heard of Lady Julia Gibbon, or of Arnold Gibbon, or of Lord Plumtree, or his wife, the sumptuous blonde Christian Plumtree. Well, no, that's not quite true, since English Sunday papers are on sale in the New Town bookshops, but, after all, who would be interested in their news stories here? The foreigners who come to Dendros do so for the sun, or for the music, or to buy furs, since Dendros has little to offer in its history or archaeology; and people who are interested in furs—or music—are generally interested in little else; which makes them dull but comfortable company for the heartsore and spiritually bruised.

We'll have lunch, thought Julia, hugging her armful of parcels in their frail, exotic foreign wrapping paper; a light lunch, just fish and salad; then we'll walk around the point to the western side of the island, where the waves are bigger, and swim—if Dirkan wants to; then a siesta; then a stroll, maybe round to the commercial harbor, where we saw the man with the radio-controlled boat the other day (damn, I forgot to mention that when I was writing Paul's postcard; must remember to tell him about it next time I write, it's just the kind of thing he'd like); then dinner—perhaps at that place on the raft in the harbor that Dikran wants to try; and then we'll take a cab out to Helikon for the concert, the heavenly Haydn baryton trios, the best concert yet. . . .

It seemed hardly possible that a day *could* contain so much straight pleasure.

She left the Old Town regretfully and walked back along the harbor front. By now she was pleasantly tired, looking forward to a seat in the shade and her first sip of ouzo. She walked past a man and thought—with an old reflex acquired during the past nine months in England—Damn, he recognized me, before recalling with relief that the man had not recognized her because she was Lady Julia Gibbon but because she had been with Dikran yesterday when they saw him—no, the day before. It was the same man who had been operating the radio-controlled toy boat in the harbor, and that was the only reason why he had recognized her; he had smiled and waved his thanks when Dikran loosed the boat from a tangle of water-logged rope and set it free to return to its owner across the harbor.

She walked past the fishermen with their dark blue boat *Aphrodite* pulled up by the harbor wall, from which, with the aid of a pair of kitchen scales, they were selling their catch in paper cones as swiftly as customers could buy the small, wriggling fish and take them away. She passed the tourist shops with their beads, pottery, and postcards, and the car-rental offices, whose beach buggies sat inconveniently in the middle of the wide pavement.

Leaving the harbor, Julia walked purposefully out along Winston Churchill Street to where the Fleur de Lys Hotel stood by itself in somewhat somber isolation on a tree-grown spit of land extending into the Aegean. The Fleur de Lys had been built in the nineteenth century and patronized at that time by royalty; since those days, it had declined but still kept three stars and the blessing of Michelin because the staff and the cuisine were French, whereas the half dozen new, high-rise creations which had sprung up like groundsel at the south end of the island during the past few years had local staff, who came and went when the orange or olive crop demanded their attention, and menus that could be classified only as mongrel-tourist. Their gardens were cement slabs and potted geraniums, whereas the Fleur de Lys had handsome old ilex trees and rose-covered pergolas; shabby it might be, but it was also stately. It possessed its own beach, too, dotted with chunks of white concrete which would support thatched beach umbrellas when the wind dropped. Julia threaded her way among these, looking to see if her husband was still on the beach. Since the hour was now one-thirty, the sand was deserted; all the hotel's sedate residents were elsewhere, studying their lunch menus. Not a soul was in sight. Julia walked through the garden and entered the dark, cool lobby. There she asked the desk clerk for the key of numéro quarante-cinq, but, as she had expected, he told her that Monsieur was *en haut*, doubtless waiting for her in their suite. Without troubling to wait for the slow, old elevator, Julia ran up the one flight of shallow, curving stairs and tapped on the door of 45.

She had to wait a moment or two; then the door was pulled open very suddenly. Dikran stood there. She felt immediately that there was something wrong about him, though she could not have defined precisely what was the matter. It frightened her, because it seemed a total wrongness. She noticed beads of sweat on his face, which looked drawn, aged by five years since she had left him after breakfast.

He said at once: "I'm all mixed up! What's happened this morning? I can't remember anything!"

He clutched both her hands violently, standing in the doorway as if he had been waiting for her there, on that spot, in a state of desperation, ever since she had left.

Julia was swamped at once by a flood of terror. So *this* is what has been in waiting! This, behind all the comfort and the luxury and pampering. I might have known it. I might have known that nothing lasts more than a few days, nothing is what it seems.

But, coinstantaneously, she was saying in a calm, confident voice, as she had so often to her children during many crises, "Come and sit down. Sit down and tell me what's the matter."

She pushed the door shut behind her and urged him through the entrance lobby into the sitting room beyond. Still clutching painfully at her hands he sat—awkwardly, sideways—on the tasseled velvet sofa and said again, "I'm all mixed up. I can't remember anything. What time is it?"

She told him and then said, "*What* can't you remember?"

She noticed that his hands were very cold, that he was shivering. On the low coffee table beside him was a mess of papers—tourist brochures, cruise advertisements, and the rental papers for the cars they had hired on the two previous days. Dikran turned these over in a perplexed, miserable, distracted way, peering at them as if they were written in Sanskrit.

"I've been trying to look through these, but I don't understand them! I can't remember anything. I'm all mixed up!" he said. "What time is it?"

"I've just told you."

"I've forgotten. What did you say?"

"A quarter to two."

"I'm all mixed up," he said again, hopelessly.

Deeply alarmed, but seizing on the nearest practical test, Julia tried to take him through their day. "Do you remember our having breakfast on the terrace? The coffee and croissants? Do you remember my saying that I'd prefer to go shopping on my own, because I thought you would be bored?"

"No, I don't. I don't remember *anything*. What time is it?"

"It's about ten minutes to two," she said once more. "I think you ought to see a doctor, darling."

"No. *No!* I don't want any doctor messing about with me!" he cried out in a wild panic. "Only, tell me what's happened. I'm all mixed up. I can't remember anything."

Julia looked at the gilt telephone, which stood on a marble table behind his shoulder. She was really terrified by now but did not know whether, if she tried to phone for a doctor, he might not physically stop her. So she suggested, diplomatically, "Don't you think you ought to put some warmer clothes on? You're shivering quite badly."

He was wearing a toweling beach shirt over cotton slacks. She noticed that his watch was not on his wrist. His feet, in *espadrilles*, were sockless. All this was most unusual for Dikran, whose sartorial habits were highly conventional; he would wear beach clothes only while actually on the beach, not a moment longer; not even in the privacy of their suite. He really disliked informal clothes.

"Did you go swimming, darling?" she asked him.

"I'm all mixed up. I can't remember," he said yet again, picking up the car-rental papers and despairingly shuffling them about.

"Come into the bathroom and get changed," Julia urged, endeavoring to hide her fear under the most soothing, matter-of-

fact tone she could muster. She picked him a clean shirt from
his closet and steered him in the direction of the bathroom. He
came biddably enough and began to pull the toweling shirt
over his head. As soon as she saw him thoroughly engaged in
this operation, she flew back to the other room, partially
pulling-to the door behind her, but not closing it completely
in case he should feel himself shut in and become anxious.

Picking up the phone, she carried it to the length of its
cord, out through the french doors, onto the balcony. Down
below, the turquoise sea sparkled and bounced; along its edge
the absurd row of short, phallic stone posts, painted powder
pink, marched around the side of the paved promenade to the
end of the point. Beyond the blue sea floated the coast of Turkey, mysterious and shadowy, with mountains wreathed in a
few gauzy clouds. Everything was just as it had been half an
hour before.

Feverishly joggling the receiver rest, Julia glanced back
through the french windows; Dikran was still in the bathroom, thank heaven.

"*Oui?*" said a voice suddenly in her ear.

"*Mon mari est malade,*" Julia murmured, fast and low-
voiced. "*Je crois qu'il a un—un coup de soleil.*" Was that the
French for sunstroke? "Please, can you send me a doctor as
fast as possible—a doctor who can speak some English, if there
is one?"

"What are his symptoms? Does he have fever?" the clerk
asked efficiently.

"No—no fever. But he is altogether confused. He does not
know what has happened. I—I am very anxious about him."

"Remain tranquil, Madame. The doctor will attend you
without delay."

"Thank you," she whispered, and put down the receiver,
feeling just a little better. At least she had *done* something;
taken some measures.

She went to the bathroom, where Dikran, having changed
his clothes, was staring in a puzzled manner at the swimming
trunks that he had just taken off.

Handling them, Julia observed that they were damp around the waist. Also, his *espadrilles*, bought two days before and so far unworn, had spots of tar and a little sand embedded in the rope soles.

"You were on the beach, then? You did go swimming? You said at breakfast you weren't sure whether you wanted to."

"I don't remember," he said doubtfully. "No, I didn't go swimming. I was on the balcony."

The balcony was now in shade, but it faced southeast and had had the full sun all through the morning. Perhaps he had gone swimming, come back, and then fallen asleep out there.

Julia said, "I think you have a touch of sunstroke."

"But the sun's not hot!" he said quickly and anxiously. "I wasn't out long. What time is it? I'm so confused." The alarm in his face was painful to see.

"Two o'clock," Julia said, looking at her watch, wondering if any quarter hour had ever gone so slowly before, and how soon the doctor could reasonably be expected.

She sat beside Dikran on the velvet sofa while he shivered, shifting restlessly, and looked with unhappy eyes around the cool, shady room with its dignified French furniture. Every minute or so he asked, with the regularity of a metronome, "What time is it? I'm all mixed up."

"Do you know who I am?" Julia rather desperately inquired, hoping to shunt his mental processes onto a new track.

But he said, "Of course I do," in an annoyed tone.

"Well, who am I, then? What's my name?"

This he would not answer; he began to fidget with the papers again, restlessly turning them over and over as if he hoped to find among them the clue to what had gone wrong with him. And she sat beside him, asking herself: Who is this man I lightheartedly married four weeks ago? Who is this stranger? What is going to happen next?

Within fifteen minutes there came a light tap on the door, and Julia, hugely relieved, hurried to open it.

The man who stood outside was dark, slight, and dapper; he was, Julia noticed absently, dressed with great neatness and elegance; he carried a black doctor's bag. He gave her a look which contained solicitude and unfeigned admiration of her own appearance, nicely blended. "Mrs. Saint? I am Dr. Achmed Mustafa Adnan. The hotel inform me that you are anxious about your husband."

"Oh, I am! Do please come in!" She shut the door behind him and then, leading him into the main room, said to Dikran, "Darling, here's Dr. Adnan, who wants to talk to you."

Dikran instantly shrank back, alarmed and reluctant; his glance moved swiftly from one to the other of them.

"Mr. Saint?" The doctor gave him a shrewd, careful, assessing glance, and then laid down his bag on a gilt-and-marble table. "How do you do, Mr. Saint? How are you feeling now?"

"I'm all mixed up," Dikran said, for about the twentieth time. "I can't remember anything that's happened to me."

"So? We will soon fix that. Don't worry about it."

Dr. Adnan spoke English with great fluency and rapidity but with the slightest touch of an accent. He was evidently not Greek; Turkish, perhaps, Julia thought, or Lebanese. Quietly and efficiently he began to examine Dikran, testing his visual reflexes, face reflexes, and blood pressure.

"What's the *matter* with me?" Dikran kept asking miserably.

"We will soon find out. Tell me, what is your name?" Adnan inquired, banging on Dikran's patella, which responded sluggishly.

"Dikran."

"Dikran what?"

"Sareyan."

"He's changed it to Saint, actually," Julia murmured.

"You are nowadays called Mr. Saint?" Adnan suggested.

"Yes, Saint, Saint," Dikran agreed testily.

"Your age, Mr. Saint?"

Dikran gazed at him blankly, and after a pause Julia came to the rescue again.

"He's fifty-one, Doctor."

"Nationality?"

This time the answer came readily enough. "American."

"So? With a name like Sareyan, I had thought you to be Armenian. Of Armenian extraction, perhaps? And who is this lady?"

Who, indeed? thought Julia. But Dikran looked at her and replied, "She's Julia."

Adnan nodded. "So. She is Julia. And who do you think I am?"

"How should I know?" snapped Dikran fretfully. "What's the matter with me?"

"You have a slight touch of sunstroke, Mr. Saint, that is all, I am glad to inform you."

"*Sunstroke?* But the sun's not hot! I wasn't out very long!"

"None the less, sunstroke is what you have. The sun here is treacherous, when the wind blows especially, as today. Our air here on Dendros is so very clear that the ultraviolet rays come through like laser beams and can knock you cockeyed before you realize what is going on. Your case is by no means uncommon, if that is any comfort to you, Mr. Saint. Every summer, we have visitors suffering from this."

"Will he be all right?" Julia murmured anxiously. But the doctor's air of imperturbable confidence was already doing her good.

"Sure, he will be all right! His blood pressure is up a little. I will give him now an injection to fix that, and to relieve his anxiety. It will make him sleep. He will sleep maybe five hours, then he will be right as rain, Mrs. Saint, don't you worry. He will just have to take things easy for a few days. Now just pull your pants down, if you please, Mr. Saint, and lie on your side on the bed."

Obediently Dikran moved to the bedroom and did so. Julia, following, watched the doctor administer what looked like a massive injection. "Largactil I give him, also Catapresan. Now also I leave you some pills, Mrs. Saint, which you make him take in two hours, in four hours, and last thing tonight before he goes to sleep. Furthermore, I think it advisable he stay in bed maybe thirty-six hours, and no alcohol at all, please, during that time. Is he a heavy drinker?"

"No, I would say moderate," Julia replied, thinking really how little she knew about Dikran's habits.

"Well, not even moderation for the time being, I beg!"

Julia accepted the pills and looked at Dikran, who was already lying back, his eyelids beginning to flicker drowsily and a more tranquil expression relaxing his aquiline features.

"You'll see; he will be asleep in two shakes," the doctor prophesied cheerfully, and led Julia back into the other room. "Now I am going to suggest," he went on in a lower tone, "that we transfer your husband to my clinic, and you too, if you wish, Mrs. Saint, for a few days. You stay in Dendros how long?"

"We have been here two weeks and are staying another fortnight."

"In the clinic he can be under my own observation and also have continual nursing care if necessary, until he is better, which is not so easy in a hotel. Better that way for you also— you are not tied to his bedside all the time. You agree?"

"Oh, I'm not sure—I don't mind looking after him—" Julia felt rather desperately that she was being hustled into an unknown situation.

"Naturally, naturally you want to look after him! You are on your honeymoon, yes? It is a most upsetting experience for you."

"Did you *guess?*" She blushed with annoyance, meeting his intelligent, plum-black eyes.

"No, Mrs. Saint. Or should I say, Lady Julia? I am not psychic! But I read the English papers. For quite a few years I was living in England, in Yorkshire to be precise; the *Sunday Times* and the *Observer* make me very nostalgic. And I recognize you at once as Lady Julia Gibbon. (May I now say that I greatly admire your work?)"

"Thank you," she murmured mechanically, trying to overcome a feeling of depression. Wherever one went, it caught up. No use trying to escape.

"Lady Julia Gibbon last month marries an American millionaire," said Dr. Adnan gaily, "and what more natural than to find the happy pair in our lovely island of Dendros, enjoying a peaceful honeymoon far from all the nuisance and turbulence of civilization? It is too bad that a small mischance like this should come to afflict you, but do not worry unduly; we shall soon have your husband again as fit as a flea."

He smiled at her with a flash of large, perfect teeth, and her spirits lifted again, as irrationally as they had sunk. In spite of his slightly odd and florid turn of phrase, Dr. Adnan did inspire confidence in her. There seemed genuine goodwill and friendliness under his aplomb.

"So do not you think it best if you remove to my clinic?" he repeated.

"Your clinic? Do you really think that necessary?" she temporized. The thought of having to shift from the comfortable Fleur de Lys to a strange clinic, with all its rules and prohibitions, was very disagreeable.

"My dear Lady Julia." Now the plum-dark eyes were suffused with sympathy and friendly understanding. "I know how you must be feeling, believe me! You have suffered already from most distressing publicity. A horrible divorce ends what were, I am sure, many, many years of happy married life. And then what? You find and marry a kind, rich man, who will take care, provide, cherish, look after all things. Your distress is allayed. And what then? He is stricken down by sunstroke, becomes, all of a sudden, like a baby. Once more you have all upon your shoulders. What a singularly demoralizing shock, just when all seemed set for comfort and security! But do not be so troubled. I assure you with all sincerity that your husband will soon be quite okay again. Only—in the meantime—how much better, do you not see, if he and you both are in the care of my clinic? He must necessarily sleep for many hours, during which you are alone and miserable in this Victorian dump of a hotel. Whereas in my clinic you have company, you have the music, you have *me*, to keep an eye on you—for I can see that you are suffering from shock, almost as much as the unlucky Mr. Saint. It is a very distressing experience that you have undergone."

"The music—?" She was bewildered. "What music? You mean—?"

"Ah—you did not know? I see you there several nights at the concerts, I thought you had known already. Yes, I run the medical side of Helikon, and my friend Joop Kolenbrander, he runs the musical side; and there, my dear Lady Julia, you shall be very welcome; we shall find a nice room for you and your husband, an orderly to sit by his bed and keep an eye on him, and this very evening you can be listening to the Haydn baryton trios, knowing that he is in good care instead of sitting here in this dismal room biting your nails with worry and loneliness. Does not this seem to you a sensible plan?"

It did, and tears pricked in Julia's eyes at his kindness. "You're perfectly right. I'll start packing right away."

"I'll phone at seven to see whether he has yet woken; and if he has, I will immediately send one of the clinic cars for you both. May I say"—Dr. Adnan contrived a neat, friendly bow while at the same time swiftly and tidily repacking his medical bag—"May I say how very honored we shall be by your residence at Helikon, Lady Julia? Perhaps while you are there our little repertory company might celebrate by performing an act from one of your beautiful plays? We should be very happy if you would consider permitting that?"

"Oh, I'm not certain—I'd really rather not have it known that I'm there—" she replied vaguely.

"Of course, of course not, just as you wish—"

Julia was wondering if the clinic was outrageously expensive—but of course such considerations were quite irrelevant, a thing of the past, out-of-date hang-ups from her previous life. The size of the clinic's fee was immaterial; Dikran could pay it with as little thought as he gave to the purchase of a concert ticket. An aged joke wandered back into her mind: "However much that doggie in the window costs, I can afford it."

"Till this evening, then," Adnan said, with another bow, another admiring glance; and he walked softly from the room.

He need not have taken such pains to be quiet, Julia reflected; Dikran was by now in a profound sleep. She covered him carefully with a cellular blanket from the closet and sat down in one of the armchairs, moving it so that she could see Dikran through the open bedroom door. She would have liked to be able to read and lose herself in a book for a couple of hours, but she had finished her own supply of paperbacks and Dikran had brought nothing but a history of gold in world financial markets, which proved totally unintelligible to her. She found a rumpled overseas *Telegraph* in the bottom of the closet and read that, but it lasted her only a short time, since she found herself unable to face the more depressing items, of which there were many, such as Yet Another Strike at Chrysler Plant, $4,000,000 Kidnapped Rittenhouse Baby Found Dead in Manhattan Basement, and Three-thousand-ton Tanker Aground on Ushant.

She decided to pack up their belongings, and was in the bathroom collecting Dikran's toilet things when he called out in a frightened voice, "Where are you?"

She went swiftly to his bedside, saying, "Here I am! It's all right!"

Taking his hand, she sat down on the bed. She was not sure if he realized who she was, but her presence seemed to soothe him; he soon sank back into a peaceful slumber. She remained sitting by him on the bed for ten minutes or so, gently smoothing the strong, thick black hair with its faint sprinkling of silver, while her memory, rebelling against discipline, conjured up for her other rooms and other beds.

Two difficult tears found their way down her cheeks.

But Dikran slept again, and presently she called Room Service and asked for a sandwich and a glass of wine.

{ 3 }

IMPROMPTU

I stood on the observation deck of the good ship *Monty Python*—which was carrying nine hundred assorted school kids along the Mediterranean to Ephesus, Heraklion, Rhodes, and other educational spots—gazing down thoughtfully into the bows and wondering what would be the best way of breaking to Mother the unpalatable news that she was not going to be allowed to take up her duties at Market Broughton School again for at least another two months.

The high sides of the Corinth Canal were sliding past us like giants' layer cake on either side. Down below, on the red-ochre foredeck, sailors darted about in a beautiful display of choreographic elegance and discipline, winding windlasses and arranging snowy-white ropes, getting the ship ready for Piraeus. The sight of their blue-clad forms against the red-brown background, among the dazzling white machinery and ropes, proved, as always, so distracting and enchanting that it prevented me from getting to grips with my problem.

Behind me Ted Toomey, the sports director, was giving a Yoga class to a batch of sixth formers.

"Breathe upward. Now downward. Now sideways. Now backward. Fill the bottom of your lungs with air," he said. "Now the middle. Now the top. Feel the air creep right up to your collarbones."

I followed his advice myself. The air crept up to my collarbones, but brought no intelligent ideas with it.

After a while Ted told his group to relax for five minutes, and came to lean on the rail by me.

"How's your mother today?" he inquired kindly.

"She's getting better all the time. It's quite fantastic how much progress she has been making! That's what's worrying me. Now she's beginning to feel all conscientious and responsible again, she hates being idle, and she's starting to make remarks about getting back to work."

It had been easy at first.

Grateful—as well they might be—for Mother's not having died when the concrete beam fell on her head and for her not even having been blinded, paralyzed, crippled for life, or showing signs of intending to sue them for negligence and parsimony, the Stretfordshire County Council Education Department had offered—indeed practically forced on Mother—a free cabin on one of their educational cruise ships, plus free accommodation for companion-attendant (me) as soon as she was recovered enough to travel—which turned out to be about five weeks after her accident.

At the time this was fixed up, Mother was still in a docile, comatose state, under a bit of sedation; she seemed quite pleased, for once in her hardworking life, to be looked after, cosseted, and planned for. "Everyone is so kind," she kept saying dreamily, as if she hadn't earned every scrap of their conscience-stricken attention and solicitude. One of the governors lent his Daimler to drive us from Stretford to Tilbury Dock, the others made sure that our cabin was supplied with books, magazines, flowers, fruit enough for a battalion of fruit-eating bats, mohair traveling rugs, portable radios, battery irons, and

all the luxuries that mean and uninventive bureaucracy, racking its brains, could summon up. For the first couple of weeks
on the *Monty Python,* while we whacked our way through the
chilly Bay of Biscay and around the coasts of Spain and Por-
tugal, this served well enough. Mother slept a great deal and
was content to rest on her bed most of the time while I read
aloud the works of Jane Austen to her.

"Are you sure this isn't a terrible bore for you, my dear
child?" she would say from time to time. "I feel anxious about
your being away from your job for so long."

But I had been able to show her letters from Eve Kransky
about the success of our production, and the clippings from
the Kent *Messenger* and other papers, even a letter from a
London manager, which had made my heart beat high when I
received it, for he asked if I'd be interested in doing some
work with his company and invited me to go and have a talk
with him sometime.

"Eve's keeping my job for me, that's all quite okay," I told
Mother. "And I've got other irons in the fire too, so don't you
fret; just concentrate on getting better. I'm planning to enjoy
this time off. And I shan't get bored. I'll do some work with
the kids to keep my hand in."

In fact, during some of the hours she spent napping, I had
organized various theater workshops and a shipboard performance of *The Tempest,* which we scraped together in record
time, cutting huge chunks and doubling parts. All things considered, it might have been worse. So Mother's anxieties in that
respect were allayed. Provided she was satisfied that I was
usefully occupied and acquiring professional experience in one
form or another, she felt that all was well with me.

In fact, I was missing my Crowbridge friends a good deal
and did, from time to time, feel lonely and cut off, but, what
the hell! it was only for two months. And my improved relationship with Mother was a continual source of satisfaction
and amazement. It could no longer be called a parent-child
bond—that, I supposed, was gone for good—but it was growing into a cautiously affectionate (if simply based on day-to-

day needs) link between two adults. Jane Austen and our joint
purpose of getting Mother well again were all we had in common, and that was just enough.

But Mother's reviving urge to return to work created a com-
plication.

The consultant at Stretford, and another who had been
fetched in from London, had been highly categorical about
the undesirability of her trying to do too much too soon. "A
headmistress's position is one of constant pressure and strain—
need for making decisions every minute of the day—long
hours—dealing with hundreds of people—and so on and so
on."

A letter giving the results of some final tests had been waiting for me at Venice. All was well, apparently, but it declared
unequivocally that she must have at least three months away
before she even began to consider going back to school.

Of course—it was true—they didn't know Mother, whose
toughness had plainly been a surprise to Mr. Wintersmain; but
still, one must defer to experts, you can't just toss their opinion out the window. And indeed it was plain to me that
Mother, although rapidly repossessed of all her intelligence
and clear-thinking capacities, had a long way still to go before
she was really back to normal functioning. Much weaker than
she liked to pretend, she still found it necessary to rest a great
deal, and, in small matters, was much more gentle and biddable
than I had ever known her. It seemed pretty plain to me that
she did in fact need several more months of convalescence.

"What's your plan for her?" Ted asked. "You're not going
home on the second leg of the cruise?"

Stretford County Education Authority organized their six-
week cruises in two halves, so as to make maximum use of the
ship while not taking the students out of school for too long.
One lot of kids had the outward three weeks and were flown
back from Dendros, where the airport was handily close to the
harbor; another lot would have flown out and be waiting
there, ready to embark. I felt fairly certain that Mother would
have had enough and would not wish to revisit any of the

places she had seen; furthermore, if we went back on the *Monty Python,* that would get her back to England too soon to return to work. Added to this, I felt sure that, once she was in England again, it would be almost impossible to restrain her urge to get back into harness. So I had made other arrangements after I received the letter in Venice.

"I've fixed for her to go into Helikon," I told Ted. "And I'm going along too, for a bit, just to get her settled in and keep an eye on her."

"Helikon? What's that? I've heard the name," he said vaguely. "But I thought it was a kind of music center like Tanglewood? Is it on Dendros?"

"Yes, it is. It's a music center and health clinic, both. They have music and drama festivals there, and students can work— they have regular seminars—but there's also a big residential clinic where people are treated for all kinds of ailments—lung and rheumatic troubles, or ulcers, or blood conditions, or overweight, or alcoholism, or heart diseases—or, like Mother, people just go there to recuperate after illness and accidents. The music and stuff is going on all the time, and the public are allowed in to the concerts and dramatic performances, so it's becoming quite a tourist attraction to the island."

"It's an odd combination—music and medicine?" Ted's round, good-natured face looked a little puzzled.

"Not at all," I said firmly. "Lots of civilizations have mixed music with healing. Aesculapius said music was a cure for many ills. The Babylonians used to cure their mad people by music—primitive tribes do still. So I'm hoping that Mother will find the combination soothing and beneficial."

She had, I knew, a kind of brisk, no-nonsense fondness for the more cheerful, less introspective areas of classical music— Haydn symphonies and piano sonatas, Beethoven quartets (the early ones), the Brandenburg concertos, most of Mozart. I thought—hoped—that she would find enough at Helikon to keep her contented. At one time, long ago, she had played quite a competent violin, and had enjoyed amateur chamber music, but she had found less and less time for such activities during her climb up the educational ladder, and her violin had long since been put away; I could not remember even seeing it during the time I was staying in her house.

"Who founded this Helikon place?" Ted asked. "Has it been going long?"

"Eight or nine years, I think. It was founded by a famous pianist, Max Benovek—do you remember him?"

Ted said yes, but I was not sure if I believed him. However, he then added, "Benovek. Didn't he die, or something?" looking a bit more intelligent.

"He died, yes; he had leukemia, I believe. But before he died he had an unexpected long remission, and during that time he had the idea to start this place—probably doing so gave him an extra lease of life, gave him something to take his mind off his illness. So he lived in Dendros for a while and oversaw its beginnings. Some local Greek Croesus helped with a lot of cash —it's a fine thing for the island, of course. Gives quite a bit of employment and brings tourists. Benovek was a rich man himself and did a lot. He paid the medical director's salary and endowed funds for poor students, and so forth."

"Who's the medical director?"

"A very outgoing Turkish doctor called Adnan—Achmed Mustafa Adnan." I smiled a little at the thought of him. "It's due to him that the diet at Helikon is vegetarian."

"How come you know so much about this place?" Ted wanted to know.

"I've worked there, when they were holding seminars, in three different summers; washing up and doing odd jobs in exchange for drama classes. They get first-rate people there, because it's such a lovely place. And of course, if you are working, you get to see and hear everything that's going on."

It had been Calliope's idea the first time; she had written to suggest it, so that I would have an excuse to go back to Dendros. We had both worked up at Helikon, which was not far from the Agnhnides' house. And that time had been so good that I had returned twice more, despite Mother's slight disapproval, and even after Calliope had married her cousin

Dmitri and had gone off to live in Elizabeth, New Jersey. The first year on my own, I had stayed with Calliope's parents, but after her mother died, and her father became very old and frail, I moved into the center itself and became quite closely acquainted with several of the staff. Adnan was also a friend of the Aghnides family. So it had been easy enough to arrange for Mother's admission, in spite of the fact that the clinic was always booked up for months in advance.

"Well, that sounds a very good plan," said Ted, turning to give his group the office to collect up their muscles and put themselves vertical. "I'd have thought from the sound that it was the ideal place to convalesce—sun and air and music and fruit and so on. And a vegetarian diet ought to suit your Mother? What are you worried about?"

"It's just that Mother's so keen to get back to her school. I'm afraid she may jib when she hears about it. I haven't broken it to her yet. And so far we haven't fallen out over any major issue."

At the start of the trip, comatose and accepting, still under some sedation, she had not asked how long the cruise lasted or when we would get back. I had hoped that this state of mind would endure until we were safely installed at Helikon. Now I was not so sure that it would.

"Above all, don't let her get upset or overexcited," Consett-Smith, the London consultant, had warned me. "Humor her as much as you can in small ways."

I could see breakers ahead.

Another consequence of Consett-Smith's warning was that I had never yet found the courage, or thought the time right, to break to Mother the fact that I had read her not-to-be-opened-till-after-death message about Father. It just did not seem a suitable conversational topic for someone in a delicate state of health.

That lay on my conscience a good deal, but my conscience would have to take care of itself. Her steady recovery was obviously of more importance. Meanwhile, I had put the note into a plain envelope and replaced it among the other papers in the desk. Mother had not, in fact, even been back to the house, since it had been felt that the sight of her home might awaken undesirable cares and responsibilities; she had been driven straight from hospital to dockside and had made no inquiries about any business or personal affairs.

Naturally I had put in a good deal of time wondering about my father—in fact a large proportion of my scanty solitude was employed in this profitless occupation. Could he be in prison? I speculated. In a hospital for incurables? An institution for the mentally incapacitated? Living in disgraced seclusion because of some frightful social offense? What could he have done? Held up a bank? Raped a mother superior? Escaped to Russia with plans for a laser beam strong enough to disintegrate the Kremlin? What was the condition so outrageously shocking that Mother felt my whole mental balance might be endangered to tottering point if I knew about it?

Whatever it was, it could hardly outstrip my imaginings; and I did long to have some plain information on the matter. But obviously this topic came high in the category of things likely to upset or overexcite Mother, and so I had not spoken about it; I tried not even to think about it when I was with her. There it lay, notwithstanding, almost visibly between us, I sometimes thought, like a heavy lump of undigested trouble.

Had Drusilla's suicide, I wondered, been because she knew this terrible thing about Father?

But if Father was alive, why had he never made any attempt to get in touch with me? Had he perhaps given Mother a promise that he would not? If so, *why?* Because she thought it possible I too might kill myself if I knew about him? It seemed almost ludicrously improbable. I am naturally of a hopeful, energetic temperament—I couldn't even imagine wanting to kill myself. And yet Drusilla *had* killed herself—in the most dreadful way, too—or so Gina Signorelli had said and I had no reason to disbelieve her. Oh, Drusilla, my poor sister, how could you have been driven to such an awful step? I mourned inwardly, thinking of her many kindnesses to me, of the strong, determined, adult person she had seemed to me when I was seven or eight. Could she really have done it? Or was it an accident, unintentional? That was another thing I could not possibly ask Mother—at least until she was much more recovered—and yet I felt I had a right to know.

There was one person, though, who might be able to give me information on these matters, and that was Calliope's father, old Demosthenes Aghnides. When Mother had written to the Aghnides asking if I could go on living with them for another year and telling of Drusilla's death, she must have given some explanation for her request, some explanation which at the time had been withheld from me. Now I was resolved to ask for it. I loved Mr. Aghnides, he was one of the people I respected most in the world, and he had always been fond of me; he was a wonderful old man, wise as Socrates and honest as bread; I knew that he would tell me the truth if he thought it right to do so and had the information. Which was another good reason for going to Dendros. I was enormously looking forward to seeing him again.

Meanwhile I read aloud the works of Jane Austen and hoped that no serious showdown would come to disrupt our tranquillity.

It did not come just yet. We saw the factories at Piraeus and the gasworks at Heraklion. We listened to lectures on the city-states and the Persian wars and the Minoan civilization. Mother put on a few pounds in weight and I gave the kids some fencing lessons. And then, on the last evening before we docked at Dendros, the confrontation came, just when I was beginning to feel foolishly secure.

I had fallen into the habit of brewing Mother a mug of Ovaltine or Horlicks last thing at night. There was a small, unused stewards' pantry next door to our cabin, where I was able to cook up snacks; service on the boat was a bit sketchy, since it was primarily a utility cruise for the kids.

Mother began to sip her milk that evening and then said placidly, "I've been thinking, dear, that I'll fly back with the group who go home direct from Dendros. I don't want to waste another three weeks going back on the ship, I've had enough time off already—and you've wasted quite enough of *your* time looking after me—sweet of you though it has been, don't think me ungrateful—"

"Oh, but you can't—" I began, appalled.

"And why not, pray?"

Mother was still quite placid, a long distance from the kind of high-strung outrage she would once have generated if I had ventured on a flat negative like that. But she sounded uncommonly firm and definite.

"Well, for one thing, because Mr. Wintersmain absolutely forbade you to travel in a plane for nine months to a year after your operation. And you have to check with him first, then. Had you forgotten that?"

Plainly she *had* forgotten; or more probably, at the time when he laid it down, she had been in such a drowsy, sedated state that she hadn't really taken it in.

I saw a look of acute distress come over her face—quite obviously she was wondering what other important information had slipped past her during that time, before she was alert enough to take hold. I felt a pang of sympathy for her. Poor dear, she was used to being so independent and decisive—and she still looked so frail and vulnerable. Apart from anything else, her hair was taking a long time to grow back, in spite of the fact that I cautiously massaged her scalp every night with olive oil and various patent preparations. She now had a sort of golden-gray fuzz that made her look piteously like a day-old chick. Since she was outraged at the suggestion of wearing a wig, I had made her several head-hugging turbans out of black jersey, and she wore them all the time. They seemed oddly formal on the ship, and made her, with her large eyes and high cheekbones, look like some distinguished, not to say formidable, character out of Russian literature. The close frame of black strongly accentuated every shade of expression of her bony, lowland features.

She said, frowning a little and compressing her lips, "Well, I certainly don't wish to stay on this ship for another three weeks."

"No, I hadn't thought you'd wish to do that—"

"What, then, if I can't fly?" she said sharply. "Can we get a train back from Athens?"

"We might do that presently, perhaps. We'll see! But honestly, love, you aren't quite well enough for long train journeys yet—think how tired you are by the end of the day. So I've fixed for us to stay a few weeks at Helikon," I said cheerfully.

But her face had turned the color of burned paper—a kind of bluish white. I watched, hypnotized, as her fingers loosened their grasp and the glass of malted milk, slipping out of them, dolloped its gluey contents over the brown carpet. I was just in time to catch her before she slumped forward out of her chair in a dead faint.

Somehow I managed to get her hoisted onto her bunk, and then phoned through in a frenzy for the ship's doctor, who came like lightning, bless his heart. He was a young, cheerful character who rejoiced in the improbable name of Dr. Albumblatt; he had been extremely kind and solicitous with his regular check-up visits throughout the voyage, having been heavily briefed, I suppose, by the board of governors and the county education department.

Thank goodness he was fairly reassuring, after he had made a careful examination of her. She was still unconscious. "Nothing the matter that I can find. She's still barely convalescent, don't forget. You say she was upset after hearing that she's not allowed to fly?"

"I suppose it might have been that."

"Might easily. She's a woman of strong character, your mother. Mortified at finding that she's not up to doing something she'd set her heart on. Don't you think that might be it?"

"I suppose it might," I said, wishing guiltily that the news had not come as such a last-minute surprise, that I had not led up to it more carefully.

"To find there's something that's physically beyond her—

after having led such an active, independent life—very upsetting."

"I shouldn't have let it come as such a shock," I lamented.

"You didn't know she'd forgotten she wasn't allowed to fly. Nor did you know what she was planning. Don't blame yourself. She'll get over it. Look, I'll give her a tranquilizing injection now. That will ensure her a quiet night. Then, when we reach Dendros, I'll phone the clinic to send an ambulance, and the whole move from ship to clinic can be carried out while she's still sedated, so as to upset her as little as possible. By the time she wakes up, she'll be there, snugly installed. Don't you think that's a good plan?"

It was certainly the easiest plan for me, though I felt very bad about poor Mother, once more practically kidnaped. She had accepted the cruise with great docility, but would she be so good-natured about Helikon? In spite of my longing to get her there and into Dr. Adnan's care, I felt it was unfair to her, though I knew Albumblatt meant it for the best.

"Well—I suppose you're right," I said slowly.

"Of course I am right," he said.

So he gave her the injection. I suppose things would have turned out very differently if I had not allowed him to do that.

{ 4 }

BOURRÉE

The room allotted to Dikran and Julia at Helikon was, by
Hotel Fleur de Lys standards, fairly austere. But it was comfortable enough. There were plain, low, flat twin beds, each of
them simply a mattress set in a kind of wooden box. There
were two plain Scandinavian armchairs, a writing desk, and a
chest of drawers fitted against the wall. No balcony, but two
windows, each with a window seat. An abstract picture on the
wall and a plain, thin carpet. There was a tiny bathroom,
functional but highly utilitarian.

Julia wondered how Dikran, accustomed all his life to luxury, would react to it when he woke. But Dikran was still
asleep.

The outlook, though, was superior, she had to admit, kneeling on the window seat and leaning out to catch the early-
morning air, which was deliciously fresh. Their two windows
were at right angles, facing different ways. The one from
which she was looking faced out over a stretch of intensively
cultivated hillside, beyond which lay the sea. On her right

grew a large and beautiful lemon orchard. Straight ahead the terraced vegetable beds dropped down the hillside, then came a narrow blacktop road, then a section of tomato plants protected from the wind by thick screens of reeds. Then a strip of beach, then the sea, today a pure, angelic blue. Across the sea the Turkish coast, far off today, a hazy, floating mirage. To the far right, beyond the lemon grove, a rocky hillside rose up to a saddlebacked headland. The hillside was all a mixture of dark and light foliage among rocks—dark little shapely cypresses like exclamation points rising from some low-growing gray shrub almost the color of lavender. Perhaps it *was* lavender, Julia thought happily. She resolved to go and investigate it at the first opportunity—after breakfast perhaps. If one was allowed breakfast at Helikon?

Dr. Adnan had told her the night before that it was a vegetarian establishment. "You prefer to share fully in our regime, I hope?" he said, strolling back with her after the concert. "Doing so will make you feel more one of our family while you remain here?"

"Certainly," Julia bravely replied, wondering what the regime involved.

"Good! Excellent! We meet at ten tomorrow and I show you round. In the meantime Zoé, our dear warden, will assign you your diet and treatment sheets."

"Do I really have to have *treatments?*" she said anxiously. "After all, I'm not ill!"

"You will be surprised!" He gave her his wide grin—it was beginning to remind her of Mr. Jackson in *The Tale of Mrs. Tittlemouse.* "Aha—you think yourself in perfect health now. But—I can assure you—after three or four days here you will feel so different that you will be sorry for the poor self you brought here, with the big hollows under her eyes and the shaking hands"—he took one, held it a moment, then shook his head at her—"the pain in the back, the stiff neck, the bad dreams, the headaches, the sour taste in the mouth—"

"Stop, stop! All right, I'll take your treatments. I might as well, I suppose, while Dikran is recovering."

"Valiant lady! You will enjoy them, you will see. There is nothing at all to fear."

Just the same, she had gone to bed somewhat apprehensive, slept badly, worrying about Dikran, and waked early, wondering what the day's program held in store. She felt as nervous as on her first arrival at boarding school.

Ravished by the sudden sound of music, she looked around for its source and moved to the other window, which faced out, rather unexpectedly, into the quadrangle of Christchurch College, Oxford, England.

"Or, at any rate, as near as we could get it," Dr. Adnan had explained cheerfully. "We left out one side of the quadrangle, firstly to give a sight of the sea, secondly because we ran out of money. The quadrangle was the idea of Mr. Capranis, a local landowner who has endowed us very handsomely—indeed he gave all the land that the clinic stands on. The Christchurch layout was his idea; he is very attached to Oxford."

"He went to one of the colleges?"

"No, his first car was a Morris. It gave him a curiosity to go and see the place. And he liked it."

"The quadrangle seems very much at home here," Julia remarked thoughtfully. "I suppose, when one remembers that the design of English colleges is based on early ecclesiastical architecture—"

"And that the early religious orders modeled their monasteries on forts and crusaders' castles—just so!"

"It's not surprising that it fits so well into this landscape. Though I *am* surprised that you have got grass to grow in your quadrangle."

"Well, we are lucky to have a spring behind the clinic that seldom dries up. Very good water! There is a most pretty path up the little valley—trees and waterfalls and nightingales. You must by no means neglect to take that walk. But in midsummer, I must confess, our grass does not always survive. We do have, though, a fish in our fountain—very proper, just like the one in your Mercury pond at Oxford."

Looking out now, Julia could see an early-rising contingent of recorder players perched around the rim of the Mercury pond, playing some cheerful music by Handel, while a trio of dancers performed a series of intricate modern dance movements, standing on one spot close together and achieving their effects by skillful, controlled leanings and bendings. The statue of Mercury, waving his broken staff in the middle of the pond, seemed anxious to join them. "They look like willows," Julia thought. "Perhaps that is the intention." And then, "I'm going to like staying at Helikon, I think."

A light tap on the door deflected her attention from the dancers.

Dikran still slept. She went to open the door quietly and discovered that two cards had been tucked into the metal slot on the outside. They were marked with the day's date and, respectively, MR. D. SAINT and LADY JULIA SAINT. Mr. D. Saint's said simply: "Bedrest. Massage. Consultant, Dr. A. Mustafa Adnan." Julia's had a whole lot of hieroglyphics which were meaningless to her, and presumably denoted various kinds of treatment. There was a square at the bottom marked *Diet*, which on both cards had the figure 1 added in ink.

Dikran stirred, mumbled something incomprehensible, and opened an eye. Julia went to him quickly. "Hullo, darling! How are you feeling today?"

He had waked briefly the previous night, had submitted in a somnambulistic way to being dressed and driven to Helikon, had swallowed a glass of fruit juice, and, as soon as he was back in bed, had fallen again into a profound and apparently restorative sleep. A student had been told off to sit by him, with orders to summon Adnan at once if he stirred or seemed distressed, while Julia, guilty but relieved, attended the Haydn concert. But the boy's report when she returned was that her husband had never moved, and he had passed the rest of the night in the same womblike repose.

Now he was looking very much better, and more like the man with whom she had so lightheartedly started on her honeymoon. His dark eyes had regained their flash, and his mouth its firm line. But this appearance of being in control was considerably impaired when he looked around the Spartan little room in which he found himself. "Hey?" he demanded, staring about in astonished disbelief. "What's going on? What the devil's happened? Where are we?"

"Don't you remember?"

"Remember what?"

"You don't remember what happened yesterday?"

"We drove up to Skimi and then went on and had lunch at that fish place—Kalkos—Kalikos—"

"No, that was the day before, darling. Today is Thursday."

"*What?* . . . What do you mean?"

For a long time he refused to believe what she told him—that he had completely lost a day. He almost flew into a rage over it. But finally the plain fact that here they were, in completely new surroundings, vanquished him into a kind of grudging acceptance that *something* untoward must have happened.

His reaction then seemed strange to Julia. His main emotion, she thought, was terror—not so much of what had happened to him, but of what *might* have happened—what he might have done in his amnesiac state.

"It was perfectly all right, darling," Julia kept reassuring him—poor dear, perhaps he was afraid he might have committed some act of undignified folly—"I was with you almost the whole time, and you didn't do anything silly. You just seemed very miserable and confused."

Then she remembered that in fact she had *not* been with him yesterday morning, when, it seemed, from the evidence of his *espadrilles* and swimming trunks, he had gone out on the beach and perhaps swum—but she resolved to minimize this part of the episode, since the thought of it seemed to upset him so much.

"What caused it? What happened to me?" he kept saying.

"Well, Dr. Adnan thought you probably fell asleep on our balcony at the Fleur de Lys and were in the sun for too long. It's very sheltered there, it could have been really hot, out of the wind."

"But that's very frightening—very frightening!" he muttered, staring past her, out the window. "Now there's a part of my life that will always be hidden from me. I shall never know what happened."

Julia soothed him as best she could, and so did Adnan when he came in for a morning visit, but all their reassurances left Dikran only half satisfied. Julia was glad to escape from his anxieties for a little and slip away for her promised tour of inspection, leaving Dikran in the hands of a masseur.

Adnan had arranged to meet her in the quadrangle and, while waiting for him, she amused herself by studying a large number of statues that were placed around the rim of the lawn. Not much attempt had been made to choose pieces in keeping with the island's classic past; the statues were mostly ornate products of the nineteenth century, and she could only assume that they had been selected as examples for patients to aim at; the females tended to opulent bosoms and improbably sylphlike waists, the males bulged with muscle and virility. Here Hercules grappled with the Hydra, there Psyche simpered over a dove. Centaurs galloped, nymphs held modest, protecting hands over their exposed persons, gods and goddesses adopted strenuously athletic positions. Somehow she suspected that they had all been chosen by Dr. Adnan.

"Ah, here you are! I am sorry I keep you waiting," he said, bustling up to her. Today he was even more elegantly dressed, in a white denim suit with remarkable piping. There was something about it that reminded Julia of mashers in the eighteen nineties.

"Now—our concert hall you have already several times visited, so I will not take you there," he went on, waving a hand toward the impressive building at the upper end of the quadrangle. "I proceed. This wing to the right is all sound-proof practice rooms for the musicians and dancers—" he flung open a door and displayed a monastic cell with nothing but a piano and a music stand. Another room beyond it, somewhat bigger, contained a *barre* and a floor-length mirror across one wall.

"Small recital hall here—lecture hall—two classrooms, which can also be joined by removing a partition."

All these rooms were in vigorous use. A string quartet was practicing a modern piece in the recital hall, four singers were attempting Barber's *Hand of Bridge* in the lecture hall, accompanied by a single, harassed-looking pianist, a mime class was being conducted in one of the classrooms, and two jugglers were seriously working in the other.

"Now we go below," Adnan said. "What you have seen so far is only the tip of the iceberg."

He led her to the northeast corner of the quadrangle and down a flight of stone steps, following a sign that said TREATMENT AREAS and a pointing arrow.

At the foot of the steps they entered a large, cool, circular stone hall brilliantly illuminated by concealed strip lighting. A carved marble font in the middle was wreathed in ferns and creepers. Twenty or so benches, wide and low and comfortably upholstered in white leather substitute, were disposed against the curving walls. In between these, passages led off in all directions, and a loudspeaker system was in operation.

"Mr. Klint to physiotherapy, please."

"Mrs. Helstron, Mrs. Psaros, Miss Jones, Mme. Jardine, to sauna."

"Herr Schneider for a mud bath, please."

"Mr. Kefauver for radiotherapy."

"Mrs. Mandelbaum for a wax bath."

"Miss McGregor for acupuncture."

"Mme. Beck for ultrasonic ray."

Around the walls, on the white seats, patients in terry-cloth robes sat waiting for their calls. The atmosphere was relaxed and cheerful. They chatted, read, the women knitted, children played on the floor. Some faces there were familiar, some were even famous. Julia recognized an English poet (as famous for his alcoholism as for his poetry), an Italian operatic tenor, and two members of the National Theatre Company. A pair of students, sitting cross-legged with their backs against the font, played softly on flute and guitar; the sound of their playing filtered gently away into the cavernous space.

Every minute, patients came and went to their various appointments.

"It seems extremely well organized," Julia said.

"We have now a computer," Adnan told her proudly. "Our local benefactor, Mr. Capranis, gave us that; it cuts down the waiting time. So patients seldom have more than ten minutes between one treatment and the next. If they *should* by chance have longer—then they can go upstairs and listen to somebody's recital, or watch a dance practice—or just sit in the sun."

"How civilized that is!" Julia thought of gloomy hours spent in the out-patient departments of English hospitals.

"Now, if you like, I show you some of the treatments," Adnan said, and led off along one of the passages, which were distinguished by numbers. The passage he selected was Number Three, which, according to a sign, led to Inhalation, Wax Baths, Sauna, and Steam Baths. It took them, after a short walk, into a large, pillared region with a vaulted roof that was painted mustard yellow. The whole area was divided into cubicles of variable sizes by painted wooden screens. The atmosphere was warm and steamy, and smelt of soap and eucalyptus. Heavy rubber cables trailed and looped hither and thither. The colors of the screens, Julia noticed, were the same as those used on the Greek houses—brilliant, powdery blues, dazzling greens and lilacs and pinks. They, and the smell of eucalyptus, contributed a gay nursery-like air to the scene, which was completely different from the treatment areas of a hospital. Carefree, youthful-looking attendants in white smocks darted in and out among the screens. Uninhibited sounds came from all about the unseen regions—cheerful yells as patients encountered the heat of sauna or steam bath, the cold of shower or seaweed; splashes of water; the vigorous slip-slap, pummeling sound of massage; scraps of talk and expostulations:

"Take care, Mrs. Carmichael, that's my gouty toe!"

"Shall I turn over now, Mr. Elkin?"

"Is my five minutes up yet?"

"Hey, that's *cold*—much colder than you gave it to me last time!"

"Oh, how delicious!—can you pour it just a little higher up?"

Everybody seemed to be having a good time.

Julia was shown patients lying on their stomachs, wrapped in hot wax; patients immersed in mud; patients with their lesions being broken up by ultrasonic rays ("We have to be very careful with them," Adnan said. "More than fifty seconds and it melts your bones." Julia resolved on no account to have this treatment and to dissuade Dikran from having it either); patients apparently lying asleep with their exposed torsos stuck full of little bamboo darts.

Passing through the steam-bath area, Dr. Adnan paused by an elderly man who was completely encased in a large white enamel box about the size of a dishwasher. Only his head protruded, with a white towel swathed over it, turbanwise, and another wrapped around his neck and chin.

"*Bonjour, M. Destrier, comment ça va?*" Adnan inquired, and received a flood of French loquacity in return.

Julia moved on a few paces, out of politeness, but looked back with considerable interest.

"Is that *Annibal* Destrier," she inquired when Adnan caught up with her, "the composer?"

"He himself!" Adnan said with tremendous satisfaction. "Is he not a great old boy? He comes to us for a month every spring. This year will be his eighty-fifth birthday, so we plan to do him honor by a performance of one of his operas. A nice idea, no? I hope you remain for it?"

"Well—that depends on how soon you do it, I suppose, and how well my husband gets on. Which opera have you chosen? Will Enrico Gaspari be singing in it? Didn't I notice him back there in the waiting area?"

A slight cloud overshadowed Adnan's brow, she noticed, at this inquiry. He hesitated, then said, "It is not yet finally decided which opera is to be performed. We have difficulties at present. Now—here are Scottish douches. Here, doctors' consulting rooms. And here the stairs which lead to the Yoga and spinal exercise rooms. Such treatments are given aboveground."

They climbed up a different flight of steps into a kind of outside loggia, set about with more statuary and furnished with bamboo tables and chairs.

They were now, Julia realized, on the west side of the quadrangle—the treatment area occupied the whole of the space underneath it.

"We thought it cooler to have treatments underground, since in the summer it is so hot here," Adnan explained.

"Now I see what you mean about the tip of the iceberg."

He looked at his watch (which was amazingly ornate, studded with rubies; doubtless the gift of a grateful patient) and said, "At this hour the patients take their morning refreshment. You care to partake also?"

"Yes, thank you," said Julia, whose breakfast had consisted of a half glass of lemon juice.

"Our regime is small meals, but frequent, so that no one becomes dehydrated," he said seriously.

At one end of the loggia liquid refreshment was being dispensed by Zoé, the warden, whom Julia had already met. She was a pleasant, capable French girl with a round, dark face, upcurving mouth, and short, toffee-brown hair cut in a smooth cap. A marble table in front of her was set out with trays of little glasses and cups. There appeared to be a choice of lemon juice, grape juice, or a dollop of a brown, gluey substance onto which Zoé poured hot water from a huge brass can when requested to do so by a patient. Residents, wearing a motley mix of garments from formal wear to bikinis or bathrobes, assembled in an irregular queue to receive their drinks, and then stood or sat, sipping and chatting in the warm sun.

"What is that brown stuff?" Julia inquired.

"It is a vegetarian composition of my own invention called

Rybomite—highly nutritious and beneficial. It contains no end of vitamin B, besides niacin, riboflavin, and thiamin."

"I'm sure it does," Julia said politely, and chose a glass of grape juice. She noticed that Adnan did likewise.

A stately old lady in a jade-green dressing gown was being pushed toward them in a wheelchair by another patient. She held a cane in her hand, which she waved commandingly at Dr. Adnan.

"Well, *Monsieur le Médecin*, are we going to have *Les Mystères d'Elsinore?* Has Enrico made up his mind yet?" she asked. She had a handsome, vigorous, hawklike face and bright, dark eyes; her white hair hung down her back in a thick plait.

"I have to discuss the matter with Joop, Mme. Athalie," Adnan replied. Julia thought his expression was somewhat evasive.

"What has Enrico decided?"

"Enrico does not wish to take part. He is on the point of leaving us, in fact. So all depends on whether Miss Farrell is able to come to us."

"You must persuade her, *mon cher Docteur!*"

"I will try my best," Adnan said.

A fat little woman was darting about, taking photographs. Julia was reminded by this of Dikran, who hated having his picture taken. "I must be keeping you from all sorts of important tasks," she said to Adnan.

He gave her his brilliant smile. "Please! My dear Lady Julia! What task could be more important than making sure that one of the most beautiful and distinguished visitors who has ever honored our clinic feels thoroughly at home? Besides," he added practically, "our staff are highly efficient; the place runs itself almost without my interference unless some slight crisis should arise."

"Then—if you still have time—I would like to ask you about my husband. Now that you have examined him more thoroughly, do you still think that it was a sunstroke?"

Around the perimeter of the quadrangle there was a wide

path paved with flagstones; having finished their drinks, they turned and paced along it.

"May I, in return, ask you some questions about your husband, Lady Julia? Having examined him more closely, yes, I do still think it was a sunstroke, but it might have been augmented by some kind of shock. But, as to this, I am not able to be more explicit unless I know whether he is very susceptible to shocks. Can you give me a little background about him?"

She remained silent, looking at Adnan with troubled eyes.

To help her, he said gently, "For instance—please forgive my suggesting it if it is wide of the mark—but had you perhaps had some kind of quarrel or dispute before this happening?"

"No *indeed* we hadn't!" she answered in relief. "Unless you count my telling him that he would only be in the way while I was buying presents for my children. But he took that quite placidly."

"Then, we must look further for our explanation. Can you explain him to me a little?"

Somewhat embarrassed, she replied, "No, that's the trouble, you see. I can't. I really know very little about him. We have been married only four weeks. And before that, we had known each other only another month—which we did not spend together, though we were seeing each other very often."

"How did you come to meet?" he inquired, still in the same kind, quiet, solicitous manner. Since she remained silent, he added, "All that I know of you, Lady Julia, I read in the papers. I know that you were married for many happy years to the art critic Arnold Gibbon, that suddenly you are divorced because he wishes to marry the wife of a Labor peer—Lord Plumtree. So, without protest, you allow your husband his divorce, and he keeps the children too—which is uncommon, surely? Now that I see you, I understand this a little better, I think; I see that you are a gentle, chivalrous person who will not fight for your rights even in such a case of flagrant injustice. But still—*why* did you not fight for those rights?"

"Oh—" she said. "Various reasons. The children are nearly grown up in any case, they will soon be out in the world—I can see them when I like—I didn't want any more disgusting publicity and fuss, I wanted the whole thing over quickly—"

"Your ex-husband must be a remarkably undiscerning person," Dr. Adnan remarked with asperity. "I saw the pictures of his new wife when they were married—pffah!" He emitted an unreproducible noise of scorn. "A bourgeois British pig-blonde!—However, that is not to the purpose. You did not then agree to a divorce for your own ends?" And, as she looked puzzled, he added, "Because you had already encountered Mr. Saint?"

"My goodness, *no!*" She sounded completely taken aback by this idea, as if it had never entered her head that anyone might hold such a notion. "No, I didn't meet Dikran until after I was divorced."

"And—permit me to ask again—how *did* you meet?"

"Why," she replied slowly, blushing a little, "it was a pickup, really."

"Indeed? You surprise me!"

"We were both at a concert in the Elizabeth Hall. I'd moved out of Palace Gate—out of my husband's house—into a service flat. I was pretty lonely and miserable—I used to go to concerts almost every night, to cheer myself up. Didn't feel like seeing my friends. And, at this one, Dikran—Mr. Saint—happened to be sitting in front of me, and he dropped an envelope on the floor when he was getting program notes out of his pocket. He wasn't aware that he had dropped it, but I noticed it, so I picked it up and gave it to him—I was charmed by his name on the envelope, Dikran Salvador Saint—and made some remark about it—he was polite and grateful; it turned out that the envelope contained a very valuable stamp —he collects stamps among lots of other things—so he asked me to come and have a drink in the interval and—and we never went back for the second half of the concert."

"So you became acquainted. He will have recognized you and known who you were, I presume?"

"I—I'm not really sure," she said. "Well, of course, we soon exchanged names—so then he knew—and he asked me out to lunch next day, he knew by that time. I suppose he'd read about the case . . . I don't know," she ended, rather unhappily. "We didn't talk about that. We were both fond of music, we were both lonely—Dikran's first wife died years ago and he has no children, he couldn't have children—so we just gravitated together."

"Very natural," Adnan said. But then he added, "You did not feel he was drawn to you because you were a rich and well-known woman, several of whose plays have been performed in the West End? This was not your attraction for him?"

"Well—perhaps—a little," she said, deliberating in her mind with slow, careful honesty. "But not from the worldly or financial point of view! Dikran is a very rich man himself, absolutely rolling in money, in fact. He's certainly not a fortune hunter. Since we've been married he hasn't even allowed me to to buy a packet of cigarettes. Up to yesterday."

"Indeed. Then you must forgive me for making such an ungallant inquiry. Irrelevant, too," he added. "No man who had seen your face would bother his head about your income." Julia blushed again. "Now," he pursued, "if it is not too prying—from what does your husband derive his wealth? Is it inherited? A business empire? Or what?"

"You'll find this almost incredible," she said. "I'm afraid you'll think me very dumb—but I simply don't know. I have a vague idea that he has a good many different business interests, mostly in America—so I suppose it is a kind of empire. I know it must seem uncommonly ignorant and unenterprising of me not to have found out—but Dikran is very uncommunicative about things like that. He came from an Armenian family, you see, and I suppose they have quite oriental ideas about the things that are and are not discussed with women. At any rate, he never *has* discussed his business affairs with me."

"So, for all you know, he is a leader of the Mafia," Adnan said cheerfully.

Julia laughed.

"Well—what kind of a man is he?" Adnan pursued. "If not about money—then, what *do* you talk about?"

The look he gave her was both quizzical and intent; for a moment, the space between them was heavily polarized by sexual currents. But then Julia said coolly, "Well—music a good deal; he's very knowledgeable about it. And my plays, which he has seen; he's interested in the theater. Books—poetry—Dikran writes poetry himself."

"Any good?" Adnan inquired briskly.

Really, he has a lot of *chutzpah*, this Dr. Adnan, Julia thought, why do I allow him to grill me like this about Dikran? But she had to admit that his intention seemed perfectly benevolent and disinterested; she answered in a moderate and considering tone, "Yes. Yes I think it is rather good."

"Not published, however?"

"He's never even bothered to try. He didn't need to. He just wrote for his own pleasure. But of course I know a good many English publishers. I'm going to show some of his work to— What is all this *about?*" she demanded, turning to face Adnan.

"Just trying to acquire a little background to the problem," he replied imperturbably, giving her a sphinxlike smile. "So, what it amounts to, really, is that you know precious little about your Mr. Saint—except in honeymoon terms; you cannot therefore be expected to predict how he may behave in a situation of stress."

"No—not really," she agreed, strolling on. "I think I'd expect him to be quite tough—after all, he has either made or kept a very large fortune."

"True. You have not, however, seen him with business colleagues or employees? Does he have a house in England?"

"No, just a service flat in a big London block. He told me he has a house in Iowa—or do I mean Illinois?—I always get those American states mixed. But he doesn't seem to spend much time there and I haven't been over yet. Well, there hasn't been time."

"Of course not! It is a whirlwind romance. So, while he is honeymooning, this empire looks after itself? He does not make long-distance phone calls? Display anxiety about it?"

"Not in the least. But he does display a great deal of anxiety about his present state: he gave me to understand that he feels he simply can't afford to get into amnesiac conditions."

"This I can readily understand. So do most of us feel, but especially so a man who runs many large and complicated affairs. Though probably he has the least need to worry, having, no doubt, many capable subordinates."

"I suppose so," she said doubtfully. "Do you think this state is likely to recur? That's what worries him, of course."

"No—I do not think it at all," Adnan said. "Knowing so little of him makes it less easy to predict, but his general health is evidently good; physically he is in excellent shape. In better shape, I should judge, than most men who have been through what he has."

"You mean the sunstroke?"

"No, I meant the concentration camp." She stared at him in such total surprise that he said, "You did not know this? Did you not observe the number on his arm?"

"Yes, but I didn't—I didn't—he said something about the Navy—"

"My dear Lady Julia! No navy in the world brands its ratings in such a way. For a lady of genius you seem singularly unobservant; but perhaps," he added thoughtfully, "that is what ladies of genius are like. I have not before encountered one. No, Lady Julia, that is a *Stalag* number."

"He never told me," she whispered.

"Then, I suppose I should not have done. No doubt he prefers to forget about it," Adnan said mildly. "But it seems certain you would have discovered sooner or later. There is nothing shameful about having been a prisoner of the Nazis. On the contrary! And—as to the amnesia—I do truly think that your husband has no cause to worry."

"I'm very glad," she said, relieved, though still startled at this new revelation of how very little she knew about Dikran.

Reaching the upper corner of the quadrangle, they entered a stone tunnel that led through past the concert hall. It was defended by a PRIVATE sign and brought them into a small walled garden which had been cut into the fairly steep hillside behind the hall.

"This is my private place," Adnan said. "I come here now and then for a little peace and quiet."

Julia looked around her in amused surprise. The garden was laid out in the English manner; there were no blazing cascades of color such as she had seen through doorways in Dendros Old Town; the atmosphere was quiet, and, in spite of the hot sunshine, a little melancholy. Wisteria grew on the walls and crept over a trellis; there were small rosebushes and stone-cobbled paths in a formal pattern; there was a sundial; lavender and other bushy, silvery, sweet-smelling flowerless shrubs grew profusely in the beds, but there were few flowers, except for small, inconspicuous things: rockroses and dwarf white cyclamens and daisies. In the center bed there was a small piece of sculpture on a marble plinth. It was very different from the opulent statuary in the quadrangle. It seemed, after a fashion, to represent a human figure, a person sitting with head on knees, hands around ankles, but the outline was rough and indistinct; the only feature directly recognizable as human was the pair of hands with fingers interlaced, which seemed to extend out of the stone base as if pleading for the rest of the figure inside to be released.

The statue vaguely reminded Julia of birth scenes in films—of a foal she had once helped deliver which had emerged feet first from its mother. There was something unhappy and claustrophobic for her about the carving—she did not like it at all. Underneath, on the plinth, she noticed that the name LUCY was carved, but, even if she had felt inclined to inquire about it—which she did not—a touch of melancholy and reserve in Adnan's expression as he stood regarding it would have prevented her from doing so.

"What a charming little place!" she said instead, looking around the garden. "You must often be thankful to have such a hidey-hole."

"Please, Lady Julia, feel free to visit it whenever you wish! I do not have time to come here much. But I shall be honored if you will make use of it." He picked a cluster of miniature pink roses and tucked them behind the statue's stone hands. Then he looked at Julia and smiled with great charm. "For you, I think, not the sweet roses but something more subtle. Such as this—" he picked a couple of sprigs from a feathery, sweet-scented gray shrub and added a couple of white rockroses with yellow centers. "There! That seems more appropriate for the author of *Sharp, Flat, and Slightly Sweet*."

"Thank you!" Julia said, laughing. Her slight feeling of depression was dissipated. She sniffed the posy and said, "It's delicious." Suddenly the warmth and quiet of the secluded little place and the spicy, aromatic scent of the tiny bouquet imbued her with a feeling of elation and hope. Dikran would be all right—everything would turn out all right. "Do you know," she said, "it's odd, but yesterday I had a real premonition that I was going to be unhappy here. I could hardly bring myself to accept your invitation. Wasn't that silly? Now that I am here, I am sure that I was wrong."

"Ah, you English are always so full of superstitions," Adnan said indulgently. "That—it must be acknowledged—forms one part of your mysterious appeal. It is like the scent of these flowers—haunting, indefinable, and very, very far from logic!"

"What good English you speak," Julia remarked as they turned and strolled back through the stone passageway. Overhead, the bell in the clock tower could be heard striking ten.

"Ah, well, I have had many very good English friends— very dear friends," Adnan replied. Julia was aware in herself of a slight feeling of hostility toward these friends, whoever they were.

Re-entering the quadrangle, she saw that the bikini'd and terry-robed patients were now all making off purposefully in the direction of practice rooms and treatment areas. The trays of drinks had been removed from the loggia, and Helikon's routine was getting under way for the day. However, out on the grass, seven musicians were amusing themselves by racing through a Beethoven septet at breakneck speed, while two girls in leotards, equipped with staves, attempted to carry out a sequence of lunging exercises in time to the music. Julia lingered, amused, watching them, reluctant to leave the pleasant, sun-warmed scene.

But Adnan said briskly, "Now I am sure that you must wish to return to your husband; he will at present be resting after his massage. And I know that Zoé has a series of treatments worked out for you which I hope that you will enjoy and find of benefit. So I will say good-by for the moment—" He broke off and, looking across the grass, exclaimed, "My goodness gracious!"

Julia could see nothing remarkable in the girl walking rapidly toward them, who appeared to have been the cause of his ejaculation. She was on the small side, thin to scraggy, and wore the usual jeans and T shirt. Her short black hair was untidy, worn in no particular style, just pushed back off her forehead. She had a lot of freckles, and a pair of noticeably blue Irish eyes; her best feature; otherwise one could certainly not, Julia thought, call her pretty, though there was something cheerfully engaging about her expression.

Adnan, however, seemed quite enchanted at the sight of her.

"Mike! My dear little Mike! But how you have *grown*—how much you have improved! What a transformation!" He enveloped her in a tremendous hug, kissed each cheek, and, holding her off by the arms, surveyed her from top to toe and exclaimed, "But you are now so pretty! It is downright amazing!"

"That's not very polite of you, Uncle Achmed," the girl said gaily. "Wasn't I always pretty?"

"Are you kidding? At sixteen you were too fat—hideous! And the glasses and the spots. At seventeen, too skinny, and wearing that atrocious brace on your teeth. At eighteen—still too skinny, the hair died and frizzed, the eyebrows plucked away to two bald patches—and as for the *clothes*—may Allah preserve me from English girls wearing dirty cotton night-dresses and wooden-soled shoes!"

"I dare say he will."

"But *now*—just right! It is wonderful what four years can do."

"Just you wait till you see me at twenty-four," she suggested.

His manner changed to kind solicitude. "And your mother? Has she made the transfer successfully? Is she settled in her room? I was sorry to hear that she had a fainting spell on the boat, but I feel sure it is no great matter. We will soon have her right as rain here, you will see. In one moment I will visit her. But first—let me introduce—" He stepped back so as to include Julia, who had politely removed herself a step or two, in the conversation. "Lady Julia, this is little Mike Meiklejohn, who has helped me on several summer seminars in the past and has now brought her mother here to be assisted back to health. And, Mike, my child, this is Lady Julia Gibb—Saint, whose plays, *The Blasted Heath*, *Midwinter*, and the rest, you without doubt know by heart and have seen many times over."

Julia saw the girl's eyes widen. "Oh, I have!" she said. "I—I'm very happy to meet you, Lady Julia."

She looked as awe-stricken as if she had bumped into Shake-speare himself, which allayed Julia's slight feeling of anti-climax.

"Come, then, Mike my child," Adnan said, retaining the girl's hand. "We go to see your mother."

"Good-by for now, then, Dr. Adnan. And thank you very much for the interesting conducted tour," Julia said politely.

He bowed briskly, kissing the fingers of his left hand (the right still held that of Mike), and Julia walked away in the direction of Dikran's room, sniffing at her aromatic posy.

{ 5 }

MINUET & TRIO

The ambulance which had been sent from Helikon for Mother was tiny but efficient, about the size of a horse box. There was just enough room inside for Mother, the attendant, and our luggage. So I sat in front, with the driver.

It was heaven to be back in Dendros again; despite my feelings of guilt and anxiety over Mother, I couldn't withstand a bursting sensation of happiness. Besides, I was sure that, once he got to work on her, Dr. Adnan would soon put her to rights. And Dendros was exactly its beautiful self, as I remembered it and had so often dreamed about it in the past four years: the honey-colored stone ramparts of the Old Town, the wide street near the harbor covered with bicycles and crazy little Fiats, the harbor water blue as the Greek flag, great big glossy orange and magnolia trees casting pools of shade, wafts of wonderful scent coming from the public gardens through the dry, hot, spicy air. All the old, black-dressed ladies were there along the quayside with their wise, wrinkled faces and their stalls covered with postcards and leather articles. I

couldn't wait to get away and roam around, visit the Aghnides, eat an orange, swim in the no doubt icy Aegean.

"What's happening at Helikon?" I asked the driver, who
was a cousin of Calliope's, a music student called George. I
had been at school with him for a year. Now he was studying
in Athens, but, of course, came back to Dendros for the holidays.

"Oh, things are much as usual. They still haven't fixed the
leak in the swimming pool. A woman broke her collarbone
diving in and threatened to sue the company, but Zoé talked
her out of it. Adnan was very annoyed about it all. And he fell
in love with an Italian film star last summer."

"Oh? Which one?" I asked suspiciously.

"Ghita Masolini—she was here losing weight after too much
pasta."

"So, what happened?"

"She fell in love back, much more, and started sticking to
him like glue. So then he got fed up and went off to Athens to
buy ultrasonic-treatment equipment for six weeks. And she
lost a lot more weight than she bargained for and went back
to Rome."

"That's a good thing. Suppose he'd married her! She'd never
have fitted in at Helikon. And he *couldn't* leave. I should think
Helikon would just about collapse if Uncle Achmed weren't
there to keep an eye. What else? Have they got any interesting visitors at the moment?"

My Greek was coming back in leaps and bounds, I was glad
to find.

"Yes, we've got old Annibal Destrier, the composer who
won the Hammarskøld Prize for Music. Uncle Achmed wants
to put on one of his operas to celebrate his eighty-fifth birthday."

"What fun!" Instantly I wondered if there would be a
chance for me to do the sets. Helikon had a small but well-
equipped stage with several nice gadgets including a revolving
bit in the middle. But of course the old boy's birthday might

fall after Mother's and my departure. "Which opera are they going to do?"

"Well, old Annibal wants *Les Mystères d'Elsinore*, which is his favorite, apparently, but that's a bit awkward."

"Oh, why? Surely he ought to have the one he wants? After all, he may not be around for many more birthdays. What's the matter with it?"

Les Mystères was short, but very meaty, as I remembered it from reading the score and listening to radio productions. It was an operatic version of *Hamlet*, very emotional, Gallic, Gothic, and overwrought. Gertrude was a kind of belle Otero-cum-Phaedra, who yearns after her son and is filling in by having an affair with Polonius; Claudius a frozen French businessman-villain-cuckold, and Hamlet perfectly epicene and schizo. His part, I remembered, had been arranged for either male or female, tenor or contralto; in both the radio productions I'd heard, it had been sung by a woman.

"So, who'd sing Hamlet?" I asked, toying with a notion I'd been nursing for a long time of sets for *Hamlet* adapted from the paintings of Piero della Francesca. I can't remember what had originally given me the idea but, once conceived, it seemed ideally suitable—wide, watery landscapes filled with low hills and lakes in the distance, a few nobly plain buildings near at hand, such as the ones in his perspective drawing of an ideal town, and, for each scene, two or three Piero figures depicted as huge, impassive bystanders—the watchers from "The Flagellation," perhaps, and some of his angels, so severely beautiful, neither judging nor pitying but just calmly observant. I thought that to see Hamlet's difficulties taking place under the eyes of these Piero people would be interesting and show the story in a new perspective. Shakespeare, after all, would have been able to see Piero's paintings; wasn't he supposed to have taken a trip to northern Italy when he was young? But, to do designs for *Hamlet* was an ambition that I had resigned myself to not having fulfilled for years to come; this chance, if chance it was, seemed too good to miss.

"That's just it," George said. "Hamlet's part is where the

difficulty comes in. Apparently there's a sort of hoodoo on *Les Mystères*."

"What sort of hoodoo?"

"After each of the last two stage productions the singer who took Hamlet's part died, each time within a month. In one case it was a man—Orlando Lipschutz, the Austrian singer —and in one a woman, I can't remember who, but she was killed three weeks later in a plane crash. Lipschutz just died of heart failure. So now the opera has got a bad name—you know how superstitious singers are—and nobody's keen to take the part. Enrico Gaspari has been staying here, but he has made a lot of excuses and says he has to get back to London to rehearse for a BBC production. So then Joop wrote and asked Elisabet Maas if she'd do it, and at first she said yes but then she said her husband didn't want her to."

"Gosh! I wish I could sing. I'd do it like a shot."

"Well, you can't, we all know that, so there's no point in wishing," George said firmly.

It was true. I love music, but, like Mother—like Trilby— I've got plenty of voice but can't keep in tune for two consecutive notes.

George drove out along Winston Churchill Street, past the square, stuccoed, nineteenth-century villas painted in faded pinks and oranges and set about with palms and ilexes and chinaberry trees. It all looked good enough to eat.

"Isn't there *anybody* at Helikon—not a great singer, I mean just someone with a reasonable voice—who could take the part?" I was reluctant to lose my *Hamlet,* now I saw it in view.

"There were one or two possibles, but once they heard about Enrico Gaspari and Elisabet Maas, they changed their minds. Uncle Achmed was very annoyed about it."

"I can imagine," I said, grinning to myself. He hated being crossed. And he had no patience at all with supernatural beliefs or any such stuff.

"So now he's written to ask Kerry Farrell if she'd like to do it. She has visited Helikon once or twice in the past, so it seemed possible that she might, if she's not too busy and booked up."

"And what did she say?"

"Don't know. Maybe she hasn't answered."

"I think I heard her do it once on the radio," I said. "She'd be all right; she'd be fine, I should think."

"Were you ever at Helikon when she came here?"

"No, I've never seen her or heard her live—only on records or radio; but I feel she's got the right kind of voice: rather pure and colorless; better for sacred music than opera, really, but I should think for Hamlet she'd be just right."

I craned out the window for a view of the beautiful Dendros landscape, for we had now left the town and were shooting up over a shoulder of hillside before descending into the valley where Helikon lay. All the flat land was cultivated to within an inch of the beach—orange groves, vineyards, olive groves, set about with thin, spiky cypresses; then, above them, the bare, silvery hillsides with gray-green wild olives and figs. And then high, white mountains. And the blue, blue sea beyond and all around.

"Here we are," said George. "As I expect you remember."

It was hardly more than a ten-minute drive from the town, really. But the intervening hill gave the estate solitude and privacy. All this valley had belonged to a local millionaire called Capranis and he had given it, lock, stock, and barrel, or rather, rod, pole, and perch, to the Helikon Foundation. Of course Mother will love it here, I thought, loving every inch myself. Of course she will. Who could help doing so?

George drove through the arched entrance under the clock tower at one side of the main quadrangle and came to a halt by a service entrance. Mother was swiftly and expeditiously carried indoors on a stretcher. I would have followed her, but I caught sight of Adnan twenty yards away, and he gave me a wave and a welcoming shout, so I went to say hello.

He was talking to a strikingly beautiful woman whose face was vaguely familiar, so I thought, Aha! old Achmed's at it again. He always made a beeline for the handsome lady visi-

tors and probably caused many a heartache by lavishing his
fascinating Anatolian ways on them; though I am bound to
admit that he was very agreeable to *all* his patients, and could
make any female feel like a million dollars.

This one had a long, pointed face with hollows under
the cheekbones, remarkable shallow eye sockets, a classically
straight nose, and a most beautiful mouth—wide, tender, curving—her best feature, and all were good. Old Uncle Achmed
does know how to pick them, I thought. Her hair, curly,
dusty-fair, didn't interfere with or detract from the lovely
mask of her face—just formed a cloudy, vague background to
it. I noticed that she had very fine, long hands, too—tragic
hands; I thought how I'd like to dress her in stiff Renaissance
draperies and have her playing some doomed part, the Duchess
of Malfi perhaps, against a lurid background of dark turrets
and flames.

I was racking my brain to think why she looked so familiar,
and when Achmed introduced her I thought, No *wonder* she
looks so haunted. I'd read about her divorce in the papers and
knew that after twenty-two years of happy marriage her
highly intelligent, distinguished, and handsome husband had
suddenly ditched her in favor of a fat blond political hostess
without any apparent graces whatever. It must have been a
terrible shock for Lady Julia. Maybe she constituted too much
competition in the home, I thought. She certainly wrote first-
rate plays, all of which I had both seen and read—and I felt
impressed by my own luck in meeting her.

However, she didn't seem disposed to be in the least impressed by *me*, which was hardly surprising, and, after a brief
acknowledgment of the introduction, said something about
seeing how her husband was getting on and went off, walking
with a long, graceful stride.

"Has she married again, then?" I said in surprise. "She didn't
lose much time, surely?"

"No, I fear she remarried in a state of shock—on the
rebound, as you would say—and may now repent at leisure."

"Why? What's the matter with her husband?"

"He is here suffering from a mild case of sunstroke."

"Poor chap." Sunstrokes on Dendros were very frequent. "But I meant, why will she repent at leisure? Is he nasty?"

"No," said Adnan thoughtfully. "No, in many ways I think he is an interesting character with many unusual qualities—judging from what I have seen of him, which is not a great deal. But their backgrounds are so dissimilar; what, I ask myself, is the magnetic force which has brought them together?"

"And the sixty-four-thousand-dollar answer to that is sex," I suggested. "Lady J. looks to me like one of those sirens who can call it out in any male unless he's actually blind or paralyzed. She's got a real aura, don't you think?"

"My dear Mike!" Adnan was scandalized. "You used to be a nice, proper young girl—demure, self-effacing, well-brought-up. What has happened to bring about this change in you?"

"I found that being demure, good, and whatever you said didn't get me anywhere. Besides, you forget that I've been out in the world earning my living for four years since I saw you last."

"Is it really four years? Well, do not let the Aghnides hear you talking about sex, or there will be the devil to pay."

"How is old Mr. Aghnides?" I asked eagerly. "I wrote to tell him that I was coming here, but he's never answered. Is he all right?"

"Not too good, I'm afraid. You will find that he is *very* old now. And he had a slight stroke last month. His sister from Athens is now living there, to look after him. But anyway, go to visit him. He misses Calliope—it will be a happy reminder for him to see you."

"I'll go right away—as soon as you've seen Mother and she's settled in."

But I was daunted to hear that Aunt Elektra had moved into the Aghnides house; she was the world's vinegar-puss.

I walked beside Adnan to Mother's room, thinking, Well, at least *he* hasn't changed, thank goodness! He was exactly the same as I'd remembered—square, dark, dandyishly dressed, teasingly cheerful, hiding, behind his big impassive dark eyes, a whole lot of secrets, but at least they were not *disagreeable* secrets. I had always felt safe with Uncle Achmed—as Calliope and I had fallen into the habit of calling him; he had a thoroughly kind heart, I knew, under his joky exterior, and, although he flirted with many, had never caused anybody permanent damage, so far as I knew. In fact, his had been the heart that got broken, long ago; apparently he had never recovered from that bygone affliction enough to become deeply involved with any other woman.

Calliope, when she was seventeen, had pined for him for a whole year, I knew, and had decided that, since he was plainly never going to take her seriously, her best recourse would be to clear out for pastures new, in Elizabeth, New Jersey. Besides, as I'd told her, he was far too old—at least thirty-four.

"Mr. Rochester was older than that," Calliope pointed out. "And I bet *you'd* take him like a shot—if you had the chance."

"Not likely! I wouldn't want to marry a blind, bad-tempered grouch with only one hand who lived in a damp thicket. Think of pushing him round in a wheelchair when he was seventy and you were fifty."

"Not Rochester; Achmed, you ass!"

"He'd never look at me. Besides, I've got to pursue my career and become one of the twentieth century's foremost stage designers."

So Calliope had gone to Elizabeth, New Jersey, and I had gone back to England. That had been four years ago.

Mother had never met Adnan, and I was marginally anxious about that, because she was such a serious person and I wasn't sure how his teasing ways would go down with her. But I needn't have worried. In no time he had her eating out of his hand.

She was just waking when we reached the double room on the ground floor that had been found for us; she seemed calm and drowsy and relaxed.

"Mother," I said, "this is Dr. Adnan that I've told you such a lot about."

"Oh, yes," she said, smiling faintly. "It was always Uncle Achmed this and Uncle Achmed that, and how kind you were —I hope you didn't let the child be a nuisance and tease you to death."

"Nuisance? She was often my right hand—even in the days when she dressed like a demented dervish! No, no, I am very devoted to this little Mike. She has been like a daughter to me. But now, my dear Mrs. Meiklejohn, let me have a look at you."

Feeling that it would be tactful to remove myself, I went out and sat on the grass in the quadrangle and listened to the sound, through a window, of somebody practicing a long, dismal setting by Respighi of a poem by Shelley about tragic love and a lady who pined for her dead sweetheart. It made me feel rather gloomy. Love, I thought, what an infernal nuisance it is, interfering with people's lives, making them rush half across the world to get away from it, or plant memorial gardens in witness to its never-fading pangs. I wandered into Achmed's little garden and then, when I judged a decent interval had elapsed, returned to Mother.

Adnan had gone and she was alone, lying on her bed by the window and gazing alternately at the beautiful lemon orchard outside and the pile of literature about Helikon that was left on the bedside table of every new inmate. There was a guest list, renewed every week, and menus of the different diets, all vegetarian and all scanty, that were supplied depending on the individual's particular ailments and problems; descriptions of all the treatments and what they did; a list of concerts, recitals, and dramatic performances; descriptions of master-classes in piano, violin, solo singing, and so on, which varied from week to week as different artists came and went; lists of lectures, communal activities available, sight-seeing excursions, and entertainments in Dendros town; and finally a short list of prohibitions: smoking, eating own food, drinking anything but the fruit juice and mild Dendros wine supplied according to diet (Achmed was a realist and knew that if he omitted the wine some guests would never return again), taking any medicines except those prescribed by the clinic, sex (not that Adnan disapproved of sex; it was simply that, he said, it played a disruptive part in the carefully controlled regime he had planned for his patients, so no sex while resident at Helikon, please), and nurturing unexpressed grudges or criticisms.

IF YOU HAVE COMPLAINTS, VOICE THEM! said a sign which was pinned prominently in the dining room, waiting area, library, and other public spots, and there was a regular period set aside after lunch every day for public discussion of any gripes that might arise, while Adnan himself was always available in his office from six to seven each evening to hear complaints that people might be too shy or nervous to voice publicly. By this means a remarkably serene atmosphere was successfully maintained, which was one of the great pleasures of Helikon. Each time I came back, I was amazed at the almost palpable warmth of friendliness and happiness that radiated from all the characters wandering about in their bathrobes and the performers whacking away at their cellos and pianos. And this despite the fact that they were all on a low diet of lemon juice, olives, grated carrot, and tomatoes! I didn't mind it for a while, but presently I did begin to long for a plate of scrambled egg or a chunk of feta cheese, or a crust of Greek bread. Adnan was firm, though: no animal foods or fats, no flour; he had a theory about expelling all the poison from the system before starting to build it up. Anyway, I knew Mother wouldn't mind the diet, as she always had been a vegetarian.

"He does seem a sweet person, I must say," she said when I asked how she had got on with Adnan. "I can quite see why you've always been so fond of him." This was uncommonly strong language, for Mother, and encouraged me very much. The worst hurdle was past.

"I really was sure that you'd like it here, once you saw the place," I said.

"Yes, I'm sure I shall too—if I'm really not to be allowed to go back yet—and you were a dear child to have arranged it for me. I think it will do me a lot of good. I only hope it doesn't cost a fortune."

"Oh, no. Adnan fixed a reduced rate because I'm going to help again. But anyway Stretford County Ed. said they'd take care of all this kind of thing."

"Well, you were a sly puss to arrange it all behind my back, but it was very kind and thoughtful of you."

Better and better! With a huge load off my mind, I asked if she'd like to come out and see the sights of the place, or sit under the lemon trees, or listen to some music, or watch some dancing. Anybody was free to wander into any practice room at any time during the day, though the formal recitals didn't begin until the evening.

But Mother said she was still drowsy and would prefer to rest on her bed for the moment and gaze at the lemon trees from where she lay.

"In that case, perhaps I'll walk up the hill and pay my respects to old Mr. Aghnides."

"Oh, do, dear; that's an excellent plan. Wait just a minute and I'll write him a note explaining why I can't come just yet."

So, presently, with a light heart, I was walking up the path that threaded its way through the little valley behind Helikon, with Mother's letter in my pocket.

The valley—deep and narrow, it was almost a ravine, really —was all overgrown with shady trees—oaks and sycamores and wild syringas smothered in white blossoms that smelt hauntingly sweet. A few cyclamens and early purple orchids were still flowering there, in damp spots by the stream that tumbled in cascades from one rocky pool to another. Nightingales in the syringa bushes were singing fortissimo, and it was all so beautiful that if I hadn't had so many other happinesses in store I would have liked to sit down by the water's edge and just spend the day there, looking at leaves and roots and ripples.

I'll come back and do that some other day, I thought, when Mother is really settled in. One of those promises that one makes to oneself and never keeps.

After fifteen minutes' climb—the path wound uphill all the

time—I came to where the stream gushed out of a crack in the
rock. I was hot by then, so I knelt and had a good drink of the
icy water. It tasted black as ink, it was so cold.

Above this point the path climbed what was almost a flight
of rock steps, then emerged from the wood and crossed a bare
shoulder of hill covered with wiry, low-growing aromatic
scrub—various thymes, and sage, and thistles. A couple of
tethered goats were grazing. Above me I could see the village
where the Aghnides had their house, perched on a ledge of
hillside, set about with dusty fig trees and dilapidated dry-
stone walls. The village was called Archangelos and consisted
of about eight houses, each painted a different beautiful color.

Presently I reached the road, which wound a slower, zigzag
way up the hillside, passed through the village, and went on
five miles farther to an archaeological site up at the very top.

I panted around a last curve under the hot sun and then
walked in among the houses, picking my way among hens and
cats, saying a polite *kallimero* to each smiling old lady that I
met. In this village they wore knee-high leather boots below
their black skirts, and thick white head scarves, and carried
themselves with stately pride, like Egyptians in wall paintings.

The Aghnides house was easily the biggest, set back from
the street behind a white wall and a large, unkempt garden full
of bougainvillaeas and cypresses. I rang the bell, and the door
was answered by the old cook, Elena, who must have been
about a hundred. She gave me a big hug and said that she
would go and tell the *Kyrie* that I was there. But he was very,
very old now, she added; I would see a sad change in him.

She left me in the central courtyard, which had a grapevine
trained across above it for shade, and swags of roses, huge red
and white lilies, geraniums and sweet williams, and something
that smelt of cinnamon. A couple of supine tabby cats gazed
at me somnolently through slit eyes.

Then, to my dismay, Aunt Elektra came stalking through an
open door. Like all elderly Greek ladies, Aunt Elektra was
dressed in black, but her dress had been bought in Athens, or
even possibly in Paris, and was draped in elegant silken folds

over her scraggy bones. She had a long, disapproving face, and her black eyes were by no means friendly.

"Ah," she said. "Priscilla. It would have been better to phone or to send a note before calling."

"I—I'm sorry," I said, much dashed. "I never thought. I was so anxious to see Kyrie Aghnides. Is he not well enough to see me?"

"He is very weak today. You may see him, as you have come, but please stay only a moment, so as not to tire him unnecessarily."

"Yes, of course. I'm very sorry that he is so poorly."

Without replying, she led the way into the downstairs room where Calliope's father lay. The room was floored with tiny cobblestones set in a mosaic pattern, and there was a sleeping platform at one end covered with handsome ancient rugs and approached by a flight of four steps. Kyrie Aghnides was not on the platform, however, but on a high, old-fashioned brass bed, reclining against a pile of pillows.

My heart sank when I saw him. He looked terribly old, white, and frail, and was breathing in long, painful rasps; each breath seemed to cost him an almost unbearable effort.

"Hullo, Kyrie Aghnides," I said softly, approaching and planting a kiss on his cold old cheek above the patriarchal white mustache and beard. "Do you remember me? It's Mike —Calliope's friend. I am sorry that you are so tired."

His eyes opened slowly and he gave me a faint smile. But I saw that the fire and intelligence which had made him such an important person in my life were now died down to the lowest possible flicker. Today he was just a frail old man, not quite certain who I was, held together only by his habits of dignity and consideration.

"I'm Calliope's English friend," I said again. "Do you remember I used to stay with you, before Calliope went off to marry Dmitri?"

"Yes, yes—dear little Mike," he whispered. "Just as pretty as ever. I am glad to see you, my child—happy to see you—" His voice trailed into silence. His eyes closed.

"I've brought you a note from my mother," I said gently. "She and I are staying down at Helikon. Shall I read it to you?"

"Later, thank you, my child," he whispered after a moment. "Put it by for the moment. I am, just now, a little bit tired. Please thank your dear mother, however. Do not omit to do that. Is she as charming as ever?" he added vaguely.

Since I knew that he and Mother had never met, my heart sank still further. I could see now that there was not the slightest hope of my ever extracting any useful information from him about my father or Drusilla. Feeling bitterly grieved and disappointed—and also ashamed because now that I saw him my plan seemed so self-interested—I went back to the courtyard. I grieved for myself and I grieved for him, because this was just a travesty of the man I remembered.

Aunt Elektra was in the yard, grimly picking dead heads off the geraniums.

"Is he—is he always as tired and vague as this now?" I asked.

"Yes!" she snapped. "He is old, young lady. And he has had much to try him."

"I'm very sorry," I said truly. "What is his best time of day? I'd like to come again when he is not quite so tired, and then perhaps we could talk about Calliope."

"If Calliope had done her duty and stayed to look after her father, there would be no need to talk about her," said Elektra sourly. I could see this was a main part of her grievance, that she had had to leave Athens and return to this uncivilized spot because Calliope had gone to America. She added, "Visitors are not good for him, young lady. It is best that you do not come again."

"But I wanted to bring my mother—she so much wanted to meet him—to thank him—"

"No. There would be no purpose in his meeting a stranger."

Aunt Elektra ushered me, very definitively, out of the courtyard.

Just inside the front door I found Elena. "What's biting Kyria Elektra?" I whispered.

She gave a shrug, crossed herself, and made the sign to avert the evil eye. "Who can tell what gets into that one's head? All I know is that she does not approve of your family. But whatever faults your parents have are certainly no faults of *yours*, my little one. I find her exceedingly unreasonable. Alas, though, she has forbidden me to let you in again. I shall always be happy to talk to you in the street, though, or in the *taverna;* send a message by Apostoulos Adossides—or anybody you see about—and I'll come out and have a chat and tell you about the *Kyrie.* I fear he is not long for this world. Eh, me, those were happier days when the mistress was still alive, and you and Calliope were tumbling about the place like two young goats, upsetting my cooking pans and pulling the cats' tails. . . ."

She probably would have gone on in this vein for a long time, but Aunt Elektra appeared in the hallway and gave me a baleful glare, so I hugged Elena once more, opened the big, chocolate-colored double doors, and slipped through, feeling both sore and puzzled.

I suppose I should have tackled Aunt Elektra then and there. It seemed quite out of the question, though, that she would be prepared to divulge any useful information. But what, in heaven's name, had made her so hostile? Why did she disapprove of my family? What had we done to earn her condemnation? Mother worked hard at her profession and thought of little else; I worked hard at mine and lived a fairly thrifty and circumspect life; Drusilla was long dead; so who was there to disapprove of except . . . Father? If he was still alive?

I simply have to ask Mother about this soon, I resolved. Not while she's still prone to faint, obviously; I'll give her, say, a week at Helikon, and then tackle her about Father. This ought to be just the right environment in which to discuss the whole affair calmly and unemotionally; there will be Adnan to keep an eye on her, too, if she gets upset. I'll do that. Much better than trying to squeeze information out of old Aghnides.

In retrospect that plan now seemed an underhanded approach and I felt I had deserved Aunt Elektra's rebuff.

Having reached my decision, I felt better about the situation and walked lightheartedly back to Helikon, taking the longer way, down the road, which zigzagged down in acute, hairpin bends. It was a dangerous road to attempt in a car, because there was no room to pass and excursion buses were liable to come tearing down at mad speed, having visited the archaeological site up at the top of the hill, which was called Mount Atakos. The buses were supposed to make the ascent every other hour, but they were liable to become delayed when their passengers wandered off and got lost among the various Hellenic, pre-Hellenic, and early-Christian ruins up on the top, so it was never really safe to assume that a bus was not due. In fact, as I walked down, one of them roared past me, taking the outside of the bend with true Greek abandon, but as I was on foot I was able to dash up the bank and hold on to a wild fig while it whirled past leaving a wake of white dust six feet high.

Strolling slowly after it, leaving the white cloud time to settle, I occupied myself by trying to put together all my childhood memories of Father. This was the first period of true solitude and peace I had had since Mother's accident, since I'd read her note, and it seemed an appropriate time for such an exercise.

Such odd, disconnected things one remembers about people —I sometimes wonder how biographies or memoirs are ever put together, how the writers possibly manage to assemble all those correct, suitable, and dignified recollections which appear to have gushed out on demand, like turning on a tap and releasing a flow of Earl Grey?

Scraping the bottom of my mind for memories, I came up with the fact that Father would not change his socks nearly often enough to please Mother; she was always scolding him about it. There was some family joke about how as soon as he took off the socks the cat would rush to them and start trampling on them. "Othello's sucking Father's socks again!" we used to shout. He got very impatient with me once when I would not drink my milk, and emptied a whole mug of it over my head. His anger was quickly roused, quickly gone. Jokes. He made a lot of jokes—puns, ridiculous rhymes, spoonerisms, just bits of nonsense. "Da bakeda bean!" when it was beans on toast for our tea, he'd go into an Italian opera routine, hand on heart, eyes to heaven, twirling an imaginary mustache. But he worked very hard, used to come home late, hoarse and exhausted from his teaching; we didn't really see much of him. He had a wonderful gift of improvising on the piano; sometimes, at what seemed dead of night (really I daresay it was only half past eight or nine) on evenings when I'd had to go to bed before he got home from work, I would wake up hearing the piano, and lie comforted, knowing that he was in the house, listening to the tunes he was rattling off on our tinkling, sweet, old shallow-keyed piano. His tunes, I later realized, were considerably influenced by the school of Scott Joplin, but still they had a touch of true invention about them and a happy exuberance that carried me, entranced in my bed, to extremes of pleasure that I don't think I have ever since reached. I used to think that heaven could have nothing better to offer than lying in bed listening to Father play, on and on, forever. Socks, baked beans, tunes on the piano—he'd had a mustache but later shaved it off; he'd smoked a pipe, then cigarettes, then stopped smoking altogether; he'd drunk beer from a pewter tankard, then gave it up in favor of vermouth; he liked his eggs boiled for one minute only and was very fond of fish, "Fishes is delishes," he used to say and taught me how to expertly bone a mackerel or kipper. "James, just *do* it for her, we're in a hurry," Mother would say impatiently. "She's got to learn some time, Barbara," he would answer mildly, continuing to supervise my unskilled efforts. He called the cat Spinach—some private joke of his own.

Gentle—cheerful—fond of jokes and music—it was hard to imagine such a man in prison, in a madhouse, escaped behind the Iron Curtain with some disastrous secret? Yet my imagination would provide no other solution to the puzzle.

Arrived back at Helikon, I went to our room to check on Mother but found a note there that said, "Having seaweed bath. See you at 1.00."

Delighted at this evidence of initiative, I went out to where I'd seen Zoé sitting at a table on the terrace, sorting herbs into bundles and labeling them. She said, "*Allo, allo, Mike, mon vieux—comment ça va?*"

I sat down to help her and we worked together while having a comfortable gossip. Zoé was very unlike everyone's stereotyped idea of a French girl: she was squarely built, with a round, dimpled, smiling face, and not particularly talkative; after we'd caught up on the basic information we fell into friendly silence. I had always felt great liking and respect for Zoé; she did a marvelous job as warden, looking after the whole establishment with amiable, serene, businesslike, unhurried efficiency.

From an open french window behind us we could hear the directions for a meditation class floating out. I glanced back inside the room and saw fifteen or so patients laying peacefully on straw mattresses.

"Think of a lake," the instructor said. "In the middle is an island. On the island grows a tree. Under the tree's roots lies a casket. In the still waters of the lake, mountains are reflected upside down. The tree, also, is reflected upside down. In the casket . . ."

In the casket, I thought. What is in the casket? Everybody has a casket inside them and its contents are unknown to anybody else.

I let my thoughts drift away in a different direction, to the *Mysteries of Elsinore*. Hamlet was really a homosexual, I (and evidently old Annibal, too) had decided; he discovers this unrealized identity in the course of the play: "Why did you laugh then, when I said 'man delights not me'?" "What should such fellows as I do crawling between heaven and earth?" And to Ophelia—who, of course was played by a boy: "You jig, you amble, and you lisp, and you nick-name God's creatures."

And, later: "Give me that man . . . and I will wear him in my heart of heart, As I do thee." . . .

Poor Ophelia! No wonder she couldn't take it, had a breakdown, and threw herself in the river.

Old Annibal had obviously teetered between making Hamlet a man and a woman. Suppose he had been a girl? What would she have been like? As things were, no wonder he was queer, after an upbringing by Gertrude, not one of the world's shining examples of maternal intelligence and devotion.

"Now, imagine yourselves in a rose garden," said the instructor. "All the roses are yellow—that is the color of philosophy. Now the roses are red; that is the color of love. Now they are white—snow white; that is the color of peace."

He let the meditators rest on that for a while; then he played the Air for the G String, and the recumbent forms slowly came to life, picked themselves up, and ambled out into the sunshine. It was almost time for lunch; lemon juice for those on Diets 1, 2, and 3; shredded carrot and pulse for the lucky ones who had progressed to 4, 5, or 6.

Among the emerging meditators was old Annibal Destrier, clad in a striped bathrobe of great age and limping along slowly with a long staff. His beard and the robe made him look rather like Father Time.

Seeing Zoé, of whom he was very fond, he lowered himself with care onto the bench beside us.

"*Les jolies demoiselles s'occupent en plein air . . .*" he said gallantly and sniffed at a bundle of marjoram.

"Has it been decided which of your operas they are going to put on, M. Destrier?" I asked.

"*Les Mystères, ma petite.* Without doubt, *Les Mystères.* It is my wish. If they can only find a singer for Hamlet. Achmed has written off to Mlle. Kerry Farrell, but it seems she is traveling and cannot yet be located. If she can only come, there will be no difficulty, for she knows the part well and has sung it several times before on radio."

I thought of commenting, "She can't be superstitious,

then?" decided not to, and asked instead, "Why did you design the part for a woman, monsieur?"

He launched into a disquisition about *castrati* and counter-tenors, and then into an analysis of the epicene qualities of Hamlet which so closely paralleled what I had just been think-ing that I became very excited. We had a long argument about the play, agreeing and disagreeing with almost equal violence, while Zoé listened to us indulgently and got on with the herbs.

In the end, flown with the excitement of talking to him, and the warm sun, and the pleasure of being at Helikon, I hauled up my courage by its suspenders and asked if I might possibly be allowed to design the sets for the production. If they did *Les Mystères*, that was to say.

Old Annibal smiled at me benevolently. "I certainly have no objection, *mon enfant;* I shall be most curious to see what you do! But you must ask Joop Kolenbrander, of course."

"You'll tell him, though, that you don't mind? Oh, thank you, thank you, monsieur!" I could have hugged him, but re-frained, out of consideration for his age and celebrity.

"Oh, to be twenty-two again!" he sighed.

"If I were as creative as you are at eighty-four, I wouldn't worry about being twenty-two," I said. Then I saw Mother coming up the stairs from the treatment room, so I ran to meet her and grabbed her arm.

"M. Destrier says that I can do the sets for his birthday opera; isn't that *something?*"

"Oh, splendid, darling; I'm so pleased that you're finding plenty to occupy you," she said vaguely. The word *opera* al-ways turns her off at once, as she can't stand it. But, still, she was very pleased for me. What she really wanted to do, how-ever, was describe her seaweed bath and the wonderful mas-sage that had preceded it. So I listened happily to her descrip-tions, while we drank our lemon-juice lunch, and managed to think my own thoughts as well.

⑥

NOCTURNE

"Won't you come out into the sunshine, darling?" Julia said to Dikran. "It seems a shame to spend such a lot of time in this room when it's so beautiful outside. Do come for a stroll!"

"No I won't!" he said snappishly. "It's too hot. Do you want me to get another sunstroke?"

Julia sighed. "It is seven o'clock in the evening," she pointed out. "Really, the sun can't be dangerously hot by now. I'm sure it would be safe enough. But if you like I'll call Adnan and ask him?"

This suggestion seemed to annoy Dikran still more. "What use would that be? If he said it was too hot it would just confirm what I've told you. And if he said it wasn't, I wouldn't believe him! When are we going to get out of this wretched hole?"

Helikon was not suiting Dikran. After three days of its regime he was still protesting furiously. He did not care for the diet, he hated the lack of drink, he despised the accommodations, and in spite of undergoing every kind of treatment, he complained of headaches, constipation, claustrophobia, eye-strain, backache, and a dry mouth.

"But *every*body has a dry mouth for the first few days; they all say so," Julia told him. "I do too. It's the reduced diet. Then, after three or four days, your mouth clears and you feel like a million dollars. Everyone says that too. By tomorrow I'm sure you'll be another person." As the words left her mouth she cursed herself, wishing she had chosen them more carefully. It was difficult to be tactful with Dikran at the moment; he was making her nervous and jumpy.

"By tomorrow I'll more likely be dead!" he growled. "I don't *want* to stay here a few more days. I want to leave now!"

Julia looked at him in worried silence. She was deeply troubled about him. He seemed so totally changed from the exuberant, gay, good-tempered man she had married that she frequently felt as if she were sharing the room with a complete stranger. In a way, she was.

Adnan had done his best to reassure her. "The aches and the eyestrain are some residual effects of the sunstroke; they will soon pass, have no fear! We must just keep him quiet and calm for a few days more."

It was all very well for Adnan to say that, Julia thought. He didn't have to spend his days and nights with her husband.

"Come into the orchard?" she said hopefully. "There's the most heavenly breeze blowing off the sea."

If he went out at all during the day, Dikran did sometimes venture into the orchard, which was usually shady enough. But this evening he snarled, "Bloody Prokofiev! I'll stay where I am, thank you. It's bad enough here!"

Outside, under the lemon trees, Joop Kolenbrander was taking an enthusiastic group of students through *Peter and the Wolf*, while an old lady in a wheelchair, with a long plait of white hair trailing over her bathrobe, read out the narrative in ringing tones.

Julia would have liked to go out and listen to them at closer quarters. She started for the door, but Dikran said, "Come back and sit down! I hardly ever see you—you're always off having some goddamned treatment or talking to that bloody Turk."

Reluctantly, capitulating, Julia sat down on her bed. She told herself that she could hear *Peter and the Wolf* equally well from there.

"'*And what kind of a useless bird are you, if you can't swim?' said the duck.*"

A spirited duet broke out between the bird and the duck. Julia listened in delight. If only Dikran would get better, she thought, what a perfect spot this would be in which to spend a honeymoon.

After a moment or two he came and sat by her on her bed, and put his arms around her. "I'm sorry to be such a bear, my dear," he said miserably. "I don't mean to be—specially to you! It's just something that gets hold of me in this place."

He began kissing her, gently at first; soon, as she responded, with ravenous, demanding intensity. Then he pushed her back onto the bed, yanked off the loose cotton shirt she wore, and began fondling her breasts. There seemed something truly desperate about his passion, she thought, as if he were trying to submerge his identity in hers.

"Take your trousers off!" he ordered irritably, finding the fastener beyond his power to shift.

Obeying him, Julia listened dreamily to the velvet notes of the cat crawling through the long grass in Prokofiev's forest. Now Dikran was pressing her violently back against the hard Greek bolster, nuzzling her, biting her neck. Her body was automatically co-operating with his, she felt herself drifting nearer and nearer to the extremity of pleasure; without conscious intent she arched and clung, twined and untwined, clasped and unclasped. But all the time her mind remained disengaged.

She continued to listen to the narrator's voice outside.

"Soon after that, a great gray wolf *did* come out of the forest . . ."

Dikran tossed her farther down the bed, moving her body as easily as if it were a sack of straw.

Julia found herself imagining the joyful expressions on the faces of the three horn players as they waited for their cue to play the wolf theme.

"But the bird flew up into the tree . . ."

Dikran's face above her, furious, acquiline, and intent, looked like that of some avenging angel about to swoop down.

"Then, quick as a flash, he swallowed her up!" declaimed the old lady down below, in ringing tones.

"Who, who can this man be?" wondered Julia, her body vibrating like an aspen leaf whirled down a weir. "What have I let myself in for?"

She cried out sharply in a voice not her own, as if possessed by devils; but her cry was lost in the clash of drums and kettledrums outside. Dikran lay spent and motionless on top of her while the hunters (shooting as they went) came marching through the forest, left, right, left, right.

Slowly Dikran's breathing leveled off, quieted down, became long and even; his heartbeats slowed, his head slumped down over Julia's shoulder into the pillow. His grasp relaxed. He slept.

Lying inertly under his weight, Julia heard Peter's tune break suddenly into lilting, perky waltz time: "Don't you worry! We've already caught the wolf!"

Flat, empty, almost anesthetized, she was surprised to find tears sliding backward out of her eyes and through her damp hair.

By degrees Peter's triumphal procession wound its way into the distance, through the forest.

"But what about the duck?" thought Julia in sudden agony. "He's forgotten about the duck!"

And then the parting line came back to her: "In his hurry the wolf had swallowed the duck while she was still alive!"

It's a cruel, *horrible* tale, she thought—barbaric, just like the Russians themselves. They are a peasant race. They aren't civilized yet.

She waited until Dikran seemed totally oblivious, fathoms deep in sleep, then, carefully, inch by inch, slid herself out from under him. It took her a very long time. But he did not wake, and she knew that if she left him now, he would very likely remain asleep for eight or nine hours. Then he would probably get up and wander out by himself into the dark. That was the pattern of their life at present; exhausting bursts of passion, sleep, tension, quarrels, and more love-making. Often at night he went for long, roaming walks, she did not know where; he refused to accompany her to the evening concerts, grumbling that he never listened to amateurs, or some other excuse obviously hatched up on the spur of the moment: he hated cellos, he couldn't stand French composers; he abused her because she would not join him on his night rambles, but she felt, just the same, that he was quite pleased to get away on his own. Likewise, although he complained about Helikon constantly and said he wished to leave, he took no real initiative about doing so; in a way, she suspected that he was finding the place as much of a refuge as she was herself.

For if they left Helikon, where could they go? To what kind of life could they return? To his flat in London? To hers? To New York, where he said he always spent part of his year, staying at the Plaza? To the house in Iowa (or was it Illinois)? They seemed to have no piece of the world that belonged to them both.

Standing under a cold shower, vigorously toweling herself, brushing her hair, putting on makeup, Julia admitted to herself, not for the first time, that she was both homesick and terrified. She longed for her lost husband, her lost children, her lost home.

Dikran seemed, sometimes, so totally irrational.

As when she had made the joke about the sunflower seeds.

She had discovered a small trail of them on the hotel bedroom carpet when she was packing up their clothes in the Fleur de Lys. Dikran had been sleeping off the effect of Dr. Adnan's tranquilizing shot.

A small trail of sunflower seeds across the carpet.

As if, she had said later, laughing, an absent-minded squirrel had passed that way. "I never knew that you had a secret passion for sunflower seeds!" she had teased Dikran. "Why didn't you let me know? I'd have kept a supply in my luggage."

But his face had turned so dark with rage that she was seriously afraid he might rupture a blood vessel.

"I hate sunflower seeds!" he roared at her. "I *hate* them. And don't you forget it!"

Next minute, he was cradling and fondling her, calling her his flower, and apologizing for scaring her. "Just don't ever mention those sunflower seeds again, that's all."

Trembling, Julia promised that she would not.

And, on another occasion, when she had offered to type out his poems—for she had brought a portable typewriter with her and a plot for a play, which was now sinking back into the sand—he had flown into another frightening paroxysm of rage. She had not even stretched out a hand toward his portfolio of papers—had not even glanced toward it—but he shouted at her, banging the table so savagely that a glass of lemon juice was jolted onto the floor.

"Don't you ever *touch* my papers, d'you hear? Don't you dare to go near that case!"

"I wouldn't dream of it!" she answered indignantly. "I wonder you dare talk to me in that tone!"

For, after all, she had her pride; who was she, Julia Gibbon, to be addressed in such a manner?

And again, at once, he was all contrition, caressed her and wrapped his arms around her, burying his face in her hair and calling her his English rose. "Forgive me, forgive me; I don't know what I am doing. It is this damned sunstroke, that is all."

But was it really the sunstroke? she wondered again, wrapping a shawl around her shoulders. Was it *only* the sunstroke? Or would he have become like this in any circumstances?

Softly pulling the door to behind her, she ran down the stone stairs to the ground floor. It would be pleasant to encounter Adnan—who had, on several occasions, found time to play tennis with her or take her for walks when Dikran was sleeping or sulking—but the evening concert had already begun and he was probably in the hall.

At the foot of the stairs a paved passageway led right into the quadrangle, or left toward the orchard and vegetable gardens. She turned left, then right, and walked past the PRI-

VATE notice into Dr. Adnan's little formal garden. Preliminary chords from Schubert's *Magic Harp* overture were coming from the lighted windows of the concert hall above her; practically everybody would be in there, attending the main music program of the evening. She could be alone here, to listen in peace and privacy.

Or, no: her heart leaped, then sank again. Somebody else was here in the small, dusk-filled place; somebody was at work. She heard the clink of a trowel and—peering through the twilight—could just distinguish a figure which seemed to be kneeling beyond the center bed, pulling plants from the ground and dropping them into a basket. The person, whoever it might be—child or girl—was too small to be Adnan.

"Oh, hullo," said Julia, rather put out but deciding that, since she had come so far in, she could hardly walk out again without making *some* remark. "Isn't it rather dark for weeding?"

"Yes, it is; you're right," said the girl, effortlessly straightening her back and standing up. It was the skinny child, what was her name, Mike something, who seemed to be a kind of protégée of Adnan's. "The dark creeps up on you when you're busy," she added. She looked down at the area she had cleared, stooped to remove a dying thistle, and explained, "I was just tidying up Lucy's flowerbed. Achmed has so little time."

"Lucy?"

"The statue."

"Oh. Oh yes. Who was she? Was Dr. Adnan married?"

"No, no. Or not that I ever heard," the girl said, sticking her weeding implement upright into the loose earth beside the statue's pedestal. "No, Lucy was a girl he fell in love with years ago. In England."

"Oh, I see. What happened? Did she die?"

"Yes. It was very sad. She was a gifted pianist; Max Benovek was teaching her—or was going to teach her, I'm not quite sure of the details, but anyway he thought she was due to become a great player—and Uncle—Dr. Adnan fell in love with her and asked her to marry him. But she had a heart trouble, and before any of these things could happen, she died. She was quite young—younger than me, I believe."

"Poor Lucy." For the second time within an hour, Julia was surprised to find tears in her eyes. Why? What had produced in her this easy sensibility? Why should this simple and not uncommon tale affect her so?

"Did you know Lucy?"

"Oh, goodness, no! I expect I'd only have been about ten at the time. It was long before he came to Deldros. I didn't know Dr. Adnan then. Some Greek friends of his here told me about it once. He doesn't talk about her much—but he has mentioned her. After she died, he and Max Benovek wanted to make some kind of memorial to her, and that's how Helikon was started. Benovek donated quite a lot of money, and they fetched in a Greek millionaire called Capranis, who gave them this site. And Dr. Adnan sold a lot of very valuable pictures that he had. The girl's—Lucy's aunt was a painter, a primitive. Her name was Fennel Culpepper; maybe you've heard of her—"

"Oh, good heavens, yes. Some of her pictures are in the Tate, aren't they? They go for astronomic sums if they ever come on the market."

"Right. Adnan had acquired quite a lot of them, so he sold them all to the V & A and gave that money too. And that's how this place began."

"Quite a good memorial for little Lucy," Julia said rather drily, defying her own unreasonable emotion of two minutes before. "After all, she might never have become a great pianist."

"No. That's true," said Mike, in a mild and reflective tone.

"I wouldn't object to having such a memorial dedicated to me."

"No? But you," said Mike, "you don't need anyone's memorial, Lady Julia. Your plays will be enough to make people remember you."

Julia made no answer to this, only sighed, looking at the dim outline of the sculptured figure on its pedestal.

After a moment, Mike added diffidently, "I do hope you

won't be offended—I suppose it must be very boring, people must be saying things like this all the time—but I would like to tell you how *very* much I admire your plays."

"Thank you," Julia answered mechanically.

Despite this lukewarm reception the girl went on. "They are so beautifully constructed. And—what I like best—they have such a marvelously condensed, suffocating feeling of *place*—that awful farm in *The Blasted Heath*, and the old man's flat in *Midwinter*, and the room over the station in *Sharp, Flat, and Slightly Sweet*—you can almost *smell* the trains—your plays don't really need sets at all, I can see, but just the same, I'd love to do the sets for one of them, some day."

"Is that your profession—stage design?" Julia inquired. In fact she had a vague memory of Adnan saying something about the child, but at the time, preoccupied and worried about Dikran, Julia had not paid much attention.

"Yes it is. I don't suppose I'll ever get to the top," the girl said resignedly. "There's a lot of competition. But I love it. Are you working on a play at the moment, Lady Julia?" She added, after a moment's hesitation, "If you are, it—it would be the most terrific privilege to hear you talk about it a little."

Julia's attention had been wandering again, but now it occurred to her that this child was actually the first person who had made any inquiry about her work since she had come to Dendros—since she had left England. Among all the actors, musicians, singers, and other artists assembled at Helikon, not one, except for this girl, had manifested the slightest interest in whether she was working on anything. Dikran certainly had not.

As a general rule Julia disliked talking too much about any project on which she was engaged—discussion of it often seemed to diminish the impetus—but now, touched and amused at finding professional interest in such a wholly unexpected quarter, she began to describe the play that was in her mind. And, as she did so, it moved sluggishly from its submerged domain, showing new features.

"It's called *The Buildings*. It's about a rich woman's bad relationship with the inhabitants of a tenement block near her house—in some northern industrial town—she's a kind of dried-out widow—"

"Hah!" Mike's attention was instantly engaged. "That sounds great! A big, tall, gaunt block, overlooking her house? Full of angry, suspicious, resentful people?"

They had turned and were walking out into the orchard, away from the ambagious strains of music bouncing out of the concert hall above them. Schubert had by now got well into his stride.

"That's it," Julia said. "I want there to be a number of different friction points—slum children climbing her fence, balls breaking her windows, arguments about loud music and dogs and motorbikes—added to which the widow has a rebellious son who wants to leave the university and join a circus and learn to be a tightrope walker—"

"A tightrope walker—oh, terrific!" breathed Mike. "I suppose you couldn't have him actually walk his tightrope on the stage?"

"I rather doubt it!" Julia said, laughing. "Though it would be a novelty! No, I had more in mind some kind of Ibsenesque downfall, offstage, where he gets killed, you know, in the last act—"

"Yes, I can see it would be too farcical to have him do it in full view," Mike said wistfully. "But what a scene! Maybe they can have it in the film version."

The orchard was all around them now. As they strolled, they could feel the dry, soft grass crackle faintly under their feet. Huge stars flashed here and there among the dark leaves; the air was filled with a sharp scent of leaves and lemons.

"Do you like *Peter and the Wolf?*" Julia asked irrelevantly.

There was silence for a little while Mike reflected. "It's a job of work," she answered at length. "Lovely tunes. But I think Prokofiev never decided whose side he was on."

"Does that matter?"

"In a folk tale—or a children's story—yes, I think it's important, don't you?"

"Perhaps. I hadn't thought in those terms."

"But about your play—are you writing it now?"

"I'm thinking about it."

"When will you have finished it? When will it be put on?"

"I don't really know," Julia answered rather forlornly. "I've just got married again, you see; it's hard to plan ahead, with a new husband; one can't tell how much time there will be for work."

Beside her, in the dark, the girl gave a chuckle. "I suppose not! I hadn't thought of that as a reason against getting married, but now I see it must be quite a strong one."

"More so at my age, when time's beginning to get short. You're all right, you've still got plenty." She added, half idly, half enviously, "Perhaps you'll be designing sets for this play someday—heaven only knows how long it will take me to get it finished. By that time you may be halfway through your career."

"Oh, wouldn't that be marvelous!"

"Tell me what else you've done—what experience you've had. Where are you working now?"

Talking, discussing, reminiscing, they walked to and fro under the lemon trees.

Presently the moon rose and threw long shadows over the limp, silvered grass.

"Do you know," said Julia, peering at her watch, "that we've been out here for two and a half hours?"

"Have we really? Gosh, I'd better go and see if Mother wants settling down for the night." She added diffidently, "I *have* enjoyed this talk."

"I have too. —Where are we?" Julia said. "I've clean lost my sense of direction under all these trees."

"Oh, I know where we are. We're right down at the bottom of the orchard—near the Dendros road—by the sun-bathing area. There's a path back to the main drive, if we go on in this direction."

"The sun-bathing area?"

"Nude—didn't you know? They've got two precincts—one for men, one for women. Uncle Achmed's a great stickler for propriety," Mike said, chuckling again. "You'd never think he was such a lady-killer in his private life. Here—this is the men's sun-bathing enclosure on our right, now, behind the bamboos."

They had reached a rock path. On their right, a barricade of bamboos and rushes, plaited and packed tightly between stakes, similar to the screens protecting the tomato beds, rose to a height of about nine feet.

"That's to keep out peeping Thomasinas," Mike explained. "Nobody from here would bother, of course. But I believe there are tales of people from Dendros—tourists probably—trying to poke spyglasses through the barricade. Silly, isn't it? I certainly can't imagine wanting to peep at male sun-bathers; most of the men who come here are no great shakes as far as looks go. Of course I'm not including your husband, Lady Julia. He's dreamy!"

Julia laughed. "The females aren't much better, if it comes to that. Who's the very fat woman with a blond bun who gets wheeled around in a wheelchair by a skinny dark boy?"

"That's Marion Hillel."

"The pianist? Whatever happened to her? It's years since she played."

"Some kind of spinal illness, I think. She couldn't even sit up, let alone walk. But Adnan's treatment is doing her so much good that she's begun practicing again—she plays Beethoven every morning," Mike said with pride.

"Hullo—what's that?"

Julia had stopped by the gate of the male sun-bathing enclosure. A large sign, white in the moonlight, said MEN ONLY. The gate stood open, and just inside it something light-colored had caught her eye.

"Nobody sun-bathing at this time of night," Mike said. "Unless they're moon-bathing."

She walked inside, glanced around, and stooped down.

"Somebody's clothes," she said, coming back. "But the

somebody can't have been here for hours—the clothes are all damp and dewy. *Espadrilles*—jeans—T shirt—wonder how he got back to his room without them." She chuckled again. "Maybe he's a streaker! Anyway, I'll put these in Zoé's office —she can make an announcement about them at evening drinks or stick a note on the board."

"He'll probably remember and come back for them himself in the meantime," said Julia. "Most likely he had swimming trunks as well, and went down to the beach for a swim, and forgot these."

"Yes, probably that's it. Good night, then, Lady Julia," Mike said, and ran off in the direction of the office.

Nice child, Julia thought absently, looking after her. Tansy would like her. Seems to know what she's talking about.

And then Julia's attention was deflected from Mike by the sight of Dr. Adnan walking briskly toward her along the wide, flagged path among a group of emerging concert goers. He wore a velvet evening jacket and a flowered cravat. He was looking exceptionally pleased with himself. "Ah, there, Lady Julia! You do not attend our concert?"

"No," Julia replied coolly—but pleased that he had re-marked her absence. "It was such a beautiful night that I've been walking with Mike in the orchard. You look very cheer-ful, Dr. Adnan?"

"Cheerful, yes indeed, I should say so. I have secured the services of Kerry Farrell for our small opera. Here at last is a singer of international caliber who is not subject to silly super-stitions and shibboleths. She will sing the part extremely well —and the old Destrier will not be disappointed on his *jour de fête*."

"Oh, that's very good news—I'm so pleased," said Julia, not with total truth, because she had never taken the least interest in opera. But she was pleased for Adnan's sake and added with sincerity, "Old Destrier's a splendid old boy, isn't he. Will you be able to get it rehearsed in time? When's his birthday?"

"In ten days from now. And, yes, I think so; we have re-hearsed the minor parts already, in hopes. Joop knows the piece very well. I myself will take the part of Horatio. But of course it has been an anxiety not knowing if we shall be able to proceed with it."

He suddenly burst into exuberant song.

> "You can't do chromatics
> With proper emphatics
> When anguish your bosom is wringing!

> When distracted with worries in plenty
> And his pulse is a hundred and twenty
> And his fluttering bosom the slave of mistrust is,
> A tenor can't do himself justice!

Julia laughed, thinking what an unexpected character he was; all serious professional consideration one minute, all light-hearted fooling and nonsense the next. What had that girl said —something about his being a lady-killer in private life?

He proved her point by dropping his musical-comedy manner and asking with the utmost kindness and gravity, "How is your husband this evening, Lady Julia? Do you think he is settling more to our ways?"

"Oh, I don't know, Dr. Adnan—sometimes I'm really puzzled and worried about him!" she burst out. "He seems—he seems in a rage against life itself sometimes—"

"That *would* seem ungrateful, just when life has presented him with such a beautiful partner," Adnan remarked, with a return to his former manner, but added more seriously, "Patience, my friend! He is a complicated character, that husband of yours. A few more days of our diet, though, a few more treatments, and we shall see a change, I am sure. You cannot expect recovery to be so simple in a man who has such a number on his arm."

"What kind of a number on whose arm?" Mike had come running lightly back along the flagged path from Zoé's office and now stood beside them. She spoke with casual friendliness, not from curiosity so much as to inform them of her arrival.

But Adnan, perhaps embarrassed at having been overheard speaking in a public place on a confidential matter, answered rather sharply, "My dear little Mike, small pitchers should not have enormous ears!" He pulled one of hers, not too gently. "Lady Julia and I were speaking privately."

Even in the moonlight, Julia could see Mike flush at the snub. "I'm sorry!" she said, trying to keep a quiver of hurt and anger out of her voice. "I didn't have the least intention of eavesdropping, I assure you! Zoé's wanted on the phone in her office—I only wanted to ask if you knew where she was."

"Down in the steam room; somebody reported that the lid had jammed on one of the steam baths, and the plumber has come."

"Thank you," said Mike haughtily, and ran off toward the stair that led to the treatment area.

"Greek plumbers work long hours," Julia remarked.

"The plumber's cousin is a nurse here."

"I see. —What a nice child that little Mike is."

"Is she not?" Adnan agreed eagerly. He added with some remorse, "I am sorry that I spoke to her unkindly—because I myself was caught in indiscretion! I will make it all right with her tomorrow."

"Oh, by tomorrow she'll have forgotten all about it. Is she your goddaughter?"

"*Goddaughter?* No, indeed." He seemed taken aback at the suggestion.

Julia said good night and walked away in the direction of her bedroom.

I'm sure a touch of sunstroke wouldn't make *him* disagreeable, she thought, sighing. He never seems worried about anything. And yet plenty of responsibility must rest on his shoulders.

I hope we'll be able to fit in a game of tennis tomorrow. Or a walk. Or a drive.

She opened the door, fervently wishing that she might find Dikran asleep. Or, better still, gone out on one of his walks.

But he was wide awake, lying with open eyes fixed on the ceiling.

⁅ 7 ⁆

VARIATIONS

At least part of what I had hoped for now came to pass: Mother really did get into the spirit of Helikon, appreciated what it had to offer, and spent her days darting from one treatment to the next—seaweed baths, massage, manipulation, acupuncture, heat, cold, wax, mud—she was always in some mix or other. If I wanted to talk to her during the day, I had to thread my way through the treatment area, serenading like Blondel in search of Richard, and would find her behind some curtain, covered in hot wax and crinkly paper, or stuck full of bamboo darts and having a long conversation about education with kindly Mr. Twang, who did the acupunctures. She throve on the lemon juice and grated radish. She borrowed a violin, went to master classes, and practiced trios with two enthusiastic Latvian girls. Not a word of Latvian did she speak, they no English, but nonetheless they all managed to communicate as much as was necessary.

Apart from the Latvians, though, and me, and friendly consultations with Adnan, Mother did not involve herself in the social life of the place, which bubbled up among performers and patients in the form of lemon-juice parties on people's bedroom balconies and long, terry-robed gossip sessions on the lawns. Basically both shy and reserved, Mother was by no means a ready mixer; in fact she found it easy to talk to people only in her own professional slot. Nor did people find it easy to talk to her; they were frightened off, I thought, by her somewhat formidable appearance. She was also, I was saddened to discover, growing a little hard of hearing; alone with somebody in a room she could hear perfectly well, but put her among a chattering group and she was sunk. She would shrug, look defeated, and go back to her own room.

So, during the day, I did not see a lot of her, for I was quite busy myself, but I always gave her a scalp massage in the evenings. She would be tired by then; she never attended the main concerts, preferring to go to bed early and read. I hoped the scalp massages were doing some good; her shaved hair was taking its time about growing back, and she still wore the black turbans, which did add a daunting air of formality among all the bikinis and bedroom slippers. By now she was fairly tanned (unlike me; all I do is freckle), but she looked frail and big-eyed and unlike herself, so that I still hesitated to burden her with questions relating to the tragic past (and the possibly disagreeable and upsetting present). Besides—amid all the peaceful harmony and virtuous activities of Helikon—my wish to find out seemed like vulgar and selfish curiosity. So I delayed and procrastinated and let it all lie fallow.

"I am a 'dull and muddy-mettled rascal, peak, like John-a-dreams, unpregnant of my cause,'" I thought sometimes, dropping in to watch the minor characters at their rehearsals of *Les Mystères d'Elsinore*. George, who had quite a pleasant light tenor, was standing in for the part of Hamlet, as their main singer hadn't arrived yet. She had some engagement in Berlin to fulfill first, but was due to appear any day. And there were still six days to go before old Annibal's birthday.

I was quite pleased with my sets.

I'd been given an empty barn as a workroom—a goat shed, I

suppose it was really—and had bought a lot of wall paint in Archangelos village. The powdery blues and greens that the Greeks use for their houses were just the thing for my Piero distant backgrounds, and I had borrowed a book of reproductions from the main library in Dendros. I needed some dark reds and blacks, though, for the interiors and the castle walls; I was thinking, one morning as I surveyed my work, that I'd really have to co-opt somebody to go into Dendros with me and help carry stuff back. Zoé and a couple of Greek students were helping me with the costumes—and we were also lucky enough to have the advice of a professional dress designer, Graziella Vanzini, who, as it happened, was having her bursitis ameliorated at Helikon. But Zoé and the students were hard at work during the day, and Graziella was undergoing her treatments and not available to run errands. They worked hard in the evenings, though, and, despite the shortness of time, we were making good progress with the costumes, which, both from choice and necessity, were severely plain. We used the formal, fluted draperies and tunics that Piero characters mostly wear, with buttoned fronts and round collars and round, fifteenth-century hats like squashed cushions; they looked impressive and were very quick to make. Fortunately there was no shortage of material, for Zoé bought Greek cotton in twenty-bale lots for the Helikon sheets and cubicle curtains; all we had to do was dye it, and there was a small dye factory in a village called Skimi, fives miles away, where they dipped all the material that was subsequently made up into shapeless garments of dazzling colors and sold to tourists in Dendros; so I borrowed Zoé's bike and cycled to Skimi and bought bags and bags of their dye powders. Then the two Greek students and I had a happy, splashy evening in one of Helikon's do-it-yourself laundry rooms, dyeing dozens of lengths of cloth and spinning them dry. By mixing and double dipping we achieved some rich and subtle shades that were highly satisfactory. I wanted, if possible, to match those shades in my backgrounds.

I was pondering over my sketches for the throne-room sets

and deciding that the painted folds of curtain must be a dark plum red, when Adnan walked in.

He wandered about the shed, inspecting my flats, while I got silently on with my planning and made lists of things I wanted to buy.

"Hey-dey! We're not speaking today?" he observed, giving me a sharp look.

"I was thinking, that's all."

He gazed at the cliffs of Elsinore. "Very nice; v-e-r-y nice! Heads of cauliflower—am I right? Covered in your English white sauce, that ubiquitous, invaluable, all-purpose medium which can be used as a poultice, a paint-base, a makeup foundation, or as whitening for footmen's wigs."

"That's body color. And the sets are the cliffs of Elsinore," I said coldly.

"Of course, of course, fancy my making such a mistake. Tsk, tsk, so they are, so they are!" He inspected them a bit more and suddenly declaimed,

> "It is the dreadful summit of the cliff
> That beetles o'er his base into the sea!

With Hadrian's villa on the top, no less! You don't think that is a *little* too classically Mediterranean for Denmark's seat of government?" He seemed extra nervous and fidgety, I thought; much more so than usual.

I said, "Certainly not. Shakespeare had *been* to Italy. He hadn't been to Denmark. I'm trying to follow *his* imagination."

"I see, I see." He began to sing,

> "Tell me, where is fancy bread?
> Or in the heart, or in the head?
> Sesame, raisin, or honey-spread?
> But shut your eyes in holy dread
> For he on every kind hath fed
> And been by an-gels nourish-ed!"

As I ignored this, he wandered about some more, balancing on toes and heels, muttering, "Not bad, not bad, they are really not at all bad. Has the old Destrier seen them?"

"Yes, he has," I said, and began gathering my brushes together.

"Hoity toity, we *are* on our high horse today, are we not? (What a wonderful expression that is, hoity, toity. What can it possibly *mean?* Now, if one were in Brooklyn one would know: hoity, toity boids, oy, gevalt! But, then, we are not in Brooklyn. And as for the high horse—I like to think of you on *that*, my dear little Mike. It is almost, but not quite, as high as high dudgeon.)"

Turning a deaf ear to his teasing, I said, "Dr. Adnan, can I have about ten pounds' worth of drachmae from the petty cash to go into Dendros and buy some more paint, please?"

"Certainly you can; just tell Zoé I said so, but from where do you get all this Dr. Adnan stuff? How formal we are, all of a sudden! Old Uncle Achmed I used to be, once upon a time."

"That was when I was a child."

"And now we are very grown up, so elderly and dignified that we have to *stand* on our dignity, hmm?" I was hoping that he might offer to drive me into Dendros in his Volkswagen, which stood idle under the lemon trees most days, and he seemed on the point of doing so, for he said, "You will need quite a lot more paint, though, won't you? How do you propose to carry it all back? You can hardly pile that on the carrier of Zoé's bicycle. Is paint all you intend to buy?"

"No, I want some plaster of Paris and some tassels and stuff for the costumes as well."

"In that case," he said, "you had better borrow my car. And why do you not take Lady Julia with you? While her husband is having his treatments, I have observed that she is somewhat at a loose end; she does not take many treatments herself and I have seen her looking as if she does not know what to do with herself. I think she would be very pleased if you invited her."

"Oh—very well," I said, rather ungraciously, because that was not at all what I had had in mind.

He looked at me intently and said in a reproving manner, "Lady Julia is lonely and homesick and very sad and worried also. It would be kind in you to do this. —Besides, she likes you."

I had liked Lady Julia too, actually, and after our late-evening talk in the orchard, had rather hoped that I was going to have her for a friend. But during the past three or four days she and Adnan had seemed to be very much in each other's pockets. I sometimes wondered what her husband, the mysterious Mr. Saint, thought about this. Saint seemed of all names the most unsuitable for him, and plainly it was not his original designation—he looked more as if it should have been Saladin or Iskandar or Sheikh Somebody. He was a sultry-looking fellow, with a heavy blue jowl, Napoleonic, dark treacle-colored eyes, a thin, rather cruel (I thought) mouth, and a short, curved, beaky nose that seemed on the thin side for his fleshy face. I had remarked on this once to Matthieu, the masseur, when he was giving the shin I once broke in sixth-form hockey a bit of a rub, and Mat said at once, "Plastic surgery."

"Eh? How can you be sure?"

"O, *peuh*, I have seen dozens. In my father's health spa in Brussels we are all the time looking after ladies who have their noses improved or their double chins eliminated—there is a look—how can I say it?—some stiffness, skin not elastic—I can tell, always. Is like a drawing when lines have been rubbed out and redrawn."

Mat's father had sent him to Helikon for experience so that he could later on return and take over the parental business, but Mat himself intended to fill the gap left by Breughel's passing. He was keen to help me with my sets, but although I was glad of his help I had to be constantly on the watch, to restrain him from suddenly putting in some feature that his inventive fancy had suggested: demons riding through the air, eggs exploding into monsters, touches of Bosch-like fantasy. "In Shakespeare's time, after all, folk believe in such things!" he would protest reproachfully.

"Mat, this is *Hamlet*, not *A Midsummer Night's Dream!*"

However, about plastic surgery and its effects I thought his knowledge was probably sound enough, and his observation had enhanced the sinister and mysterious aura that Mr. Saint seemed to carry around him. I'd cast him as Rochester, or Mr. Murdstone, I thought, or one of those fiends in Restoration drama. I could hardly imagine that he would take kindly to being neglected by his wife in favor of a smooth-spoken Turkish doctor. But perhaps he didn't realize what was happening; like Mother, he did not mix much; outside of his treatments, he seemed to spend a lot of time in his room. One saw him with Lady Julia in the big, light dining room, eating his little mounds of shredded nut and carrot with a look of disdainful, incredulous disgust; sometimes he could be seen briefly in the downstairs waiting area clad in a black robe of silk so stiff that it would have stood upright on its own—I longed to ask if I could borrow it for Hamlet. Otherwise Mr. Saint was not generally visible. Perhaps he was hardly aware that his wife played tennis and swam and so often went for strolls and evening drives with Adnan.

But, strangely enough, *I* found myself minding for him. Also, I had taken a liking to Lady Julia, and if Adnan was regarding her as one of his regular flirts, I knew she would be in for a painful letdown. On the other hand, if it was more than a flirt, then everybody was in for trouble.

But why should one need to flirt on one's honeymoon?

None of this was my business, however, and I said to Adnan, who was now observing me very acutely, with a look that I did not greatly care for in his plum-dark eyes—ironic, patronizing, quizzical—"I like Lady Julia too! And I admire her plays. If she wants to go into Dendros, that's okay by me. If she wouldn't prefer to swim or play tennis, I'll be glad to take her."

"Good," he said briskly. "Then, you can certainly borrow my car."

"Why don't you take her in yourself?" I couldn't resist saying.

He looked at me under his eyelashes—which were as thick

and dark as a Jersey cow's—and said silkily, "Believe it or not, my dear little Mike, I have work to do, keeping an eye on Helikon. Besides, it is *your* trip to Dendros that is in question."

I wasn't going to pick that one up. Suddenly I felt tired of this conversation—tired altogether—in fact, really fatigued. I sat down on a packing case and said, "Very good. Tell Lady Julia—if you should see her—that I'd love her to come along if she wants to, and I plan to start about two o'clock. Dr. Adnan there's something I wanted to ask you about Mother."

Immediately he was kind, serious, attentive—a changed person. "What is it, Mike? Something is worrying you?"

Then of course I found it hard to go on. I looked down at my paint-stained fingers and rubbed at a patch of explosive green on the back of my hand.

Seeing my difficulty, he, too, sat down on a box and said, quietly and sympathetically. "Do not look so distraught. Whatever it is, we try to fix it, hmn? It probably is not so bad as you imagine. Tell Papa Mustafa all your trouble."

I said, "You are a great friend of the Aghnides family. Did they ever tell you—anything of my family history?"

He looked at me very gravely and said, "No, Mike, they did not. Old Demosthenes Aghnides is the very soul of honor and discretion. Even supposing I were his blood brother, if he had been entrusted with any secret about your family, he would not tell it unless he had permission to do so. I do know that there was some tragedy connected with your family—that your father and sister both died, and that was the reason why you spent those years in Dendros when you were a child—but more than that, I do not know. It was long before I came to this island. But why do you ask?"

I could not tell him about Father being still alive—about my having read Mother's note. It wasn't my secret to give away; if old Mr. Aghnides could keep silent, so could I. But I did say, after a moment or two—during which he sat immovable, unspeaking, looking at me with the most penetrating attention —"I wasn't trying to *find out* from you—what happened to my father and Drusilla, I mean. It's just that there's this great, awful, undivulged secret which has always come between my mother and myself. It really has just about wrecked our relationship. Until now."

"You mean to say that *you* do not know what happened?" At this he did look really startled. His eyebrows—which were black, thick, and bushy—shot up like forklifts. He said, "She never *told* you what happened to your father and sister?"

"No."

"Ah, you English, you English!" Adnan exploded. "Never will I understand this race, never—not if I had lived in England for seventy years instead of just seven! Here you have a mother—an intelligent, educated lady who makes a fine career for herself, as what? as a *teacher*, directing young persons how they shall grow and learn and discover how to meet experience and make the best of their life. Here we have her child—a nice, funny, creative girl (never mind that she is also cursed with a black, censorious, puritanical, churlish temper) —" Dr. Adnan threw me a needle-sharp glance—even in his kindest moments one could never be quite safe from these darts—"and what does this lady do? Does she tell her troubles to her child, avail herself of this outlet, strengthen their relationship by mutual comfort, consolidation, solace, et cetera—"

"No," I said flatly. "She doesn't. She was trying to spare me from whatever it was, because it was all so dreadful."

He threw up his hands. "I say nothing! It is just a wonder that you have turned out—as you have turned out. Certainly I realize right away when I first see your mother that here is the very quintessence of English ladyhood: self-contained, reserved, independent, up-tight, and, above all, reluctant to make a fuss. Ah, this dread of fuss! It is the motivation behind all English history. Why did the Pilgrims go to America? To avoid fuss. Why did King Charles let his head be cut off? Too much of a gentleman to make a fuss. Why was Prince Albert —but I digress! So, all this time, your mother contains this terrible secret in her bosom. Whatever it was. No wonder she still looks so thin and frail, no wonder our Helikon regime is slow to take effect on her."

"It really has helped her, quite a lot," I assured him.

"Well, she must have a constitution like a musk ox—to retain all that anguish within her, the deaths of husband and daughter—*and* sustain a concrete beam dropping on her head as well. But, without doubt, this delays her recovery. Most definitely I think you should have a heart-to-heart conversation with her about it all. 'Mother, dear Mother,' you say to her, 'it may have escaped your attention that I am now a grown-up girl'—yes, my dear Mike, I have observed how she still behaves to you as if you were a little child, age twelve or less—'Mother,' you say, 'I am now an adult and it is my right that you reveal all.' Quite simply you say it—like that."

"Sure I do. Just like that."

"Well, my dear Mike, I know it takes a little courage, but courage you have in plenty. Faults you have in plenty too I do not deny—intolerance, suspicion, obstinacy, superiority—" He was well back in form now.

"Okay, okay," I said, standing up.

"But courage—this you do not lack. You are braver than I, indeed." He stood up too.

"I don't remember ever seeing *you* scared of *any*thing."

"No? But some things do scare me, Mike, and several of them are right here in Helikon at this time."

I did not feel enough of the courage he attributed to me to ask what he meant by that, and when he said, "Come, I will give you the car key," I followed him silently to his office. This was an austerely tidy place in the main building, with a secretary's room opening off it. Looking at his orderly files, dustless desk, pencils and pens tidily contained in a pottery mug, books neatly marshaled in bookshelves, I thought that, despite his explosion about the English, he and Mother did have quite a few traits in common.

Whereas I am really very untidy.

"Here." He opened a drawer and gave me the car key. "And here—" From a cashbox he gave me a fistful of Greek notes. "Buy your paint and trimmings. With what is left, treat yourself and Lady Julia to a glass of ouzo. Now run along. Have a—" he paused and then flashed his wide, beaming grin, "Have a nice time. That is the term, is it not?"

"Thank you," I said, and pocketed the money.

On his immaculate desk there stood one photograph. It was a head, not very big, simply framed in black. The print was fuzzy, as if it had been blown up from a much smaller snapshot: picture of a girl with a wide forehead, a thin, pointed face, and a spray of untidy, flax-pale hair. She was looking intently forward, eyes narrowed as if taking aim, and indeed, in the background, the stalls of a fair could vaguely be distinguished. It was, I knew, Adnan's lost love, Lucy; when I was much younger, he had occasionally let fall pieces of information about her. Rather a plain girl, Lucy was; but I thought I would have liked her. She looked an extremely determined character, who might ride roughshod over anyone who obstructed her; but she also looked as if she found plenty of things funny. She was not smiling in the picture, she was frowning slightly, and her lips were parted as she took aim, revealing the fact that her front teeth were rather endearingly crossed. I wondered what it was that she had been aiming at so carefully when the picture was taken, and whether she had hit it.

Adnan, following the direction of my gaze, said, "She has a little the look of Lady Julia, do you not think so?"

"No, I don't," I said shortly, and turned to leave the room.

Behind me, I heard him give a brief, sharp sigh. Then his phone rang, and instantly he was involved in a vigorous discussion about students' unions and the rates of holiday pay for part-time workers at Helikon. "Not a drach more do we give until we hear from the union about it! I am not in this business to support idle, good-for-nothing dropouts from the universities!" he snapped. Adnan could be quite tough when it suited him. He was by no means a simple character. But as I was going around the turn of the stairs, he put his head out of the study door and shouted, "Mike! Don't forget about the hand brake!"

I remembered then that the hand brake in his car, if applied too violently (and you had to apply it quite a bit, since the foot brake was not up to much) had a habit of opening the passenger door, which had caused unwary passengers to be catapulted out on bends. "All right, I'll remember!" I shouted back.

I went out into the sunshine with plenty to ponder about.

People were already assembling in the loggia for their lunchtime lemon juice. (Patients who were not yet on solids were not subjected to the torture of going into the dining room and watching their better-fed companions chomping chick-peas). I picked up a glass of juice and sat on the grass, waiting for Lady Julia to appear.

In the middle of the quadrangle Joop Kolenbrander was taking a batch of his compatriots through a Mozart wind octet. They were all different heights, and somehow, with their bulbous and tubular instruments, they looked irresistibly comic, like the Seven Dwarfs. Joop himself, pink-faced and egg-headed, was the shape of a stick of celery and had an outsize Adam's apple—an Adam's pineapple—which rushed up and down his throat all the time he conducted, as if it were some kind of glottal stop and wanted to be in on the act.

In between their bursts of carefree music I could hear conversation of the usual kind as patients wandered out of the dining room with plates of salad and sat on the grass crunching their carrots and sipping their juice.

". . . swelling's really going down at last."

". . . *always* comes in two bars early . . ."

". . . sore from all this harp practice—if I could possibly borrow your surgical spirit . . ."

". . . can't stand the woman who does the saunas—the big strapping one . . ."

". . . wind! I just fart *all* the time here . . ."

". . . Who doesn't? Adnan would say it's evil humors being released . . ."

". . . still haven't fixed the fourth steam bath. Greek plumbers . . ."

". . . first full rehearsal of *Elsinore*, now Miss Farrell's . . ."

". . . what wouldn't I give for a big steak and a plateful
of . . ."

". . . joke if Kerry Farrell dropped dead in the part like the
last two . . ."

". . . didn't actually die *during* the performance?"

". . . well, you know what I . . ."

". . . only ever sleep about four hours a night here—beds like
planks—and as for dreams . . ."

It was true that one's sleep was thin and light on the low
diet. But it did not seem to matter. Adnan's theory was that
the life of stress and anxiety and regular overeating that most
people subjected themselves to also caused them to sleep for
unnecessarily long, even harmfully long periods of time, as a
kind of escape. "Oversleeping is as bad as overeating," he
often said severely. As a solace, or reward for the non-sleepers,
he had a projection room at Helikon where early silent films
were shown from midnight to 5 A.M. I seldom bothered to go
in there; I quite enjoyed the sleepless hours and either went
for night walks or lay on my bed peacefully planning the sets
for all Shakespeare's plays.

Lady Julia came strolling out on to the grass wearing a
plain, straw-colored silk dress and a big natural straw hat, and
looking like a million dollars. It's no use, I thought; having a
whole lot of money *does* make a difference, there's no getting
away from the fact; expensive materials are just better than
cheap ones.

But it was true that no amount of cash could have improved
or made any difference to her long, beautiful face, framed by
the cloudy, pre-Raphaelite hair.

For once, her husband was with her, and he stood regarding
me impassively while I made my suggestion of the trip into
town, feeling rather shy and foolish about it. Politeness im-
pelled me to include him in the invitation: "And you too, of
course, Mr. Saint, if you would like?"

"Thank you, but I'd better not," he said. "Walking around the streets of Dendros in hot sun is probably not what Dr. Adnan would recommend."

Did I imagine the sarcastic note in his voice?

Lady Julia, however, said that she would love to go, and vanished indoors to fetch her purse. I had thought her husband would go with her, but to my surprise he remained by my side and we kept up a slightly stilted conversation, waiting for her to return.

He asked how I came to be so well acquainted with Dendros, and I explained about my childhood visits. Then he said, "I hear that you are painting the sets for this *Hamlet* opera?"

Out of politeness, I think, he asked me about the job, so I described my Piero idea. Unexpectedly, he turned out to be very well informed about Piero; he did not, somehow, look the kind of man who would know about painters—I can't help it if that sounds snobbish—and our discussion had become quite animated by the time Lady Julia returned. It appeared that he had traveled all over Italy looking at Piero pictures in remote country churches, and had seen the great "Flagellation" at Urbino before it was stolen; he seemed as familiar with it as most people are with "When did you last see your father?"

"Do come and see my sets, any time," I said. "I'm sure you could give me lots of advice about them," and he said that he would very much like to.

Lady J. came back at last with her handbag and more lipstick on.

"Take care of yourself, my darling," she said, giving her husband a hasty peck, and then we went off to the corner of the lemon grove, where Adnan's unassuming little auto lived. It was the same he'd had ever since I'd known him; many were the excursions I'd taken in it with him and Calliope. The smell of warm dust and gasoline and dirty upholstery gave me a queer, nostalgic feeling.

I remembered to warn Lady Julia about the handbrake, and we swung off up the road into town, passing a bus in which an old lady was holding up her dead husband's picture to the window so that he could enjoy the ride too. I suddenly thought that we should have brought Lucy along. Perhaps that's what Adnan would really have liked.

"I can see that my husband has taken a big fancy to you," Lady Julia said as we came within view of the flat, white roofs of Dendros town and the Aegean shining beyond them. She went on, "I do hope you'll talk to him some more. I don't think he knows any people your age and he's very shy with them. He's never had any children of his own, though I suspect he would have liked to very much."

Why didn't he, then? was the obvious question, but as there was presumably some sad reason for this I didn't ask it.

She added thoughtfully, more to herself than to me, "Perhaps, in a way, it's just as well. Millionaires' children must be in such a position of risk all the time."

"You mean kidnaping?" I said, working the car carefully along Winston Churchill Street, which had acquired several sets of traffic lights since last I'd been there. "Like the Getty boy, and that wretched little Rittenhouse baby that they found gnawed by rats."

She shivered and said, "I can't *bear* to think of that case. I really just meant spoiling—the danger of having everything within reach, always—but there's kidnaping too, it's quite true."

I drove on past the post office and along the harborside. "Shall I park here, or would you like to go straight into the Old Town?"

"Whichever suits you better. I haven't anything special that I want to do," she said. "I just thought it would be nice to get away for a bit. I'll come and help you with your errands."

{8}

WATER·MUSIC

As usual, when she got back, Julia found Dikran lying on his bed.

"I don't know why you didn't make an evening of it," he said in a surly tone. "Why didn't you go to a nightclub? Have dinner somewhere? Stay the night at the Fleur de Lys?"

"Mike wanted to get back and hear the Hamlet rehearsal," Julia replied coldly, affecting to be unaware of his sarcasm. "Kerry Farrell has arrived, and she's going to be singing tonight for the first time. I thought I'd go and listen, later on—do you want to come along?"

"You know I can't stand that man's music. Now," he said. "now, I suppose, what time you have left over from that little Turkish pimp is going to be spent puttering around with the girl—is that it?"

"Oh, Dikran—*don't!*"

"Don't what?"

"Don't *be* like this! She's a very nice girl—you liked her yourself, didn't you? You thought she was interesting—I could see. I just like her, that's all. What's wrong with going shopping with her?"

"Nothing—nothing—nothing!" he snarled, and, turning away from her, lay curled up with his face to the wall, sullen and silent. Julia gave a long, impatient, unhappy sigh. For the past two or three days Dikran's temper seemed to have been deteriorating hourly. He alternated between morose gloom and fairly active rage. Was it unreasonable that she wished to spend as little time as possible in his company?

Since she could think of nothing to say that was conciliating, she turned to leave the room.

"*Now* where are you off to?" he demanded.

"I'm due for a sauna in half an hour. I thought I'd go and listen to some music first. Why don't you come along?"

"Because I don't want to listen to any more goddamned amateurs!"

She shrugged and left him. No use to point out that many of the performers to be heard at Helikon were not amateurs at all but top-class professionals; in this mood Dikran was unsusceptible to reason.

Actually it was the amateur side of Helikon that Julia chiefly enjoyed. She loved to walk past a window, hear a burst of music, and, looking in, see three long-haired young persons in swimsuits playing a trio entirely for their own pleasure, lost to everything but the enjoyable noise they were making.

She loved being able to drop into any room, sit and listen to the music that was going on there, then, when she pleased, move on and dip elsewhere—or lie out under the lemon trees, with a distant, leaf-checkered view of the Aegean, and hear snatches of organ, flute, strings, or choir, from open windows or distant groups. The sense that all this joyful sound was free, given and taken purely for pleasure. added to her delight in it. Whereas for Dikran she feared that it worked in exactly the opposite way: his appreciation of anything went up in direct proportion to its cost; in a month's marriage she had already discovered that, and she occasionally asked herself, with unwonted bitterness, whether her own value to him had anything to do with personal attraction at all—or was it solely based on her status as playwright, celebrated ex-wife of a celebrated critic, well-known TV beauty of panel fame, much-photographed newspaper and magazine subject, conspicuous central figure in a notorious divorce case?

Perhaps, she thought gloomily, that was why Dendros had turned Dikran so sulky—because there were so few observers here to appreciate the prize he had acquired.

Running down the stairs, she turned right at random—she had really come out with no other intention than that of escaping from Dikran—and encountered Joop Kolenbrander carrying a suitcase and escorting an unfamiliar female with eager deference. His red face and unwontedly flustered demeanor aroused Julia's curiosity—could the newcomer be the much-discussed Kerry Farrell, the dauntless candidate for the part of Hamlet?

So it proved.

"Oh—Miss Farrell—have you met Lady Julia Gibbon—er—Lady Julia Saint?" Joop said. "Lady Julia, this is Miss Kerry Farrell, who has come so kindly at short notice to help us out of our difficulties."

"How do you do, Miss Farrell," Julia said, smiling. "I can't tell you how anxiously everyone here has been waiting for your arrival!"

"And sorry I am I couldn't be here sooner," said the singer. "'Twasn't the will that was lacking, I can tell you—if I had the choice I'd spend every minute of my time in this blessed spot. But I had a concert scheduled for last night in Berlin that I couldn't be cutting."

She spoke with a slight Irish lilt which Julia's sensitive ear diagnosed as being half artificial—a theatrical flourish. Though it was true that Kerry Farrell looked genuinely Irish. Despite the accent, she seemed pleasantly unaffected; she smiled frankly at Julia, putting out a large but shapely hand.

"And aren't you the clever one, Lady Julia, to be writing all those beautiful plays, each one of them better than the one before? Glory be to God, the time I've had, trying to get back to see them all, and I, as likely as not, stuck in some god-forsaken corner of the globe singing my soul out to a lot of heathen who don't know Monteverdi from Monty Python."

Julia laughed. "Well, you won't find audiences like that here, I can tell you! Everyone's just panting to hear you."

"No, faith!" said Miss Farrell, rolling her eyes in mock despair, "it's terrified I am entirely at the thought of singing in front of such a set of experts."

"Oh, what nonsense you talk, Kerry," said Joop. "Come along with you now and meet M. Destrier."

The Irish accent seemed to be catching, Julia reflected as they went on their way.

The sound of piano and strings coming from a recital room caught Julia's attention as she wandered idly along the flagged path, and she turned through a door that stood open. Finding a canvas seat placed handily in a cool current of air near the entrance, she settled down to listen.

A woman sitting on another canvas chair gave her a welcoming smile; she was a fat little person with bright, rosy cheeks, and a row of black curls across her forehead, whom Julia had seen around for the past few days, taking a vociferous part in the talk of the livelier groups and using her immensely elaborate camera as a means of getting into conversation with others who might have wished to avoid her, which Julia had hitherto succeeded in doing. But she looked harmless enough. She wore a pink shirt and an ill-judged dirndl which did not suit her bun-shaped figure.

Julia smiled back with caution and turned her head in the direction of the players.

A quintet consisting of two violins, cello, viola, and piano were performing a work unfamiliar to Julia, but, to her chagrin, and as so often happens when one turns on radio music, she had no sooner settled herself than the piece came to its end.

The players all gathered around the piano to discuss the difficult passages.

"What *was* the quintet they were playing?" Julia murmured rashly to her neighbor.

"It's by Franz Schmidt—it's arranged for—" The little woman poured out a profuse flood of *sotto voce* information, not one word of which could Julia catch; her neighbor's voice, a kind of soft, chuckling coo, combined with a Missouri drawl, rendered what she said almost wholly incomprehensible.

Julia hopefully smiled and nodded and longed for the music to begin again.

The string players settled themselves to rest, and the pianist began on a solo. The music he played now was thoroughly familiar to Julia—the Bach-Busoni chaconne; nonetheless, there seemed something odd about it. For a few minutes, Julia found it hard to determine what was making her feel so uncomfortable; then she realized that the pianist was playing with his left hand only. He sometimes moved his right hand, as if unintentionally, toward the keyboard; then hastily checked himself and lowered it sharply to his side again. In spite of these hesitancies he played remarkably well; with considerable virtuosity indeed; if Julia had closed her eyes she would not have been able to believe that such a flood of complicated contrapuntal music could be produced by five fingers only. But she could not close her eyes; she watched in rather tense fascination as the pianist pounded and slashed his way through the work; and she had a feeling of immense relief when he finally reached its end. After joining in the polite applause of his fellow players and the fat little woman, she was glad to make her escape—it was almost time for her sauna, in any case.

"Isn't he just wonderful?" To Julia's annoyance, the little woman had followed her out and now accompanied her toward the loggia. "Henk Willaerts, you know; he has such bad arthritis in his right hand that he had to give up playing with it; but Adnan thinks that with the treatment here he can get back the use of it. That's why they were playing the Schmidt, before; that's arranged for left hand also."

Out in the open she spoke at normal pitch, and was intelligible; she continued to pour out a cascade of unwanted information about the players they had just left. Julia glanced at her watch, wondering how to get away.

"Oh, excuse me? I'm Miranda Schappin, I'm a professor of research into Social Divergences at Baton Rouge. Of course I know who *you* are: You're Julia Gibbon, aren't you? I'm just so *happy* to meet you; will you please allow me to say how much I admire your plays? They display a wonderful knowledge of human nature, if I may say so. I'd like to take your picture if you'll permit me?" Without waiting for verbal authority, Ms. Schappin extracted the elaborate camera from her large, loaded shoulder bag and took half a dozen snaps, darting about the terrace so as to get Julia from different angles. "You're a wonderful subject—but you must know that, of course! These will be developed in a couple of minutes if you've time to hang around," the little woman went on, twitching damp prints out of the camera. "Of course the full tone doesn't come up for half an hour, but you can see the outline. . . . I got a couple of your husband the other day, too; he's very photogenic, isn't he? Marvelous bones. Want to see?"

She rummaged again, among scarves, enormous pink sunglasses, quart-size containers of moisturizing cream, fly repellent, and the scores of late Beethoven quartets, and finally produced a large bundle of prints.

"There he is—see?—under the lemon trees. Isn't he just darling?"

Julia was amazed that the little woman knew they were husband and wife, still more that she had succeeded in taking pictures of Dikran, who was exceedingly camera-shy and greatly disliked being photographed even by his wife, let alone by a total stranger. Possibly he had not noticed what was happening on this occasion, for it was a distant shot of him, taken probably from the driveway.

"I'll send you a print," promised Ms. Schappin, beaming. "*And* the ones of you, too, of course. This camera doesn't do color prints, but it does give a negative, so useful. . . . Now I must take all those gorgeous people—" for a stream of dancers were emerging from a nearby practice room.

Julia, with polite thanks and excuses, made her escape.

She ran down the stairs to the treatment area and heard her name called for a sauna just as she reached the circular waiting room.

The steam baths, seaweed baths, and sauna were all adjacent to one another in a big, vaulted region some distance from the central lobby. It was under the guest wing, and some basement windows looked out toward the lemon orchard but were kept curtained so as to preserve a dim, cosy gloom. The six steam baths stood in open-fronted cubicles screened by curtains along the wall. In front of the steam baths came a row of showers, accessible from either side. The three sauna cabins were in the middle, then another row of showers, and along the opposite wall, similarly cubicled, the row of marble tubs for seaweed baths. The whole area was illuminated by a dim infrared light in which patients and attendants flitted about softly like peaceful ghosts. The dim light made it possible for people to slip from tub to shower and back without anxieties as to nudity or propriety, since they were only visible at all from about five feet away and recognizable only at very close quarters.

Here vague figures wreathed in towels sat steaming peacefully on benches or lay in cocoon-like hammocks; soft music came from the ceiling; the whole scene, Julia thought, resembled a sequence from Gluck's *Orpheo*, a greatly slowed-down Dance of the Blessed Spirits.

Passing in front of the steam baths (one of them still labeled OUT OF ORDER; evidently the plumber-cousin had not yet been able to fix whatever was wrong) Julia reached the saunas. These were sturdily constructed log cabins, their walls rising to the vaulted ceiling, with thick, insulated doors and an unrobing room at the side of each. The sauna bathers, in batches of four, first stripped and showered, then, wearing nothing but towels, entered the cabins, which contained wide, slatted wooden seats arranged in tiers like flights of stairs. The highest temperature was up at roof level, but the top step was seldom used; the bathers sat or lay on the other three benches, and the last one to enter, after having shut the door, poured a bucket of water onto a brazier full of electrically heated firebricks just inside the door, which instantly filled the cabin with steam. The bathers stayed in for about five minutes—or as long as they could stand the heat—then emerged for a cold shower, then returned to the sauna again, and so on, half a dozen times over. After that, wrapped to the chin in towels, they reclined in hammocks which were slung in a space beyond the cabins. They sipped lemon juice, dozed, or listened to the music from the ceiling, which was a taped recording of the previous night's concert. Julia found this ritual positively beatific; since her arrival at Helikon she had become greatly addicted to saunas and took one whenever there was an available slot. It was generally possible to fit in one every day.

Two supervisors were in theoretical attendance, for fear any patient should turn faint, but since these attendants also had charge over the steam and seaweed baths, the sauna users were mostly left to their own devices, and it was possible to steam, shower in cold water, and steam again, lulled by the peaceful fragrance of hot, wet wood and clean, damp toweling, without any outside disturbance. Much, of course, depended on one's partners in the ritual; the enjoyment of a sauna could be greatly impaired by an uncongenial or intrusively chatty fellow bather, but Julia had hitherto been lucky, or else Helikon had put her into a friendly and accepting frame of mind. She had shared saunas with the old pianist, Marion Hillel, and Zoé, the warden, and little Mike, and a batch of girl dancers, and a harpist from Tel Aviv, and three teachers from a Paris music school; she had enjoyed sleepy, fragmentary conversations and undemanding silences, lying draped in towels or naked and relaxed on the baking, aromatic pine planks.

Today her fellow bathers were the two violin-playing Latvian girls, who were excellent company, in her opinion, since they seemed to speak no English at all. Blond and slender as

Nordic goddesses, with their hair plaited in coronets, they restricted their communication to beaming smiles, friendly gestures, and a flow of soft, guttural conversation between themselves. The last member of the quartet was another Englishwoman, Mrs. Meiklejohn, the mother of little Mike. In the course of the past two days Julia had struck up a mild friendship with her, confined mainly to smiles and brief remarks about music. Certainly, her appearance when seen stripped was a little daunting, for she was haggardly slender and still wore on her head one of the black jersey turbans that she kept on all day long. This gave her a strangely incongruous appearance; all she needed, Julia felt, to complete the image of a Moulin Rouge dancer was black, elbow-length gloves and black stockings. But Mrs. Meiklejohn's expression did not recall the Moulin Rouge.

"Won't your turban get very wet?" Julia suggested, but Mrs. Meiklejohn answered with her usual reserve and brevity, "It doesn't matter. I have several."

She sat down primly on the bottom bench. Julia shrugged, and was about to climb to the middle bench when Mrs. Meiklejohn, evidently feeling that she had perhaps been too unforthcoming, added, "I have an ugly scar on my head, you see. I'm wearing a pad of medicated lint over it to keep it cool, and the turban helps. I had a head injury."

"In that case," said Julia, "you won't want the temperature too hot?"

"No—if you don't mind."

"Not a bit," said Julia, and altered the thermostat, having conveyed her intentions by signs to the two Latvian girls, who made agreeable, assenting gestures. She then poured water on the brazier and closed the door. Just like Renoir, she thought, surveying the shiny, pink, steam-wreathed forms dimly visible in the light from the thirty-watt red bulb.

"It really makes you feel good, doesn't it?" she murmured when she had settled herself on the middle bench.

"Very comfortable," Mrs. Meiklejohn agreed.

"No—I mean more than that—really *good*, as if all your imperfections are being sweated out of you."

"Er—what kind of imperfections did you have in mind?"

"Oh—all the useless, destructive ones: guilt, remorse, anxiety, hate—"

"Hate?" The other woman turned her black-swathed head on its thin neck and regarded Julia with thoughtful appraisal. "You don't—if I may say so—give the impression of a person who is capable of a great deal of hate?"

"Oh—I can hate, all right!" said Julia cheerfully.

"Whom?"

"Whom? Reviewers who say horrible things about my plays—people who prevent me from doing what I want—odious officials—people who take things away from me—my ex-husband's new wife—stupid people—rude, disagreeable people—"

She fell silent, thinking about Dikran. Sometimes, these days, she felt that she hated *him*—for letting her down by being other than she had expected, for imprisoning her in his cell of gloom.

She went on: "Come, now, Mrs. Meiklejohn, you must hate somebody in the world, surely? You are in the educational field; there must be all sorts of obstructive people, reactionary bureaucrats, dogmatic, hellfire, punitive people—?"

"Yes, but I don't hate them," replied Mrs. Meiklejohn in her precise, Scots voice. "I—just take what steps I can to make sure they do the minimum of harm."

"Ah, well—of course you are in a position of power, aren't you? If one has power, I suppose there is no need to hate. But, in the past, before you had the power—?"

"In the past, yes, that's true," Mrs. Meiklejohn murmured thoughtfully.

"You're a Scot, I assume? I thought Scots made a specialty of long-standing feuds?"

"Feuds?" the Scotswoman took it up in her literal, repetitive way. "Eh—no, I don't believe I've ever had a feud with anybody. But I suppose I have hated; yes—there is one person whom I might say that I hate."

"That's the spirit!" Julia said encouragingly. "Why? What did he or she do to you? Is it a personal hate or a professional one?"

"Are you interested in *me*, Mrs. Saint, or are you collecting material for your plays?" Mrs. Meiklejohn inquired with her usual prudence.

"Oh, how can I divide that up?" Julia answered impatiently. "Of course I'm interested in you! And of course everything I see and hear all day long may—will—have its influence on my work, but never directly; rest assured that you won't ever find your character in any play of mine! What did this person do to you?"

"Stole something from me."

"You can't get it back?"

"Oh, good heavens, *no!* What was stolen was part of myself —and part of *them*, too; twenty years of my life."

"Ah—I see." Julia thought of Arnold Gibbon, of her own marriage. But she said, "Don't you think that's being a little unfair? An overemotional statement of the case? After all, you *had* those twenty years, while they were going on; and you still have the memory of them."

"You don't understand at all. The case is quite different from what you imagine." Mrs. Meiklejohn spoke with a cold, controlled intensity that did carry conviction.

Julia threw out her first hasty impression of a self-pitying injured wife determined to be a martyr; and indeed it had hardly accorded with Mrs. Meiklejohn's general demeanor. "What happened to this twenty years, then?" she inquired, more sympathetically.

"Oh, they were really lost—they were all turned inside out, in the most disgusting way imaginable."

"How?"

"You really are very inquisitive, Mrs. Saint," the other woman remarked, looking at Julie with a kind of unresentful surprise.

"I do like to know about people, it's true. Why not? It's my profession. Geologists study rocks, botanists look at plants. I'm interested in character. I don't think I use my knowledge harmfully. And I never indulge in gossip. Go on," Julia urged her, "spill the beans. It will do you good. Tell me what happened."

But Mrs. Meiklejohn still could not bring herself to do that. She thoughtfully crossed one thin, elegant leg over the other and said, "Imagine you thought you were living in a house—your own, private place—doing your normal job, pursuing your ordinary life, peaceful and unobserved—and suddenly you found that all the time you had really been a—a kind of exhibit at a zoo, with people studying everything you had done through a glass wall, laughing at you and everything connected with you, because it was so grotesque and peculiar?"

"I find it hard to imagine anybody laughing at *you*," Julia said, studying her with curiosity. "You have such a lot of natural dignity."

"Dignity! Hah! Nobody has dignity when they fall down in the street and the whole world can see they've forgotten to put any underclothes on! Nobody has dignity when they're on the operating table with twenty medical students peering up their vagina."

Yes, she can hate, all right, Julia discovered with surprise. The jerky force with which the last words had come out told of a terrifyingly banked-up resentment burning underneath.

"You're very good at metaphors, Mrs. Meiklejohn. But couldn't you tell me what actually happened? —Was it a long time ago?"

The other woman remained silent.

"Where is this person now? Is he or she still alive?"

Mrs. Meiklejohn said bitterly, "Alive? Oh, yes, very much so. Flourishing like the green bay tree."

"Do you ever see them?"

"See them? I'd sooner *die*. It would be like—it would be like going back to some house where you had lived and been happy—and discovering that it was a brothel. *Had* been a brothel all along—"

Now, who'd have thought it? Julia reflected. Who would have expected that this quiet, controlled, elegant professional woman would have such a burning core in her?

Julia's professional curiosity was really roused by now; she longed to know Mrs. Meiklejohn's story. But the wretched woman was beginning to show distinct signs of strain, twisting her fingers and biting her lips. Filled with a certain compunction—for this was hardly the ideally relaxed atmosphere suitable to someone recovering from a head injury—Julia therefore slid the conversation sideways to quarrels based on misconceptions, hatred of tyranny, and the motives that make people cruel to one another.

She was resolved by one means or another to find out what lay behind these powerful feelings, but it would be kinder—and more practical—to proceed slowly. Besides, there was always the possibility that she could get it all more easily from the daughter.

They took cold showers, came back for further steam sessions, and presently migrated to the hammock area, where an attendant helped them wrap up in layers of toweling and then lie back, totally relaxed, with their beakers of lemon juice in easy reach. Muted strains of Mozart's Twenty-ninth Symphony came from overhead, and the dim red light lay over them like a soft extra covering. This is really back to the womb, Julia thought; I could spend half of every day like this with the greatest pleasure in the world. . . .

Mrs. Meiklejohn was being assisted by the nurse into the next hammock. Julia extended a lazy, friendly hand to help, and was surprised by the strength of the other woman's grip. The hand that caught hers was big-boned and firm; that impression of fragility that she gives is highly misleading, Julia mused; I bet Mrs. Meiklejohn is really quite a tough nut.

I wonder if Mike is fond of her mother? There's not much sign of affection between them. A bit of the mother in the daughter—feeling of resilience, a vigor—but Mike's got the creative streak; this woman has vitality, but she doesn't seem at all imaginative. I suppose the imagination came in with the father. Wonder who or what he was . . .

She closed her eyes, taking in through ears and pores the dreamlike, ethereal beauty of Mozart's adagio movement.

"Perhaps you're right," said Mrs. Meiklejohn's voice abruptly from the next hammock.

"Mmmh?"

"Perhaps it would do me good to get it off my chest. To tell you what happened."

"Of *course* it would." Julia was fully alert at once. "It *always* does good. Go ahead! There's no one in earshot. (Except the Latvians, and they don't understand English.) We're as private here as if we were in the vaults of the Bank of England. And you can trust me not to repeat a single word."

"Yes, I daresay." Having come to her decision, the other woman seemed hardly bothering to pay attention to Julia's words. She took a deep breath. "Well—you see, it was like this: I married at nineteen—"

But at this moment the screams began.

⟦9⟧

FANTASIA

A queer and haunting thing happened to me after I had returned from the excursion to Dendros with Lady Julia.

The first thing I did when I got back was to leave the things we had bought in my workroom. She had gone off to see how her mysterious husband was getting on. Then, feeling hot and dusty from town, I thought I would go and swim. So I collected a swimsuit and towel—Mother was having a treatment somewhere, presumably; at any rate, she was not around —and walked down to the shore, taking the sandy path between the rush-screened beds of tomato plants. This led out onto the flat, white beach, which, as ever, was completely empty; because there was a swimming pool alongside the practice rooms, the visitors to Helikon mostly appeared to think it not worth the trouble to walk five hundred yards for a dunk in the real McCoy. I had the Aegean to myself and it was wonderful; an afternoon breeze had sprung up, as it often did in Dendros, so that the waves rolling in from Turkey were quite large, and yet the water wasn't cold, just invigoratingly brisk.

I rolled and floated in the troughs of the waves, and let myself be slung and heaved over their tops, and gazed at the blue sky above me, and thought about how much I enjoyed the company of Julia Saint.

Away from the opposite sex, she became quite a different person, easier, more relaxed, and, it seemed to me, happier; she didn't bother to turn on her devastating sex appeal, or, rather, I thought, reconsidering that, it switched itself off; it was just an automatic response to the presence of any male. When she was with one of her own ilk she was highly sympathetic, intelligent, and very entertaining, too. She could be funny in a farcical, primitive way that reminded me of my friends at school or the Crowbridge Rep. But also I became more and more convinced that, under her composed exterior, she was a sad and lonely woman.

I had enjoyed the trip to Dendros—and I thought she had too. We had strolled, and shopped, and gossiped; we had stood for a long time in front of a baker's oven in a back street, watching the people bring their food to be baked. It was a big, communal place, a huge hole in a wall, with three men operating long-handled, flat spades—"Like Hansel and Gretel," said Lady Julia—shoveling people's loaves and pies and legs of mutton in and out. Then, when we had bought all the things I needed, we had spent the rest of Adnan's money on ice cream, sitting at a table under a huge laurel tree on the harbor front, stroking the skinny, agile harbor cats and talking about Jane Austen.

"She ought to have written plays," said Lady Julia. "Have you ever thought by what a narrow squeak she didn't? English literature only moved from plays to novels about fifty years before she began writing; it's probably thanks to Jane Austen that it has stuck at novels ever since. But she would have written plays equally well; think how naturally all her books fall into scenes between a few people. That's why they adapt so well for television. And all her main points are made verbally; her characters hardly ever indulge for long in deep introspection or private agony."

"Emma does," I said. "She cried all the way home in the

carriage. And there is a point you've missed—how about Jane Austen's habit of condensing all her denouement and unraveling the whole plot in a huge letter from the offending villain—the one from Darcy, the one from Frank Churchill? That's not very dramatic." I thought about this a bit more, and added, "I bet she did that because of some awful happening in her own life that we don't know about. Probably the mysterious person she's supposed to have been engaged to, who jilted her, explained all *his* unfaithfulness in one long, dreadful letter, from which it took her nine years to recover. I think those letters in the novels are her greatest weakness—she makes use of them to shirk the real dramatic climax."

"Perhaps that's because she never had the real dramatic climax herself," said Lady Julia. "Or," she went on thoughtfully, "perhaps she couldn't bear to remember it. —But there isn't any letter in *Persuasion*."

"Yes there is! He proposes by letter. But also, perhaps by *Persuasion* she was beginning to get over whatever it was—the heartbreak. If she had lived long enough to finish *Sanditon*, perhaps she'd have done a real live denouement."

I finished my swim and wandered back up the dusty track, thinking about *Sanditon* and the enjoyable time Jane Austen had had setting up her scene in the seaside resort, setting her characters on the treeless, wind-blown hilltop with Waterloo Crescent in process of building, females sketching on camp-stools, and the sound of a Harp to be heard here and there from an upper Casement. Harps must have been a great deal easier to come by in 1817 than they are nowadays, for farther on in the story the Miss Beauforts, having overspent their allowance on clothes, are obliged to be content with a frugal holiday in Sanditon plus the hire of a harp and the purchase of some drawing paper.

It must, I was thinking, have been very pleasant to stroll through such a watering place as East Bourne or Brighthelmstone and hear the sound of all the young lady visitors practicing their harps behind the open casements. I wonder what kind of music they played?

Engaged in these speculations, I walked up the path between

the practice rooms and the swimming pool. The faint sound of music coming from an upper window had probably, as Jane Austen would have said, given a turn to the course of my reflections. But as I came closer to the sound, and it grew more distinctly audible, it gave such a twitch to the course of my reflections that I forgot *Sanditon* entirely, and stood stock-still, suddenly overwhelmed by a huge wave of nostalgia. For the music that came from the upper Casement (in actual fact a piano was being played, not a harp) took me back eighteen years to those nights of childhood when I had lain in my bed hugging Othello, looking at the shadowy slope of my bedroom ceiling, and listening to my father improvising his catchy, plaintive jazz tunes on the piano downstairs.

I stood still to listen. The tunes were, in fact, *extraordinarily* reminiscent of those Father used to play. How could anyone have picked up so exactly his very twirls and twiddles, his ornaments, flourishes, and hesitations? Perhaps this was a person who had also heard him? Perhaps . . .

And then came a tune that was unmistakably, irresistibly familiar, part of my whole childhood world; I felt as if it were unrolling inside me like an old phonograph cylinder; I could positively feel it emerging from the depths of my buried memory. I had always, to myself, for some probably Freudian reason called this tune "Tapioca"—something to do with the rhythm—not knowing Father's name for it, or even if it had a name . . .

Tum tiddle-tiddle-tiddle, tum tiddle-tiddle tum . . .

Surely *no one* but Father had ever played that tune?

Anybody watching me from the swimming pool would have been justified in thinking that I had suddenly gone crazy. Having stood riveted under the window, with my mouth open, I suddenly broke into a wild run. There wasn't an entrance to the practice block on this side. I had to go around two corners, along the path that circled the quadrangle, and in at the main entrance, which was halfway along the other side of the building. Then I had to go up two flights of stairs, for the music had been coming from the upper story.

Nobody was in sight. Upstairs, a gallery ran the length of

the building, giving access to the doors of the practice rooms. But which room had it been? I was not sure. The fourth or fifth from the end nearest the sea, perhaps. I began at the beach end and walked along, softly opening the soundproof doors and looking inside. Two rooms were empty. One had three absorbed men with a lot of electronic equipment. One had two flautists. One had old Marion Hillel playing Schumann—I was pretty sure that she was not my unknown pianist. Another room was empty, but the piano lid was open. Had somebody just left? I could have cried with disappointment and frustration. The next room had a pair of girls giggling their way through a Mozart duet—surely it had not been them? Now I was almost certain that I was too far along, but I went on. More empty rooms; a pair of guitarists . . . a couple who were making use of their proximity on two piano stools for a ten-minute kiss. And that was all. I had come to the end.

Feeling absolutely bereft, I ran down the stairs again at top speed. Perhaps somebody had just gone outside? In the lobby at the stair foot I found Adnan, looking, contrary to his usual habit, slightly irritated, as he stuck up on a board a notice relating to bulk purchase of honey from Hymettos.

"Has anybody just come down the stairs?" I asked him hastily.

"Who?"

"I don't know!"

He looked so very unreceptive and inaccessible to what I had been about to say that my impulse evaporated. "My dear Mike, have you gone off your chump?" he inquired tartly, "You look like Il Distratto."

I supposed I did, with my sandy hair, trailing a damp bathing towel.

"What is the matter?" he said.

"Nothing, nothing. It doesn't matter." For a moment, again, I considered telling him my wild idea, but it sounded too lunatic. Dejectedly I said, "It isn't important."

"Did you have a pleasant time in town?" he inquired courteously.

"Very; thank you," I rejoined with equal politeness. "Thank

you for the loan of your car. I left the key in the ignition."
(He often did, himself.) "And I bought all the stuff I need."

"Did Lady Julia also enjoy herself?"

"So far as I know. She seemed to," I said, and hurried out
into the quadrangle to see if anybody still in the neighborhood
looked as if they might have been the originator of my music.
Two ladies were standing in the middle of the lawn having
their pictures taken by the fat little sociology professor from
Baton Rouge. A boy and girl were sitting on the grass arranging manuscript music. The nearest other person, strolling
away at a measured pace, was Mr. Saint. Could some exchange
with him have occasioned Adnan's annoyed expression? Could
I ask Mr. Saint if he had been playing the piano? I walked rapidly after him, not certain of my resolution. Although in our
brief exchanges he had been quite pleasant to me, there was
something about him that made me very nervous. And when I
saw his face, my courage failed me entirely; his thick brows
were knitted, his thin lips were compressed in a tight line that
boded no good to somebody. Not his wife, I hoped.

However, he greeted me civilly enough and, like Adnan,
asked if I had enjoyed myself in Dendros. Lady Julia's company was a guarantee of attention from everybody, it seemed.

I replied in kind. "Yes, thank you, we had a very pleasant
time. I am sorry you couldn't come."

He looked so incredulous at this remark that I wondered if
he suspected that his wife and I had slipped off to some den of
assignation. In consequence, without having the least intention
of doing so, I found myself launched into a description of our
innocuous shopping and the baker's oven.

He listened, still with that same look of sour disbelief, as if
he wondered whom I expected to take in with my far-fetched
tale: baker's oven indeed! Who would want to stand for half
an hour watching loaves of bread slid in and out on spades?

"You and my wife have made great friends?" he remarked
with unmistakable distrust.

"Yes, isn't she nice?" I replied idiotically. "It's wonderful
for me to have a chance to talk to her."

Quite evidently he was wondering what the devil *she* saw

in *me*. This nettled me so much—though, of course, it was quite a reasonable point of view—that, without meaning to do so, I invited him to come and have a look at my sets. Now it was his turn to seem taken aback. But, to my great annoyance, he said, "Thank you. I should like that."

Gritting my teeth, I led him away to the workroom.

And then—as sometimes happens unexpectedly when two people are both ruffled and upset, but from causes not involving each other—we found that our relationship had, for reasons that were not in any way apparent, suddenly lifted from a very unpromising level to much more cordial terms.

He walked around examining my sets, praising, criticizing, and discussing them in a most knowledgeable manner. He asked what had given me the idea for using Piero in this way, and from that, by degrees, we found ourselves embarked on a general discussion about the effects of realizing that one's troubles and difficulties are being observed by strangers.

"Hamlet at least was in his own family," he said, which I found rather touching. "This aspect of Helikon I do not like at all. I am a private person, Miss Meiklejohn. I like to be alone with my wife, not to be all the time in a crowd of strangers. But she, I now begin to think, is a public person."

I felt for him very much in his difficulties, but I wasn't prepared to discuss Lady Julia with him, and when he said, "This Dr. Adnan, now. What kind of a person is he?" I limited myself to replying that Adnan was a man of high principles and a very good doctor and that he had always shown me, personally, very great kindness. Then, wishing to change the subject, I said that Lady Julia had told me Mr. Saint wrote poetry, and that I was very fond of poetry myself; what kind did he write?

To my great surprise, he said, "I write sonnets; nothing but sonnets. I have written a whole novel in sonnet form."

"Good heavens! That must have been very difficult, surely?" I thought also, privately, that it would be even more difficult to get such a work published.

He said, "Not difficult when you are, as I am, in the habit of the sonnet form," and quite matter-of-factly began to recite the last one he had written. It was very sad and complicated; it seemed to be about a dead child and a faithless lover; or perhaps the dead child was the sad, starved love that had perished prematurely and been devoured by the scavengers who lurk in darkness just out of sight, ready to prey on human weakness . . . his imagery was impressive and frightening and it shook me unexpectedly.

I made some appreciative, respectful comments, but I felt very strongly that I did not wish to hear any more of his verses just then, so I looked at my watch and said, "I'm just due for a spinal exercise class. Would you care to come along?"

I thought that might get rid of him; but also I vaguely felt that his mixing so little in all the activities of Helikon must account for some of his evident malaise and grouchiness; if he could only be beguiled into more participation, he might come to relax and enjoy himself a little.

To my astonishment—I had quite expected a fearful snub— he said, "All right, if it is not too athletic." He added, with a kind of nervous gloom, as if already wondering why he had made such a rash concession, "What do we have to do?"

"It isn't at all athletic," I reassured him. "Come along. It's in here."

I led him back to the quadrangle and into one of the downstairs practice rooms, where half a dozen people were lunging about in a lackadaisical way with staves in their hands. A fierce-looking old Scandinavian lady in a white chiton was calling out directions, but her class did not pay much heed to her; spinal exercises were a subject that few people took seriously, and the participants talked to each other freely as they lunged to left and right, or raised their staves with both hands above their heads. I collected a couple of staves and presented one end of each to Mr. Saint.

"Here. You take these. Now push and pull alternately with me, like pistons."

An unwilling smile replaced the scowl on his face, after a few minutes of this rather infantile exercise.

"What is it supposed to do?"

"Goodness knows. Loosen the shoulder blades, maybe."

Even if his shoulder blades weren't loosened, his expression certainly relaxed, as he watched an immensely fat man performing the piston exercise with a tiny, scrawny girl.

After ten minutes with the staves, we were instructed to take to the machines, nine or ten of which stood at the end of the room. They were hammock-shaped affairs made of jointed metal tubing, on which, after fitting hands and feet into holds at each end, one could, by dint of a certain amount of exertion, jackknife back and forth, bending one's spine forward and backward, which was supposed to benefit the hip and pelvic joints.

As there were not enough machines to go around, I sat out and watched Mr. Saint while he did a few, not very enthusiastic, jackknife exercises, and then he sat out and watched me.

"What do you and my wife talk about?" he inquired rather deliberately as I arched my back and then bent it. "What is the subject of your conversations when you are together?"

This was a bit of a facer. He really *is* suspicious of her, I thought. On their honeymoon! How very sad! And what a question to ask me! Is it because he is an Armenian—or whatever he is? Women's conversation not considered private? Or because he is a tycoon—anxious about vital secrets she might have given away? Or did he just envy our facility? Find conversation with her difficult? Maybe he wanted a bit of guidance? "Well—gosh—let me think—this afternoon we talked about plays quite a lot; and novels; and bread; and cats; and fishing; and life" (Life, I remembered, had also included Marriage, the desirability or undesirability of; but as that seemed a risky topic, I omitted it); "oh yes, and Jane Austen."

"*Jane Austen?*" For some inscrutable reason, this innocuous topic seemed to make him doubly suspicious. Perhaps he just plain didn't believe me. "What do you find to say about Jane Austen?"

"Oh," I said blithely, "let me think what were we saying. Lady Julia was talking about the dramatic structure of her books—how they might just as well have been plays."

"Ah yes. So she would." His expression relaxed. "My wife

sees a buried play in anything she looks at. That, already, in so few weeks of marriage, I have discovered."

"It must be quite strange, being married to someone like that," I remarked, bending my back forward, and then backward. "All the time, you must feel they have a whole inner life inside them to which you have no access; like a locked room and you haven't got the key." Though everybody is like it, really, I decided, thinking of Mother.

"That is so, indeed." Mr. Saint regarded me with surprise, and even a certain amount of respect, I thought.

I went on, "But we none of us know much about each other at all, do we? I'm here with my mother, you'd think I'd know her inside out, but I don't, not in the least; I doubt if I know much more about her than I do about you, Mr. Saint."

"And that is very little!" His glance at me was full of irony.

Old Miss Bjornsen banged two staves together to dismiss us, and we walked out into the evening air. I looked at my watch again. I was feeling full of useless regrets about my missed chance with the unseen pianist, and by this time quite badly wanted to escape from Mr. Saint; in spite of his new friendliness I found a long spell of his company somehow oppressive.

In ten minutes a full-scale rehearsal of *Les Mystères d'Elsinore* was due to commence, with Kerry Farrell for the first time singing the main part. I intended to be there. But on the other hand I didn't want to offend Mr. Saint; my instinct told me that it was a good thing to keep conciliating him.

Our early-evening meal was being served from a buffet table in the loggia. As I had graduated to solids, I secured a couple of plates containing the customary nine or ten little heaps of grated this-and-that, and gave one to Mr. Saint, as he was still standing near, with an irresolute expression on his hawklike countenance.

I began nibbling fast at my carrots and chestnuts. Little time was wasted on eating at Helikon. I am fond of leisurely eating as a rule—and protein—but at Helikon one did not feel the deprivation much, because so many alternatives were offered.

"Would you care to come to the *Elsinore* rehearsal?" I

suggested to Mr. Saint, chomping away on my shredded raw beet and leeks and chick-peas and currants. I could see that he was looking around impatiently, for his wife no doubt, and she was not to be seen; Adnan was nowhere in view either, and I felt the suspicious husband was best kept distracted if possible.

"I am not sure," he said doubtfully. "I do not care for opera."

But I thought he might be willing to be persuaded, particularly if the alternative were solitary brooding about where his wife might have got to. (Of course I hoped that she was irreproachably taking a wax bath somewhere below ground.) To divert his thoughts from her, I began talking about *Hamlet*, reverting to our conversation in the workroom. "It would be interesting to see an uncut version of the play; of course in a way it's pretty irrelevant, all that stuff they usually cut out, with Voltimand and Cornelius and Fortinbras and Rozencrantz and Guildenstern and the letter to the King of England —the play stands just as well without it—"

I wasn't concentrating too hard on what I was saying, my mind had gone back to that tantalizing snatch of piano music. Who, *who* could have been playing just there, just then? "And then there's Hamlet's letter to Horatio—that's a fairly clumsy bit of business," I remarked, munching my last mouthful of chick-peas and glancing up at Mr. Saint, who was picking his way distastefully through his. "Oh, of course, that was another of the things that your wife and I were talking about— Jane Austen's letters."

"*What* do you say?"

I had tossed this out heedlessly enough, but he grasped my wrist so hard that if I had not swallowed my last chick-peas they would have been jerked all over the terrace.

"Jane Austen's letters?" I said, puzzled. "I mean the long, explanatory ones in her novels. You know, Frank Churchill writing to give an account of his secret engagement to Jane Fairfax—and so on." He looked at me as if what I was saying made no sense. Maybe he had never read any Jane Austen.

Lots of people haven't. I went on nervously, "Nowadays I expect if a writer put such a device in a novel his editor would sling it back and tell him to turn it into direct action."

Then I blushed, thinking how conceited and opinionated I no doubt sounded, airing my superior views about Shakespeare and Jane Austen. If this made Mr. Saint wonder what his wife could possibly see in me, I didn't blame him. By now his expression really scared me; I had no clue at all to what he was thinking. Whatever it was, I was glad I was not sharing his thoughts. Though I couldn't for the life of me imagine why my frivolous reference to Jane Austen's letters should have engendered them.

He looked at me long and hard, and for several minutes said nothing at all. When he did speak, his words were not related to what had passed; he merely remarked. "After all, perhaps I will come to the rehearsal," and accompanied me across the grass to the big hall. At some point he had let go of my wrist, but it still ached so badly that I rubbed it surreptitiously as I went, while at the same time I tried to sort out my scared impressions. Such an atmosphere of cold seemed, sometimes, to emanate from him that I felt, when he was around, as if some large bird of prey had flown between me and the sun. But perhaps that was an evocation from his terrible past? For when he gripped my wrist I had seen a tattooed number on his, which must—mustn't it—be a constant reminder to him of hideous sufferings. Why, I wondered, did he not have it removed? If, as Mat the masseur believed, his face had been altered by plastic surgery, it would surely have been no problem to remove or replace that small patch of skin on his arm at the same time? But perhaps he *wanted* to be constantly reminded of the bad card that life had once dealt him? Perhaps—I thought—he might find it a justification for things he was doing now?

A chattering, anticipatory group had already assembled in the big hall. Here, in imitation of some English chapel, solid wooden seats like pews lined the walls, going up in tiers at right angles to the dais at the far end of the hall. Automatically I glanced around to see if Mother was there, but she was not, and I had not really expected her; opera and large gatherings ran each other close for first place among her dislikes. How did she stand school assemblies? Presumably because they were part of her profession, and, as such, to be endured. Lady Julia was not there either, so far as I could see. In itself that was no concern of mine, but the fact that Adnan was also absent did cause me some disquiet. Since he had been so proud of the fact that his personal intervention had been what persuaded Kerry Farrell to cancel an engagement in Basel and come here, I had expected that he would be in full plumage tonight, bustling about and organizing. Perhaps he intended to arrive escorting the diva? But no; that must be she on the dais already, talking to old Annibal and Joop Kolenbrander.

Curious to see her at closer range, I moved on toward the front of the hall, along the rows of sideways seats, and Mr. Saint followed me. Because of his company I did not go up on stage, as I otherwise might have done, but settled quietly down to watch on a bench near the front. Mr. Saint sat down silently by me. I could not see his face without screwing my neck sideways, but his silence was so fraught and ominous that I did not dare try to break it up with more chatter. I just observed the people on the stage and tried to pretend that I was not aware of the unspeaking thundercloud at my left elbow.

Joop was organizing the small orchestral ensemble, every now and then crossing the dais to ask Miss Farrell for her opinion and suggestions.

He was being his usual slow, lanky, efficient Dutch self, but his long, comic face had turned a dusky red and his Adam's apple was working overtime; it was plain that he was unusually keyed up. Old Annibal, established for the evening in his wheelchair and wrapped in a big blue Greek rug, looked very impressive and patriarchal, with his beard sweeping down over the blanket and his white, bushy hair standing on end; he seemed keyed up, too; his eyes sparkled and he was chatting away volubly to Kerry Farrell and the five or six other singers who stood nearby. None of them were in costume yet; we were to have a dress rehearsal the next day, and my conscience told me that I should be elsewhere, putting in some final touches, but the rest of me was determined to stay, at least for half an hour.

Kerry Farrell seemed very composed. I studied her with interest and perplexity, as one does when seeing a screen star for the first time in the flesh. I had heard her voice on the radio, and even had a Oiseau-Lyre record with some songs of hers on one side, but she was not in the least the way I had imagined, from her voice, that she would be. The voice was unusually powerful and clear—a kind of pure mezzo, without ornament or vibrato—and I had expected that, to match it, she would be a powerful-looking person. Not a bit of it. On the contrary, she looked rather slight and frail as she stood sniffing a syringa flower that she held between her fingers and laughing at something old Annibal had said. She was not very tall—even in high heels she hardly came up to Joop's shoulder. Her hair was black, and swept back in a high, bouncy set that suited her narrow, pixyish, Irish face; couldn't see the color of eyes from where I sat. Her face—not pretty, but sparkling—was one of the most lively and mobile I'd ever come across. She never kept one expression for more than an instant; at the same time, she twisted and pivoted, stepping from side to side, joking and chatting as if she were in her element in this central situation, enjoying every minute of it. The dress she wore was dark but flared, with a flash of lace jabot at the chin, and it emphasized her incessant movement, the skirt swishing around her, the frill catching the light as she leaned from side to side. I could see that her vivacity was infecting the people around her; there was an atmosphere of hectic gaiety, of heightened excitement and enthusiasm.

I wonder what Lady Julia will make of her? I suddenly thought. Can Helikon contain such a pair, both of prima-donna status?

While part of me—the conscious part—speculated about Kerry Farrell in this manner, another part, deeper down, was puzzled by some attribute of hers that seemed confusingly familiar. Could I, after all, have seen her somewhere long ago—

on stage, on TV?—without remembering, without realizing it? Perhaps I had seen her before she was so well known—for I thought her name had only come into prominence within the past three or four years. I knew nothing about her past. She had appeared, she had become quite well known; that was all. Could she, perhaps, have taught, or given a lecture, at one of the schools I had gone to? I thought I would have remembered if she had. Unless she had come in merely for a single occasion, or judged a singing contest? Could I have seen an article about her somewhere, with pictures? I could not recall doing so; and in any case that would not account for the peculiar familiarity I felt with the way she *moved*.

The more I teased my memory, however, the less co-operation I received from it; you know how it is sometimes when you try to remember a dream and your mind seems bent on throwing up obstacles, willfully scrambling the whole message.

Matthieu came stomping along the aisle and plumped himself down on my right.

"So she is here at last, our leading lady?" he muttered in my ear. "*Mon dieu*, what a complexion! She has the appearance to use boot polish instead of makeup foundation."

"It's her voice we're interested in, not her skin!"

"Me, I know nothing about voices," he said.

"Why are you here, then? Why aren't you massaging somebody?"

"There is trouble downstairs; they clear the steam area, massage rooms also. One of the steam baths misbehaves. So I come hoping to find a place by you," he said gallantly.

"Go on! *Quelle blague!*"

"Also, of course, hoping the witch's curse take effect and the prima donna she fall down dead," Mat said hopefully.

Mr. Saint, on my other side, had been watching the performers, as they moved and chatted on the dais, with, it seemed to me, a curiously rigid and fixed attention. I wondered if he, too, like me, was pursued by some elusive, dodging memory. But at Mat's words he sat forward, looked past me, and said, "What's that about falling down dead?" very sharply indeed.

"Oh, ho," said Mat. "You do not know this tale?"

"What tale?"

"It is why they have such trouble casting this piece. The old Annibal Destrier is not always as you see him now, stuck on two crutches or in a wheelchair. No, when he is young he is very gay—I do not mean that he is a homo—"

"You mean gay in the sense of a gay Lothario," I suggested.

"*Quoi?* He is *homme du monde*. He has many *belles amies*. And one of them is a singer, a soprano called Minny Montherlant; when he is with her he compose this *Mystères d'Elsinore*, and she, she hope to sing the part of Ophélie at the first performance. Okay?"

"So what happened?" inquired Mr. Saint. He seemed greatly interested.

"*Enfin*, by the time it is put on, the old Annibal tire of this lady and leave her, as he has done all the rest. He live with her no longer, and, what is upsetting her much more, she do not get to sing the part of Ophélie, *moins plus*. She feel very bad and sad about it all, and she throw herself in the Seine, like all sad Parisian ladies."

"Not *quite* all, surely?" I said.

"But before she throw herself in, Minny Montherlant leave a note for Annibal. 'Me, I am gone,' it say. '*Et je m'en fiche*, I do not give a snap who play your silly Ophélie. But I wish, I wish from the bottom of my broken heart—'" Mat made a terrific gesture with his hands, as if he were tearing out his own heart and then breaking it like an egg—"'I 'ope from the bottom of my brroken 'earrt that bad luck come to your *opéra*; I 'ope you never 'ave a performance that go as it should.'"

"And he never has?" I said. "Really? Not ever?"

Mat shook his head. "First one thing, then another. And, *enfin*, after the two times when the 'Amlet 'e die soon after the performance, nobody care to put it on. That is why the old skunk ask to 'ave it perform here for his jour de fête, because 'e know otherwise 'e will likely not have the chance to 'ear it again in 'is lifetime."

"Surely," said Mr. Saint, "nobody seriously believes that any harm will come on account of that silly woman's letter?"

I said, "Kerry Farrell looks carefree enough, at all events."

Mat stuck out his lower lip. "*Les gens du théâtre sont toujours*—actors are always superstitious," he said, and gave a big, Belgian shrug. "*Moi, non!* I don't believe. But if somebody is afraid they will die—then, maybe, they do die. Anyway—by and by we see, *n'est-ce pas?* If the performance go well—okay, the jinx is lifted. And if the 'Amlet die—okay by me also. It is no skin off my *poitrine.*"

He did not actually say "*poitrine.*"

By now, action on the stage appeared imminent. Everyone except Kerry Farrell and the singer who was taking the Ghost's part had left and gone into the wings—or, rather, the choir stalls. The instrumentalists had finished their tuning, and the first violinist had given Kerry Farrell a note, which she sang, softly but clear as a bell.

She and the Ghost moved into their assigned positions, looking expectantly toward Joop, who raised his baton.

And then, when everybody, including myself, had reached a high point of nervous anticipation, I heard loud, clumping footsteps and the voice, from behind me, of Dr. Adnan, who called out, "I am very sorry to interrupt you, my friends, but I fear we must call a halt to this rehearsal, only temporarily I hope. There has been a very unfortunate accident in the treatment area. We have been obliged to fetch in the police, and they now wish to question everybody."

Commotion broke out at once. Everybody stood up, many people made for the exit, presumably with the idea of rushing down to the treatment area and discovering for themselves what had happened. But Adnan, climbing onto the stage, called for order through the rising buzz of nervous, hysterical chatter.

"*Et alors?*" said Mat. "Now what?"

"Please keep still!" Adnan demanded. "Do not all rush about like sheep! Captain Plastiras of the police requests that all the persons who are in this hall *remain* here unless specially requested to leave. The captain himself will be coming in here to interrogate you by and by. All the other Helikon guests are assembling in the dining hall, and the captain's assistant will be taking statements from them. What they will be wanting is any information you can give them about the steam area during the past few days. Can you therefore please try to have your memories sorted out, so as not to waste police time. This is a *deeply* regrettable occurrence, and I cannot tell you how much I wish that it had not happened. I can only ask you to be calm and patient, so that we can get through these formalities as fast as possible."

He added, "Mlle. Zoé is at the desk by the organ. Will you all file slowly past, and give her your names; then we shall have a knowledge of which guests are where."

The slow procession formed and began to move. Mr. Saint, behind me, looked very impatient. He said angrily, "It is ridiculous to keep us in here. I do not see my wife here—I shall wish to reassure her. She will find all this terribly upsetting."

"I expect she's with the other lot in the dining hall," I suggested soothingly. "She's probably just as worried about you."

He pressed his thin lips together irritably. "It is stupid. I myself have never taken a steam bath—why may not those like me give their names and leave at once?"

This seemed odd to me, as I myself had certainly seen him in the steam-bath area one day soon after I had arrived.

"I think it's not only people who have taken steam baths, but anyone who has been in the neighborhood."

However, Mr. Saint pushed off through the crowd, presumably to demand special treatment from Adnan, who was in the center of a group of vociferous inquirers.

Mat looked thoughtfully after Mr. Saint and remarked, "Always there is some guy who think he shall have all special, just for him alone!"

When, in my turn, I reached Zoé and gave her my name, she said,

"Ah, Mike. I have a message for you: you are to go to your

mother in Achmed's office. Captain Plastiras has asked it. He will question you there."

"Why?" Unlike Mr. Saint, I was terrified by special treatment, the more so as I had no notion why I should be singled out in this way.

Zoé shrugged. "*Sais pas, moi.* I just tell you what he asked."

As I slowly edged my way to the door, which was guarded by a cop, I heard a buzz of speculative conversation from the crowd waiting to give names.

"What happened?"

"One of the steam baths blew up."

". . . killed Marion Hillel."

". . . no, it was a man, *I* heard."

". . . bits of him blew about like confetti . . ."

". . . never did care for steam baths . . ."

". . . claustrophobia, okay, but not to be blown to . . ."

". . . who found him?"

". . . some woman . . ."

". . . no, it was the plumber, I heard . . ."

Everybody seemed better informed already than I was.

I left the hall after giving my name to the policeman and hurried in the direction of Adnan's office with deep anxiety in my heart, which was not allayed by the unwonted and frightening hush that reigned over the buildings and quadrangle. Normally the stone stairs and passages of Helikon resounded all day and half the night with cheerful chatter and bursts of music, but now, since all the residents were corralled in two spots, I felt a chill of isolation as I crossed the starlit, silent square of grass and then climbed the stairs toward Adnan's quarters. Loud, quick footsteps coming in my direction almost made me turn and retreat toward the safety of the crowded hall.

But it was only Adnan, looking angry and troubled. His expression did not lift when he saw me, but he said, "Ah, Mike. That's good. Your mother is in my office."

"W-why?" I stammered nervously.

"She happened—quite by chance—to be the one of the first

on the spot where the—the accident took place. She was upset."

Oh my god, I thought. Involvement in another accident—particularly one as gruesome as this sounds—is just the *last* thing she needed. This is hardly the cozy peace I promised her at Helikon.

"Is she—is she all right?"

"I think she will be so—yes," he said. "She has good stamina, your mother. But, what a thing to happen, my god! With all our safety precautions! And I am afraid Lady Julia was terribly shocked; she reacts violently to such things. It is to be expected."

"Lady Julia was there too? What—"

What *happened?* I wanted to know, regardless of etiquette, but Adnan, without paying any attention to my words, suddenly did a thing that disconcerted me very much: taking hold of my shoulders, he gripped them painfully hard, staring down at me—a long, long, piercing look—then he exclaimed harshly, "Oh, my dear Mike, why, *why* do you have to return to Helikon *now*, of all possible times? Why, if you were coming, could you not have done so three years ago, tell me that?" He almost shook me in his intensity, scowling at me as if I were too tiresome for words.

This behavior took me so much by surprise that I could only stammer, "It was because of my mother—"

"Oh, to hell with your mother!"

In the same harried and abrupt manner, he pulled me against him, wrapped his arms tightly around me, and buried his face in my hair; thus we stood for a brief, astonishing moment, with my nose jammed into his embroidered velvet waistcoat; I could hear his heart going pocketa-pocketa; I seemed myself to have lost the faculty of breathing, but that did not much matter, because I began to be convinced that I must be dreaming this whole unreal dialogue.

Then, with equal abruptness, Adnan let go of me, gave me another intent, scrutinizing look, and said, "Never mind! No matter! Forget it, please. Go to your mother."

Off he strode along the echoing passage, and I started in the other direction.

I was feeling shaken to my roots, it need hardly be said. But there was absolutely no time for self-analysis, as Mother and Lady Julia were sitting in Adnan's tidy office looking white and shocked, both of them, still wearing terry bathrobes and carrying bags of sauna equipment.

A young Greek police officer was solicitously plying them with coffee.

Mother, although she was pale and looked as if she might vomit, seemed reasonably collected and in control of herself. But Lady Julia looked deathly; her skin had a glazed, waxen shine, her eyes were dull and staring, she kept wiping beads of sweat off her forehead. The cloudy, curly hair, which usually made such a striking frame to her long, lovely face, was now a damp, matted tangle, and her mouth sagged. For once, she looked her age, which I happened to know. From time to time she jerked with nervous tension. When she did this, Mother patted her shoulder protectively, to my surprise, for Mother was not given to such gestures.

I went and sat beside them, and murmured, "What happened?" to Mother, but she gave me a bitten-off nod that signified, "Later, not now."

The young policeman poured me a cup of coffee, which, I must say, was welcome as brandy from a St. Bernard, and just about as stimulating after days and days of lemon juice. Goodness knows where it had come from. Coffee was never served at Helikon, being considered a sinful, addictive, poisonous stimulant only about one degree up from heroin. Perhaps Zoé and the kitchen staff kept a secret supply for their own use.

While I sat sipping the thick, black, delicious brew (it was Greek coffee, solid with sugar), Captain Plastiras came into the room and smiled at me. He was a long-time friend of the Aghnides family—like most leading citizens of Dendros—and had played chess with old Kyrie Aghnides every Thursday for years, so he and I were well acquainted. He was a big, agreea-

ble-looking man, the shine on his leather uniform belt equaled
only by that on his bald head. He had opaque, thoughtful
brown eyes under thick, busy gray brows.

"And so here we have the little Mike," he said cordially.
(He pronounced my name Meekay, it had been a family joke.)
"We are so delighted to welcome you back to Dendros,
though it is too bad that your visit should coincide with such a
disagreeable occurrence."

"What actually happened?" I ventured, for what seemed
like the fourth or fifth time.

Glancing at the faces of Mother and Lady Julia, he beck-
oned me into the secretary's room and closed the door.

"It seems," he said, "that some unfortunate visitor has been
boiled in a steam bath."

"Oh my *god*. How on earth—"

In the light of this grisly news, all my other confused and
untidy feelings about the earlier events of the evening—the
nostalgic snatch of music, Mr. Saint's disconcerting behavior,
Kerry Farrell's elusively haunting appearance, and—last but
most emphatically not least—Adnan's wholly unexpected act
—all these indigestible ingredients shook, and sank, for the
moment, to the bottom of my mind.

"When did it happen?" I asked.

"It seems that about one hour ago one of the attendants
downstairs, a half-trained girl called Ariadne Vasiliou, noticed
that the sixth steam bath, the one at the end of the row, was
switched on, though it had been reported as being out of
order, and the safety lid was closed down and fastened. In fact
the whole bath was covered by a tarpaulin, to remind everybody that it was not to be used—the thermostat had gone
wrong, I understand. Anyway, Ariadne, who is a careful and
conscientious girl, noticed that the switch was down, so she
switched it up. After waiting ten minutes or so, she then apparently took off the tarpaulin and lifted the lid, presumably
so as to allow the machine to cool down faster—and found
this person inside. At which point she first screamed, and then
fainted, falling and banging her head on a concrete plinth.

That was when your mother and Lady Julia went to her assistance. She has now been taken off to hospital, as it is thought she may be suffering from concussion."

"Poor girl! What an awful thing to find. And who—who—"

"Who was the person in the steam bath? We think, a man. But that is a matter for the experts. The person—whoever it was—had been in the bath for quite a long time—possibly for days."

"Was the bath switched on all the time?" I asked, horrified.

Captain Plastiras gave me an approving look.

"No, it was not. The steam baths are all on one circuit. They can all be switched on at once by a master switch. But also it is possible to switch off each one individually, and to regulate it to the required temperature—as you doubtless know."

I nodded. I can't stand steam baths myself, and wouldn't ever climb into one. To climb into a big metal box and be shut in, helpless, with towels draped around you and a bowl of water on your knees, your hands inside too, so that you can't reach to open the lid—no, thank you, not for me! It is like the nastiest kind of nightmare. But I am familiar with the setup. The master switch was in a small office at the end of the treatment area, which was kept locked outside of treatment times, so that such potentially dangerous equipment as the steam baths and the ultrasonic ray could not be switched on accidentally.

Captain Plastiras pursued, "This steam bath, number six, had been switched off and covered up some days ago, as the thermostat had become defective and the temperature inside was uncontrollable, rising to dangerous heights. The plumber had inspected it, but a spare part was required which had to be obtained from Athens."

"And then somebody turned the switch on again, so that the bath kept automatically heating up again every time someone switched on the master switch?"

"Né," he said. "That is so. It may have been switched on for most of the day—perhaps for most of several days."

I wondered what would happen to a person who was boiled in a steam bath for several days; my imagination gulped and retired from the resulting picture.

Another of his lieutenants came in, saluted, and handed Captain Plastiras a piece of paper.

He studied it thoughtfully for a while, then nodded. The man withdrew again. Captain Plastiras then looked at me in silence for a minute or two with a pondering, but not unfriendly, expression. I waited in nervous bewilderment, expecting him to go into a "When were you in the steam-bath area last?" routine, and I was wondering why he had chosen me to interrogate, for in fact I practically never went near the steam baths.

But Captain Plastiras did not ask me any questions about steam baths.

He said, "You left a small pile of clothes in Miss Pombal's room one evening."

"Oh, yes," I said, after a moment recollecting what he was talking about. "Yes, I did."

"Can you now recall which evening that was?"

I had to do a considerable amount of calculation. "Wait a minute—I'm getting there. It was the night they did Schubert's *Magic Harp* in the big hall—I know that because I was weeding in Dr. Adnan's little garden and listening to the music and then Lady Julia came in, that's right—and we went for a walk in the lemon orchard. And we found the clothes down at the bottom of the orchard by the men's sun-bathing enclosure. So it was about five days ago—last Monday or Tuesday. You can easily find out by checking the concert programs with Mr. Kolenbrander. Or Lady Julia might remember."

"Lady Julia is not in a very clear state at the moment," he said. "I will ask Mr. Kolenbrander."

He made a note on his tablets.

"But then—" the meaning of his question had taken some time to penetrate. "Do you mean—you think those were the clothes of the person in the steam bath? He has been there *all this time?*"

"We fear this may be so. You see—" Plastiras glanced at the piece of paper the man had brought him. It was a list of names. "We do now have a complete roster of all the guests and students at Helikon. Everyone is accounted for, nobody is missing. And, moreover, nobody ever claimed the pile of clothes that you left in Miss Pombal's room. They have remained there ever since."

"There was no identification on them—in them?"

"You yourself had already discovered that," he reminded me. "There was nothing at all in the trouser pockets—except a few sunflower seeds."

"That's not unusual at Helikon." Sunflower seeds were among the few permitted snacks. "But how on *earth* could an outsider, a stranger, make his way into the treatment area and accidentally get himself stuck in a steam bath?"

People did come into Helikon for single or day treatments, but it was not a practice encouraged by Adnan, who held that, in order to be any use at all, the Helikon regime, which was designed to benefit the whole system simultaneously, must be taken *in toto* for at least two weeks. And the treatment time-tables drawn up by his cherished computer were so tightly scheduled that it seemed highly improbable an outsider could wander through and find his way to a vacant steam bath. Let alone get stuck in it. The security provisions around the treatment area were not obtrusive, but they were pretty thorough.

"Ah, well, this was no accident, I am afraid," Captain Plastiras said.

"No? You mean somebody *put him in there?*"

"It was a convenient circumstance that the defective steam bath was the only one situated beside a window—one of those basement windows looking out into the sunk area."

"Oh, I see," I said slowly. "And the area runs down alongside the lemon orchard—"

"Just so. In point of fact there are bushes and shrubs growing all over that sunk area; it would not be difficult for somebody—somebody of considerable strength—to climb down unobserved and lift another person through that window. The windows are not high. They are normally kept closed, but, on account of the overheating steam bath, that one had been left ajar during the past few days."

"Aren't there bars?"

"There are bars, yes, but two of them had been wrenched away at the bottom and were merely hanging loosely. Somebody had climbed in and put the person in the bath. And, thanks to you, we shall now perhaps know when—one day early last week."

"But wouldn't he have been seen inside?"

"Not necessarily. While treatments were going on, and all the cubicle curtains were drawn, it would not have been too difficult to slip in and out again. The lights are very dim, as you know."

I gazed at Plastiras in silence, taking in the horrible implications of what he had said. He took a black-and-white photograph from a folder and showed it to me.

"Do you know this man?"

The picture was of a thin, dark, short man, wearing Levi's and a T shirt. He was walking along the harbor front in Dendros town; I recognized the Turkish arches of the harbormaster's office behind him. I also recognized the T shirt as the one I had picked up—or at least its twin; it had a design of rampant seahorses on a striped background.

"I don't know the man, but the shirt looks like the one we found."

"You have not seen this man around Helikon?"

"No, never."

"Well, if you *should* recall seeing him at any time—either here at Helikon or in the town—more particularly if you recall seeing him with anybody that you know—will you please not mention this to any person at all, but at once let me know?"

"Yes, of course."

"Very well; thank you, Mike, you have been very helpful," he said. The friendly, chestnut-brown eyes smiled at me again, and then he walked swiftly out the passage door, neat and noiseless in spite of his large bulk. I went back into the other room.

Mother said, "Thank goodness he's done. I thought he was never going to finish talking to you. And I was afraid he might want to question Lady Julia again. I'm worried about her—we ought to put her to bed."

"Do you think we're allowed to leave here?" I said doubtfully. "Should we ask the cop?"

"If someone's ill they have to be looked after!" declared Mother, with a return to old habits of authority. Fortunately the matter was resolved by Adnan, who returned at that moment.

"Lady Julia needs to be put to bed!" Mother said to him truculently.

"Of course she does," he replied, taking the wind out of her sails with his usual imperturbability. "And I have sent for an attendant and a wheelchair to take her to her room, now that Captain Plastiras has said he will not want her again. You, yourself, Mrs. Meiklejohn, have also had a bad shock; I think your daughter should take you to your room. I will visit you there presently. It is probable that, like Lady Julia, you would benefit from a sedative."

The chair arrived now, and Lady Julia was wheeled off, drooping like a Madonna lily; Adnan bustled after with a bag of equipment. All the time he had been in the room, he had not once looked at me; apart from this, which was not customary with him, he had behaved as if that odd, brief moment at the head of the stairs had not taken place. He looked pale, grim, and set-faced; most unlike himself.

I took Mother to our room. In spite of her spurt of authority, she was fairly groggy, and glad enough to lean on my arm as we proceeded slowly down the stairs and across the quadrangle to the guest wing. People were now starting to trickle slowly out of the concert hall as interrogations finished, and knots gathered together outside doorways, engaged in nervous, excited discussion.

As we passed the main entrance to the concert hall, a small but distinguished procession debouched from it: old Annibal

Destrier being pushed in his wheelchair by Joop Kolenbrander, accompanied by Kerry Farrell, walking alongside.

"Poor, poor devil," she was saying, in a clear voice that easily carried to where we were. "What a horribly bizarre way
to die! Do you think, M. Destrier, that it *could* possibly have
anything to do with the hoodoo on *Les Mystères d'Elsinore?*"

"*Ah, mais, voyez-vous, Mme. Farrell, c'est de la folie, ça!*"

At the sound of Kerry Farrell's voice, Mother had started
violently, and gripped my arm so hard that I almost yelped;
she had clutched exactly the same spot which had received
such paralyzing treatment from Mr. Saint earlier on in the
evening.

"Wait here a moment; don't move!" she said in a peremp-
tory tone.

We stood still. We were about five yards away from them,
half hidden in the shadow of a buttress.

"But you must admit, M. Destrier, that it is a bit of a coinci-
dence! I am not superstitious myself . . ."

The little procession moved toward us, illuminated by the
light streaming out the open door. Old Annibal's bush of
white hair shone like a halo, and Joop's Adam's apple was
clearly silhouetted, whereas we were in shadow. Nevertheless
old Annibal recognized me, by the side of the path, and called
a friendly good night.

"*Et alors, demain*—tomorrow we try your costumes, we
forget all this sadness and see 'ow all will go together, *hein?*"

"You mean the performance is still going ahead?" I asked,
very astonished. I had expected that all such festivities would
be canceled.

"*Pourquoi pas?* No one may leave—Captain Plastiras require
that every guest shall remain here until the inquiries are
finished; but is that a reason for *tout le monde* to sit about as
dumb as tortoises, as melancholy as giraffes?" Annibal demanded. "*Au contraire!* Everybody will need to be cheered
up and have his mind distracted."

"Oh, well, I'm very glad to hear it. Good night, then, M.
Destrier."

"*Bon soir, mon enfant.*"

They moved on.

And we went in the other direction. When we reached our room, I was alarmed to see that Mother had turned as white as lint; she looked far worse now than she had when I first saw her in Adnan's office.

"*Mother!* You look terrible. You'd better get into bed at once. I'll make you some hot milk with whiskey in."

Milk was in disfavor at Helikon, but a few goats browsed in the ravine behind, and their scanty supply was available to those in the good graces of the kitchen staff. I ran off and begged a cupful from old Arachne, who was a sister-in-law of Elena, at the Aghnides. Mother and I kept a bottle of Glenlivet in our closet; Adnan would doubtless have disapproved, but Mother is too much of a Scot to travel anywhere without a dram for emergencies, and, knowing her views, I had stocked up before the cruise.

When I got back with my hot milk, she was looking a little better, and the posset helped. But still her manner seemed terribly strange. She would not get into bed, but sat in our armchair, staring away through the dark window with a set, fixed face and eyes that saw God knows what; things far off and long ago and even worse, it seemed, than the boiled victim in the steam bath.

"We'll have to leave," she said abruptly.

"We can't," I reminded her. "Didn't you hear what old Annibal said? We're fixed here till the police have finished investigating. Besides, honestly, Ma, you aren't fit to travel yet. I'm most *terribly* sorry about this horrible affair—it's not at *all* the kind of thing that usually happens at Helikon—and it was just frightful that you happened to be first on the scene—"

Frightful, but not surprising. If screams were heard and someone was in trouble, naturally Mother would be first on the spot.

"Oh, it's not that," she said impatiently. She was not listening to me. She beat her clenched fist against the wooden arm of the chair. Then, "I'll have to stay in this room—just not leave it at all. Oh, why, why did I ever allow you to bring me here?"

With a remorseful pang, I remembered her sedated journey in the ambulance. She had really had no option in the matter. And I resolved that never again, even if it seemed to be for their own good, would I deprive anybody of the right of choice.

Which did not help in the present instance. But still I did not understand what was causing her deep distress. That, perplexingly enough, seemed not to be connected with the man in the steam bath.

"Mother, what is the trouble?" I said quietly. "I think you really must try to tell me."

I went and squatted in front of her chair and took hold of her thin hands.

"*Why* do you feel that you must stay in this room? What's worrying you so? Are you"—it seemed wildly improbable, but it was the only theory that presented itself to me—"are you afraid of somebody?"

"Afraid? No!" she said violently. "There's nothing to be *afraid* of! It's just disgusting!"

"What is?" I persisted. "Mother—I simply can't go on in the dark like this about what's making you feel so awful."

She took her haunted eyes away from the window and turned them on me. Still she said nothing.

"Who knows—perhaps I can help in some way," I said rather hopelessly.

She laid her hand briefly on my head. "You're a good child. But no," she said, as if to a stranger, "no, you can't help. You'll have to *know*, though, I suppose. I suppose I should have told you before—I just couldn't bear to."

"Told me *what?*" I asked with a fearful palpitation of the heart.

"As we were coming along," she said. "That person who was with the old man in the wheelchair—"

"Old Annibal Destrier?"

"No, not him—"

"Joop? The tall Dutchman who was pushing him, Joop Kolenbrander? Or the other person? Do you mean Kerry Farrell? She's the singer who's just come. She's taking the part of Hamlet."

Mother gave a violent shudder. A spasm twitched the corners of her mouth as if she had swallowed poison and felt it burning its fatal way into her system.

"You do mean Kerry Farrell?" I pressed, with a premonition of what was coming. "What about her?"

But inside me, as I asked, with the fearful velocity of a computer, everything began to add itself together. Digits flashed and slid, whole columns totaled up, shot themselves to the side, merged with other columns, exploded into fountains of zeros, and flung new rows of figures down to the bottom.

"*Her?*" Mother said. "Singer? That mincing, posturing, self-advertising little monster? That's not any *woman*—that's your *father!*"

I couldn't help it—the shock was too sudden and profound, the anticlimax too ludicrous—I burst into a fit of laughter, hysterical, I daresay. But I soon stopped. Mother was sitting staring at me in rigid silence, her cheek muscles tight with strain, a tear in the corner of her large, round eye; she looked like some stricken, wild creature trapped in the dignity of death.

"I—I'm terribly sorry!" I gulped. "It was such a shock—not in the very least what I'd expected." I'd had some vague notion that perhaps Kerry Farrell was his mistress—that might account for her having picked up his mannerisms, his tunes on the piano . . . "Are you *sure?*" I wanted to say. But there was no uncertainty in that frozen face, those wide, inward-looking eyes. "You've just got to tell me all about it," I said resolutely. "That's really *Father?* What happened? His sex changed, somehow?" I'd heard of such things in a vague way. But it is not the sort of occurrence with which one expects ever to be intimately connected; one reads these cases in the newspaper; they happen to chemistry teachers in Leighton Buzzard or to film actors in Los Angeles; not to one's own father.

"His sex didn't 'somehow' change," Mother snapped. "He had it done. He had an operation."

"Oh, my god," I said slowly. "I see. He *wanted* to have it done. He wanted to become a woman."

"As if any man ever could!" said Mother with a vehement sniff.

Slowly, slowly, by painful degrees, I dragged the story out of her—or at least a thin, bloodstained thread of narrative; plainly there were many terrible passages, which, though preserved intact, I was sure, fossilized in Mother's wincing memory, would never be divulged by her, or at least not to me.

They had been married very young. He was twenty, she nineteen. Father had always toyed with this fantasy of becoming a woman—he had made no secret of it, apparently—but Mother, with her blunt Scots common sense, had been sure that marriage and its responsibilities—and they did love each other, after all—fatherhood, a career, adult citizenship, she had thought, would soon knock all the nonsense out of his head.

But she had been wrong. The wish remained, the urge grew stronger and stronger; although they had an affectionate relationship, although he loved us when we began to grow, he could not rid himself of his longing.

"Didn't even *try*," Mother said, blinking furious tears away.

He was not a transvestite, not a homosexual; play-acting—wearing women's clothes—was no good to him; he was not interested in the company of queers; what he wanted was the real thing. With every fiber of his being, he wanted to become a woman; he felt that, in all the most fundamental parts of him, he already *was* a woman.

"And, would you believe it," demanded Mother, staring at me with ferocious intensity, as if she were reliving endless, bitter old scenes of dispute, "not only did he want to have this disgusting operation done to him but he *then* expected to come home and live with us all just as before! As if nothing had happened! Can you imagine anything so horrible? He actually said he could live with me as if he were my sister, and go on having the same kind of relationship with you and Dru —" She stopped, gulping.

Oh, poor Dru, I thought. Poor, poor Dru, who loved Father so much. "It was just too much for Dru?" I asked, after a while. "She couldn't bear it? Was that why she killed herself?"

"How did you know *that?*" asked Mother on a pounce. "You weren't supposed to. I always kept it from you."

I couldn't betray Gina Signorelli, so, rather evasively, I said, "Oh well, it got back to me in the end, the way things always do. I couldn't tell you that I knew."

What terrible things we expect each other to bear, I thought. Father honestly thought that there was nothing wrong in expecting them—us—to have him back at home. But was he so wrong? Perhaps we would have learned to adjust to the situation in time. People are probably more flexible than they imagine.

Sadly I wondered what Father had felt when he heard about Dru. How terrible it must have been for him!

Mother would not allow this, however. "Why should *he* feel anything?" she demanded. "He was too wrapped up in his own selfish concerns. Besides, if he did feel anything, it was only what he deserved, wasn't it?"

"But he was terribly fond of Dru. She was his favorite."

"Well? He should have thought of that sooner—before he robbed her of her father, turned the whole relationship into a horrible travesty."

In the end, I gathered, he had simply taken his own way. After settling all he could on Mother, he had gone off to a clinic in Sweden where they gave him preliminary treatment for some time—over a period of about eighteen months, Mother thought—with hormones, before the climactic operation.

"And you've never seen him since?"

"What do you take me for? I told him I'd sooner die. I told him I'd get a divorce and change my name, that he must be prepared never to see his children again, that *he* must change *his* name, and completely disappear out of our lives. I wasn't going to have you and Dru—all of us—mixed up in revolting newspaper publicity, people coming and asking me how it felt to have a *woman* for a husband. Ugh!" She gave such a violent shudder of horror that I brought a blanket from the bed and draped it around her shoulders.

"You've never heard from him since? You didn't know the name he'd taken?"

"No, I didn't." *Could* I believe her? She went on, "He did write to me once or twice; he wrote care of the lawyers, and just signed with his initial, as he always had. Then he said that he missed us badly, and asked if he couldn't come back—just for a visit. But I—couldn't. I said no. After that I tore up his letters without reading them." Again that spasm of the mouth, as if she were suppressing nausea. "I'd thought he might have kept up connections with Dendros; that's why I never cared for your coming back here."

"Never cared" had been an understatement. There had been bitter rows over my first two visits to Helikon. But I, feeling there must be *some* advantage to be derived from my distant, cool relationship with Mother, had simply ignored her anger and gone; and presumably when she discovered that I had not run into Father here (by that time, no doubt, Kerry Farrell was becoming well known and had little chance to revisit old haunts) Mother's resistance died down; she became reconciled to my visits. When I gave up going, it was not through fear of her disapproval.

She went on, "Then—when I found you had brought me to Helikon—I was terrified that he might be here—but there was no sign of him, so I began to feel my fear had been a fuss about nothing."

And so it would have been, I thought, if only Elisabet Maas or someone else had agreed to sing the part of Hamlet; if old Annibal hadn't been so set on having his *Mystères* performed; if Kerry Farrell hadn't managed to get out of her engagement in Basel—

His engagement.

What an extraordinary situation. That's no lady: that's my father.

Suddenly I felt a furious anger against both of them. How dared they rob me of my father in this arbitrary way? He had been one of the two first people in my childhood's world—someone with whom I shared happy games, songs, jokes, a whole loving relationship—and because *he* had this crazy longing, because *she* couldn't stand it—*wouldn't* stand it—because of their obstinacy, Dru must be driven to suicidal despair and I must be left to a lonely, virtually parentless childhood. Why didn't you think of *us* at all? I wanted to demand. But Mother would say that she *had* thought of us—the rigid silence, the impenetrable secrecy, the puritan reserve had been her way of protecting us. I felt that I would have been glad to exchange such protection for more love and the risk of publicity, of the world's curiosity—but how could I judge? Maybe she was right. And presumably she knew the limits of her own endurance; she knew what she couldn't stand. The drawn expression of disgust about her mouth denoted plainly enough that her feelings were still as deep and bitter as they had ever been.

What a terrible, grotesque sort of rejection, I thought. To have a man say, "I don't want to go to bed with you any more, but I'd like to be a sister to you." All right for some women perhaps—but not for Mother, with her hot, fierce, sensitive Calvinist pride. With her deep, strong, inarticulate feelings. Think of having to share your memories of early sexual discoveries and happinesses with someone who had withdrawn from you in this way. No, I could see that it was not to be borne.

"I suppose Father didn't ever—well—marry again?" I asked with caution.

"God knows," said Mother with a curl of her nostril. "I suppose there might have been some man perverted enough to —I don't know. And I'd rather not know."

Enough of *that*, said the snap of her lips.

But it wasn't enough for me. And I felt that her acute disgust was a measure of how little she had allowed herself to discuss the subject—even *think* of it, probably—during the past twelve years. It had been unhealthily buried, deep down, festering. Who knows, if Father had had his way, if he had been allowed to live with us, she might in the end have become resigned—

But no, the idea was too squalid; there I did sympathize with Mother. I could not endure the thought, and pushed it away.

Poor Father, though. He had paid dearly for the realization of his dream. And how, I wondered, had he found it, being a woman? Had it come up to expectation? Satisfied his hopes? It seemed to me the most extraordinary wish imaginable—but how could I judge, being already endowed by nature with the estate he longed for? I tried to imagine longing to be a man—a yearning for the unattainable romance of being male—but my imagination could not bridge the gap; besides, I felt that I had already within reach all the desirable attributes of maleness—freedom, a career, the right to wear trousers, travel alone, sleep with whom I chose; the only exclusive male role remaining, it seemed to me, was the sexual decision, the right to attack, to make the first move, to take the plunge—and who in the world would want *that*, with its terrible anxieties and responsibilities, terrible risks of failure, impotence, or plain rejection?

No, the more I thought about it, the more I felt a strong sympathy with Father's wish to opt out of the whole male rat race; I couldn't find it in my heart to blame him. But of course that was the last thing that Mother could be brought to understand, for hers was an intensely competitive nature. She thought that achievement was no more than one's duty, that one should be constantly overcoming challenges and grappling with circumstances. Maybe if *she* could have chosen beforehand, she would have preferred to be a man?

Maybe that was what attracted Father to her?

But there was no profit in indulging in such speculations.

"Poor Ma! What a mess!" I sighed, leaning my head back against her knees. "It was lucky you were such a good teacher and had your career to occupy you. But didn't you ever think of marrying again?"

"Not likely!" she said with terrific intensity. "Do you think I'd run such a risk twice over?"

"A thing like that would hardly happen twice," I pointed out mildly.

"I'd had enough of men," she said with finality.

I didn't trouble to suggest that Father was hardly your typical man. I just felt sad for her. All her capacity for love wasted. And what about him? Did he never miss his male beginnings? Did they never miss each other? Didn't he ever long for the name "James" said as she used to say it?

But then, when I thought of Kerry Farrell, pacing so jauntily about the stage, swishing her flared skirt, teasing Joop Kolenbrander, and laughing at old Annibal's jokes, I could not feel that Father was much to be pitied; in fact some of Mother's disgust tinged the color of my thought. He had come a long way since he left our pleasant house near Oxford; he enjoyed his feminine role; he did not need us any more. I was glad at least that Mother had not watched that rehearsal; and I began to feel that she might be right to want to stay shut up in here.

Why should she be obliged to do that, though?

She had not committed any offense. Why must she remain cloistered up like a prisoner?

"You're quite sure you don't want to meet him—her?"

"I can't *stand* the idea!" Her expression, and the passionate intensity of her words, convinced me.

"Luckily I don't think there's much chance of his having recognized you. You look awfully different from your normal self in that black turban—and you're so thin just now."

"I recognized *him* at once," she said.

And at her tone of voice, I realized with a sad, transfixing stab of pain what had been staring me in the face all along. That she loved him still and completely, and always would. *That* was why she had never married again.

But nothing could be done about that.

"I know what," I said, jumping up. "I'll ask Adnan if we can't transfer to a hotel. I'll explain that there are acute personal reasons why it's necessary—I won't explain what—" as she looked daunted. "I'm sure it will be all right; he can fix it with Captain Plastiras. As long as we stay on the island."

"Oh, no, I don't want a whole lot of fuss and special arrangements," Mother said exasperatingly.

"Of course the best thing would be if they just canceled the *Hamlet* opera—and really it does seem unsuitable to go on with it after that poor man's death. I could ask Adnan to suggest that to Annibal. If it were canceled I expect Kerry—Father —would just leave again."

How strange it was, I thought, that in all this personal denouement I had almost forgotten about the poor man and his grisly end. Yet that sinister problem still remained, waiting to be solved.

"No, I don't want you making that kind of suggestion to Adnan," said Mother, sounding even more obstinate. "I hate anything devious—underhand—"

I could have shaken her.

Luckily, just at that moment there came a tap on the door and Adnan walked in. I was unfeignedly glad to see him, though he was looking even grimmer, paler, and more fatigued than he had in his office. I felt it would be the last straw to burden him with our grotesque little problem.

"How are you now, Mrs. Meiklejohn?" he asked, walking over to Mother and laying a finger on her pulse.

I noticed his eye instantly take in the signs of our debauch: the two milk-rimmed cups, the bottle of Glenlivet on the table. The faintest possible grin momentarily lightened his expression. Then he became serious again.

"I am glad you are not too upset after such a shock, Mrs. Meiklejohn, but it is best you go to bed, I think."

"Thank you; I was about to go," said Mother with dignity. "And then I have a personal problem about which I should like to ask your advice, Dr. Adnan."

"I am delighted to be of any use," he said formally.

Well, that's certainly a massive step forward, I thought, helping Mother into bed. Though what poor Achmed will make of the business, heaven knows.

Adnan, meanwhile, had flung himself down in our armchair and was gazing moodily at the pile of paperback plays and poetry that I lug around with me, and the Piaget and Kornei Chukovsky and Winnicott with which Mother enlivens her leisure.

I was quite surprised that he acceded to Mother's request so readily, since there must be no end of horrible formalities requiring his attention.

Perhaps he was glad to escape them for a bit.

When Mother was all settled, "I have a message for you, Mike," he said. "I hesitated to give it, not knowing if your mother could spare you, but, if you do not object, Mrs. Meiklejohn, Lady Julia would be very glad to see your daughter for a few moments."

"Of course!" Mother said. "I'm quite all right now, and I'm sure Mike will be glad to go. Poor Lady Julia—is she still very upset?"

"Not good. For a person of her temperament—highly strung, imaginative—the shock was particularly severe."

I glanced at Mother to see how she received this implication that she, being of tougher, peasant stock, could be expected to weather the experience more easily, and our eyes met; she gave me a small smile, which suddenly cheered me up.

Also, I was now provided with an excuse for going off and leaving them together, which seemed a good thing; I felt sure that Mother would prefer to be alone with Adnan while she discussed the problem of her transmogrified husband with him. So I said, "Okay, I'll go right along now. Shan't be long, Mother. See you later. Good night, Ach—Dr. Adnan."

To tell the truth, I was glad to get away from that piece of revelation.

I went quietly out and closed the door on them.

❧ 10 ❧

ADAGIO

Julia lay weakly on her bed, gazing at the ceiling. Strident, random thoughts circled and collided inside her head like disordered hornets. Dikran was sitting in the far corner of the room with his back to her, as he had throughout Dr. Adnan's visit; he was being no help at all.

It was plain, thought Julia, from time to time, among the rest of her unprofitable reflections, that Dikran had never before found himself in the position of being required to look after anybody else; or not for a long time, she amended, remembering that number on his arm; for the latter part of his life his money had entitled him to all the service that was going; and he seemed as indignantly astonished and unhandy when asked to bring a box of tissues or to find her eau de cologne as if he had been expected to mop up vomit or empty a bedpan.

In consequence, Julia, on whom shock had had the effect of bringing to the surface all the buried griefs and distresses of the past two years, lay silently, painfully crying, and longing for her children, both so quiet, deft, and considerate when a parent was sick, or for her lost husband, who, with all his failings, had been a kindly, domesticated man, always amiably prepared to make a pot of tea or fill a hot-water bottle.

Adnan had provided her with a sedative, advice to stay in bed on the following day, and solicitous bedside manner but in the face of Dikran's silent, glowering hostility, he had kept his visit to the barest, polite minimum and had not stayed to supply any of the comforting, informative chat for which Julia had hoped.

"Is there anything more you need?" he had asked, casting a frowning, thoughtful glance at Dikran's unforthcoming back.

And Julia, terrified at the thought of being left to her husband's mercies for the next nine or ten hours, had said faintly, "I'd love to see Mike for a little. Do you think her mother could spare her to come and sit with me?"

"I will inquire. I do not see why she should not," Adnan said after a pause, and escaped. "Take the pill soon—try to sleep," he warned from the doorway. "I am afraid there will be police here all night long, trampling about, hunting for clues— though what clues they can expect to find in this nest of musicians, who are among the most untidy, haphazard creatures in creation—!" He flung up his hands and left the room.

"What did the police ask you?" Dikran inquired some time after Adnan had gone.

"Oh—if I had ever seen or heard anything odd in the steam room. Which I hadn't. And Captain Plastiras asked me if I knew about any feuds or antagonisms among people staying at Helikon."

"What did you say to that?" He had turned around. His face was very sallow. His dark eyes were fixed on her in a kind of angry irony.

"Antagonisms? How should I know? I said we hadn't been here long; I could not be expected to have picked up information about internal feuds."

Captain Plastiras had received that with skepticism. "Really?" he had remarked. "You have met nobody who so much as dislikes one single other person here?"

Guiltily Julia remembered that she had then—with some misgivings—mentioned Mrs. Meiklejohn's remark, brought out with such cold force: "Yes, there is one person whom I can say that I hate." But the moment after she mentioned it, she had felt angry with herself. For, after all, there was absolutely no indication that the person hated by Mrs. Meiklejohn was at Helikon; indeed, such an eventuality was highly improbable. Moreover Julia's recital of the incident had earned her a very strange look from Captain Plastiras—a look, it seemed to her, of disapproval, mixed with a sad, understanding pity. She preferred not to think about it. She had been glad to hurry out of the secretary's office, collapse into a chair, and forget about the interview.

"Was that all he asked you?"

"Yes, it was." Firmly, Julia suppressed the tale of the pile of clothes in the sun-bathing enclosure; she had never told Dikran about that, and had her own reasons for finding it too frightening to dwell on. She said, "What did Plastiras ask you?"

"Oh, nothing much. The same. About feuds and antagonisms. And had I used the steam room. I said no."

"Oh, but you have been there," Julia said incautiously. "Don't you remember the first time when you got up—when I showed you round?"

"So what of it?" he shouted with sudden fury. "Has not every person in this damned hole walked through there at one time or another?"

"I only meant—"

"Yes? What did you mean?"

Luckily, at this moment Mike tapped on the door and put her head around it, asking, "May I come in?"

"Oh, yes, do come in, Mike," Julia said with great relief. "This is very sweet of you—how is your mother? Are you sure it's all right to leave her?"

"Thank you, yes, she's better, and Dr. Adnan is sitting with her at the moment."

"Oh, so he does sit with other lady patients as well as with my wife?" Dikran observed sourly.

Mike threw him a rather startled glance and then, catching Julia's appealing expression, said, "Is there anything I can do for you, Lady Julia? We've been drinking hot milk and scotch —would you like some?"

"That's very kind of you, but I think I'd bring it up—the very thought of that awful sight nearly makes me vomit," Julia said with a gulp. "I'd love it if you'd just sit with me for a bit, though; and do you think you could possibly brush my hair? It feels such a horrible, dank mess."

"Of course I will."

Mike found a hairbrush, turned the bedside lamp so that its light did not shine in Julia's eyes, and gently set to work. Dikran watched all this with a cold, ironic eye. "It is exceedingly kind of Miss Meiklejohn to spare the time," he muttered.

"I'm glad to do it," said Mike, brushing away. "It must have been the most dreadful, dreadful shock for Lady Julia—finding that man—"

"I do not see why that stupid nurse-girl had to lift off the tarpaulin and open the machine," Dikran grumbled. "If she had waited for the engineer's arrival, like a person of sense—"

"Oh, well, it would have been bound to happen sooner or later. Let's hope the police quickly find out who did it. Poor Dr. Adnan! It's horrible publicity for his clinic."

"Such publicity often brings more customers, out of curiosity," Dikran said, and turned away again impatiently.

Wishing to change the subject, Julia asked Mike about the performance of *Les Mystères d'Elsinore*—was it still going forward?

"I think so," Mike said. "M. Destrier seemed to think there was no reason why it should not. So they will spend tomorrow rehearsing, and the performance will be on the day after, as scheduled. Perhaps the police will have finished their job by then."

"Oh, well, I'm glad you didn't have all your hard work in vain," Julia said. "I'm looking forward to seeing your sets. Dr. Adnan says they are highly original."

A closed, clouded expression came over Mike's face at that,

but her only comment was, "He told *me* they looked like boiled cauliflower."

She glanced toward Dikran's back, as if she hoped for or expected some remark from him, but all he said, in an acid tone, was, "Dr. Adnan has a great sense of humor."

Julia wished that her husband would either take a proper part in the conversation or leave the room; it created a very uncomfortable atmosphere to have him sitting there with his back half turned, doing nothing, but apparently monitoring all they said, and inserting his tart comments from time to time as a reminder that he was listening. Deliberately ignoring him, she asked Mike, "Have you been introduced to Kerry Farrell yet?"

The girl paused for a long moment before answering. The same guarded expression came down over her face; she said, "No. No, I haven't. I saw her in the hall just before the rehearsal was interrupted. I'm not really sure that I want to be introduced. It's awkward—I've found out something—" Then she stopped, bit her lip, and said, "Have you talked to her?"

"Yes, I did, before the rehearsal. You found out about her sex change, you mean?" Julia said. Without noticing Mike's shake of the head, she went on, "But that's all in the past, years ago now. I honestly don't think it would embarrass you in the least. It didn't me, a bit. I think that was such an incredibly brave thing to do, don't you? When I remember the disgusting publicity about my divorce, and how scarifying I found it all—and think what *she* must have gone through—I take off my hat to her, I really do. What a decision to make! And yet it's plain that it was the right decision, for her; she seems so *buoyantly* happy and at ease; one can see at once that she ended up where she belongs."

"You knew all about her, then?" Mike asked. "I'd never even heard—about it—I knew of her as a singer, of course. I—I suppose I was over here, at school in Greece, at the time when he—she—when it happened." She swallowed. After a moment she added, "Was there much publicity?"

"No; some. Photographs in cheaper papers—especially

when she took up concert singing; and I remember an article in one of the color supplements about sex change in general, with some pictures of her. And a bit about the clinic in Sweden where it was done. Apparently they are doing more and more of these operations—as well as other kinds of plastic and cosmetic surgery. Anyway, it's done, it's over. She's a different person now."

"Did you *like* her?" Mike's tone was neutral, but she suspended the brushing for a moment while she waited for Julia's answer.

"Yes. Yes, I did!" Dikran raised his brows and, turning his head, directed an enigmatic look at his wife. But she had her back to him now and went on, "She was so lively and friendly. She seemed like a balanced, happy, *brave* person." Mike's suspended arm returned to its brushing. Julia went on, "I suppose she's the embodiment of the truth that most of us have a mix of both sexes in us and the really intelligent person must learn to assess their own balance and rectify it if it feels out of kilter."

"So I should be a woman, perhaps?" Dikran muttered, but not very loud.

"In fact I don't remember when I've felt so immediately *comfortable* with anybody," Julia continued. "You know what I mean? One didn't have, with her, the feeling that she— that she had any sexual ax to grind. It was easy and relaxed."

Dikran's grin became even more malicious. But Julia was lying on her stomach with her chin propped on her hands, enjoying the sensation of the brush gently teasing out her hair; she was remembering with an internal grin of her own that what she had actually felt, after ten minutes' conversation with Miss Farrell, was that it would be very enjoyable to share a sauna with the singer. Here, in fact, was the perfect friend— somebody with whom one could gossip and chuckle on most complete terms, who would never attack, never be a rival, but who knew about *the other side;* who had a foot in both camps.

"I wonder where she lives?" Mike remarked quietly.

"In Ireland, I believe. Her accent's quite Irish. Of course she spends most of her time traveling from one engagement to another."

"Did the article—any of the articles you read—say anything about her private life?"

"You know something of it yourself, Miss Meiklejohn?" Dikran suddenly interjected.

Mike looked startled. "I? Why should you think so?"

"Just now you said you had found out something about her."

"Only a private piece of information that isn't my secret," Mike said quickly.

Julia yawned. "I don't remember that the article said anything about her private affairs. Dead silence as to whether she had a lover. Some vague indication that she'd had to leave a family when she took off for the opposite gender. Rather weird for them, poor things—but I suppose they're used to the situation by now. Better have Daddy turn into Aunty than find out he's really the Boston Strangler or one of the Moors Murderers."

"Cripes, so I should think!" Mike's tone was startled. "Why them? What far-out alternatives you pick!"

Dikran shot another narrow-eyed glance at his wife, but she, yawning again, rolled over onto her back and said, "Angel Mike—you really are a child of light! You've actually made me feel sleepy with your conversation and your brushing—I never *ever* thought I'd be able to sleep again after that unutterably ghastly sight—Irish stew! Ugh! Now, could you be a love and fetch me a glass of water—give the glass a bit of a rinse first, I had cyclamens in it and they're almost certainly deadly poison—"

When Mike returned from the bathroom, Julia unclenched her hand, in which she had been holding Adnan's pill since he had given it to her.

"*Now* I shall sleep," she said, swallowing it with most of the water.

"Would you like me to stay till you drop off?" suggested

Mike with a cautious glance at Dikran. Julia nodded, with a look of appeal, but Dikran again interposed.

"My dear Miss Meiklejohn, it is kind of you to make the offer, but that will be entirely unnecessary. Anything further that my wife requires, I can perform. She has taken an unfair amount of your time as it is—since your mother also is suffering—"

"Sure?" Mike was already poised to go. "Okay! I hope you'll have a good night and be much better in the morning. I'll come round at breakfast time to inquire—not too early."

"No, not too early," said Dikran, with his tightly controlled, muscular smile.

When he turned to speak to Julia, after closing the door, she lay silent, feigning sleep; and soon she was asleep in good earnest.

But Dikran sat up all night, motionless, in his chair, staring out the window, thinking. When light came, he got up and went out softly, leaving Julia still sleeping.

She woke with a start, some hours later, hearing a tap on the door, and called, "Come in!" anxiously, but it was only Mike again, carrying a glass of grape juice and some puréed fruit.

"Good morning. How did you sleep?"

"Like a log, thank you. I feel miles better," Julia said, stretching luxuriously. It was a great relief to find Dikran gone out, though she did not say so. Seizing the chance of his absence, she said, "Mike. You did tell Captain Plastiras about finding that man's clothes?"

"Of course." Mike's tone was puzzled. "Didn't you?"

"Yes—I did. I wonder *why* they were left there?"

"I've been thinking about that. I suppose whoever killed that wretched man—he must have been murdered, mustn't he? No one would put someone else's body in a steam bath unless they had killed them first?"

"Might have been unconscious," Julia said grimly.

Mike shivered. "What a horrible idea! I hadn't thought of that. But the person who put him in must have done it hoping the body would be boiled till it was unidentifiable. I suppose he left the clothes in the men's sun-bathing place temporarily, thinking they wouldn't arouse any comment there and he could go back later and collect them and dispose of them permanently. But before he could get back, we came wandering along at dead of night and happened to see them. It was bad luck."

"Yes, it was bad luck," said Julia tonelessly. "The clothes didn't ring any bell with you—when the police questioned you—you didn't remember seeing anyone wearing them—either here or in Dendros?"

"No, Plastiras asked that," said Mike. "But I didn't—I'm sure I'd never seen them before. I would have remembered that shirt."

"Oh, well—" Julia's tone brushed the matter aside. "Maybe it was some wandering hippie who got bashed by one of his mates—some of the lot who sleep on the beach in Dendros—nothing to do with Helikon. Let's hope so. Thank you for the breakfast; it was sweet of you to bring it. Now I'm going to get up."

"You're sure you'll be all right?"

"Yes, fine, thanks—and your mother will be needing you, I expect."

"She's going to stay in bed today—take it easy," Mike said, accepting her dismissal and moving toward the door.

"I'll drop around and see her later."

Julia slowly dressed and went out into the quadrangle, thinking that it would be pleasant to encounter Kerry Farrell. More people than usual were standing and sitting in groups about the statue-studded grass. The heavenly, hot sun made yesterday's hideous discovery, and Dikran's strange behavior, seem like some half-forgotten nightmare, but there were still police around, and an uneasy atmosphere of gossip and speculation, to remind Julia that it had been no dream. Fellow guests eyed her with respectful commiseration, but few came to speak to her; evidently the news had gone around that it was she who had found the body, and people were shy of approaching her. Among the nervously whispering groups the shining, white, athletic statues leaned and watched and listened, as if waiting for a chance to take part in the discussion.

The sound of horns, violins, and a clear, carrying soprano voice floating from the main hall was a reminder that normal life was still proceeding, however. Julia moved irresolutely toward the concert-hall door, but before she reached it the rehearsal apparently broke up and the participants began to come out, laughing and chatting, evidently very pleased with themselves and each other. Old Annibal Destrier was among them hobbling on his two sticks today; he sank down on a bench in the sunshine and called to Joop Kolenbrander, "Be so good, *mon cher*, as to bring me some of that disgusting pseudo-beef drink from the loggia, will you? I wait for you here and rest my aged legs." Seeing Julia nearby, he gave her his gnome-like grin and said, "Aha, the beautiful Lady Julia! Expressly sent by *le bon Dieu* to cheer me after an exhausting *répétition*. Sit yourself here by me, and tell me about the rehearsings of your plays—you will 'ave seen many and they will all 'ave been 'orrible, is it not so?"

Julia, who had been feeling rather uncomfortably conspicuous and isolated, was glad to sit by him.

"Why," she said laughing, "was the rehearsal so very bad? I find that hard to believe. The musicians all seem first-rate—and I can't imagine that Kerry Farrell doesn't know her stuff?"

She glanced around for the singer as she spoke and saw her with Joop Kolenbrander, standing in the long, straggling queue that moved toward the hot-drinks table.

"*Pas mal*," Destrier confided. "No, I joke; the opera goes on in effect very well indeed. But—you know 'ow it is—players and singers are all obstinate as mules, self-willed as pigs—each wants his own way regardless of what is best for the ensemble."

"But I am sure they pay heed to you," Julia said soothingly.

"*Comme ci, comme ça!*"

"I'm afraid you will have a long wait for your *bouillon*," Julia remarked, observing the slow progress of the queue.

"No matter; what of it, when I am in such delightful company?"

Julia felt that the only appropriate reply to this would be, "La, sir, you are a sad flatterer, I vow!" She inclined her head, smiling.

Then in the distance she noticed Adnan, coming from the direction of his office. People streamed toward him, evidently asking him about the progress of the police investigations; he shook them off impatiently and came over to pay his respects to Annibal Destrier. He seemed to be doing it primarily out of a sense of duty; he asked civilly how the rehearsal had gone, but he looked pale and worried; his usual air of cheerful urbanity had quite left him. Julia felt fairly certain that, despite his informed and courteous inquiries, he was secretly wishing the aged composer and all his works at the devil. The presence of a whole batch of international celebrities at the time when such a horrible event had taken place at Helikon must add immensely to his problems and responsibilities.

Two pink-faced girl music students had summoned up the courage to approach Annibal Destrier and gigglingly ask for his autograph. Under cover of their chatter, Julia said to Adnan in a low tone, "I'd like to ask your advice sometime when you've a moment. I have a—a private problem that's worrying me."

His usual sympathy was noticeably lacking. He answered shortly, "Oh, very well—later, I will find time. After lunch."

"You seem very bothered."

He burst out, "It is all secrets, secrets! Everything at Helikon just now is somebody's secret. It is like "The Fall of the House of Usher." If only people would be rather more communicative about their past lives, *my* life would be a great deal easier."

With which he turned on his heel and walked away, leaving Julia feeling hurt and snubbed. He had not even inquired how she felt.

But then, with a chill sensation at the pit of her stomach, she saw her husband, who had evidently arrived while she was talking to Adnan and taken his seat on a bench about fifteen yards away. He sat with his arms folded, watching her impassively.

The two autograph seekers had retreated, grateful, blushing, and stammering; Julia reflected rather disconsolately that it was a long time since she had been asked for her autograph; at Helikon, playwrights rated nowhere in comparison with musicians.

Annibal Destrier turned back to her and gave her another of his singular grins—shrewd, sharply observant, rather malicious; she fancied that, even while he was signing the girls' books, he had been aware of her overture to Adnan, Dikran's arrival, and Adnan's rebuff. He did not immediately allude to any of these events but embarked on some rambling remarks about Helikon, its beneficial treatments, and, in particular, its wonderfully serene ambiance.

"Indeed I have heard it said," he pursued, "that many, many people who come here regularly begin to find, after a while, that, in effect, Helikon is quite changing their natures."

"Really, M. Destrier? In what way?" Julia asked politely.

"They become, by degrees, more serene; less self-seeking. Now, you, madame," he said gallantly, watching her with his small, brilliant black eyes, "you are a very lovely woman, very intelligent, very creative, you are admired by *tout le monde*, accustomed at all times to 'ave your own way; but if you were many times in 'Elikon, I wonder if even you might not begin to ask yourself, 'Should not all this come perhaps to a stop? Maybe I am not to 'ave my own way so often? Maybe I should not expect to 'ave my cake and eat it quite so much?' You look upset—I think you do not agree with me?"

"I—I'm not really sure that I know what you mean." Julia was very much startled indeed, and her feelings were even more bruised than by Adnan's snub; she had expected more compliments from the old composer, not disconcerting home truths.

But he went on, gently and remorselessly, "I observe much, madame; I notice 'ow your very charming and 'armless flirtation with Achmed upset your 'usband—and this so soon after you are married, and when 'e is not well; this I find sad. Achmed *sans doute* can look after 'imself, but as to your 'usband, I am not so sure; if I were you I would treat that one with more care. Also, there are others concerned—I name no names!"

Julia opened her mouth to protest, but he checked her with an upraised hand. "Ah—ah! I am informed about your divorce, you see, also—for I am in England at that time, conducting the City of London Orchestra, and I rent a house in 'Olland Park from a lawyer who knows much about the case; I learn, what is not generally known, that it is not so much the 'usband who commit adultery, though *évidemment* 'e wish to marry 'is fat peeress, but, to my great astonishment, I find it is the beautiful, virtuous wife who 'ave commit so many indiscretions until at last 'er 'usband become fed up with 'er and throw 'er out."

Tears stood in Julia's eyes; an angry spot of color burned on each cheek.

"Now, you may say," continued old Annibal peacefully, "you may say, *et pour cause*, 'Why should this interfering old man, who 'ave 'ad many, many affairs *avec beaucoup de monde*, why should 'e presume to criticize a lovely, talented lady 'oo is young enough to be 'is daughter? Why is it okay for Annibal to commit *des folies* while I am denied this right?"

She could not speak, but swallowed and gave a slight nod, frowning to draw the tears back into her eyes. She felt wholly outraged, furious, *violated* by such an unprovoked attack; and done in public too, even in the presence of her husband!

"But, you see, it *is* different for me," Annibal ended with great complacence. "And the difference is that I do no 'arm to anybody, and I am 'appy myself."

No harm, thought Julia; what about the lady who threw

herself into the Seine? For she too had encountered this legend as it floated around Helikon.

"I am 'appy myself," repeated Annibal. "But you, madame, you are not 'appy. Anyone can see that. And in your chagrin you pull and snatch at others, you inflict wounds—"

But Julia had had enough. She stood up, trembling.

"Monsieur Destrier," she said with what dignity she could muster, "I am sure you have meant this kindly. But you are quite right—it is no business of yours."

And she walked away from him, straight out across the lawn. The old man gazed after her with a sad and speculative air.

Dikran stood up leisurely and came to meet Julia. His appearance alarmed her inexpressibly: he was pale and sunken-eyed, as he had been on the day of his amnesia; he did not seem to have shaved. His expression as she came up to him was a frightening blend of fear and hostility; as if she were his life line, but one he hated to make use of.

He said, "I cannot stand this silly place a day longer. We have to leave—"

"Dikran, we can't. Don't you remember—"

Immensely to Julia's relief, Kerry Farrell, who had been strolling in their direction carrying a mug of bouillon, at this moment greeted Julia with a friendly smile.

"Hallo! I hope you have recovered from your horrible experience?"

"Yes, thank you. I'm fine today. How did your rehearsal go?"

"Well—" The singer rolled her eyes in the direction of where old Annibal was drinking his bouillon and talking to Joop Kolenbrander; she then gave Julia a swift, conspiratorial grin. "'Deed and he's an old Tartar, bless him! It would certainly go more easily without him there conducting an inquest into every note; he has me petrified entirely—but still! He's a great old boy and it is for his birthday—I daresay we'll survive."

"Poor you! He certainly is an old terror," Julia said in heartfelt agreement. Then, feeling Dikran's powerfully silent presence at her shoulder, "Oh, excuse me—this is my husband, Dikran; Miss Kerry Farrell."

"How do you do?" said Kerry Farrell with her frank smile. She held out a well-shaped, blue-veined hand, which was small for a man's but large for a woman's; after a moment's hesitation Dikran took it.

"Haven't we met before?" Kerry asked him. "Are you a musician? Your face is so familiar; I'm sure I know you from somewhere."

But he shook his head. "No, I am not a musician," he said stiffly. "I do not think we have met."

"Really? You weren't at Drottningholm last summer? I felt certain we'd met somewhere; I never forget a face."

"My husband isn't a musician; he's a businessman," Julia said, and thought with annoyance how artificial her laugh sounded.

"Is that so? What kind of business?"

"Many kinds," Dikran answered briefly, returning Miss Farrell's look of lively interest with a lowering, frowning stare. "It would take too long to explain."

"And I've little head for business, faith!" the singer said laughing. "I'm always two years behind with my taxes, and keep my cash in an old teapot." She blew on her bouillon. "I wish this disgusting stuff would cool down; it's away too hot to drink yet, and me as parched as an old shoe after singing '*Être ou ne pas être*' thirty times over."

Mike walked swiftly across the grass carrying two cups of bouillon; she nodded, in response to Julia's wave, but did not stop, and disappeared into the guest wing.

"Who was that?" Kerry Farrell asked, looking after Mike.

"Oh, she's a dear child—haven't you met her yet? I'll introduce her when she comes back," said Julia. "She's got a lot of talent—and she's a darling, isn't she, Dikran?"

He grunted; but at this moment the two giggling autograph hunters came up, nudging each other like calves, even more pink and flustered than when they had approached Annibal Destrier.

"Oh, Miss Farrell—*could* we have your signature?"

Julia, who was feeling more and more apprehensive, looked at them with exasperation. But Kerry Farrell shrugged and laughed, accepting the autograph book that one of them handed to her.

"Would you mind, just a moment?" she said gaily to Dikran, and passed him her steaming cup. "Which page— any?" she said, opening the book and delving in her shoulder bag for a ballpoint.

"Anywhere—yes, there—*thank* you, Miss Farrell!"

They stood in worshiping silence while she inscribed a baroque, flourishing signature in each book, then shouldered each other off again, triumphantly comparing signatures. As they did so, Julia noticed that a sudden hush had fallen over the lawn, like the silence in a hen run when a hawk sweeps overhead.

Glancing behind her, she saw that Captain Plastiras had appeared and was walking across the grass, glancing about him as if searching for some particular individual. When he saw Dikran and Julia, he quickened his pace and approached their group.

"Good morning!" Julia said nervously. "How are your inquiries proceeding?"

"Good morning, Mrs. Saint. I hope you are feeling better today?"

"Yes, thank you. Much better."

He greeted Kerry Farrell politely and, turning to Dikran, said, "Mr. Saint. I just wish to ask you one question. Yesterday I show you a photograph of a man, and you say you do not recall ever speaking to him?"

"Yes." Dikran was watchful, guarded; he eyed Plastiras with the wary look of a wrestler waiting to see which way his opponent will move. "That is so."

"Now, today, there has come into my possession another

picture, taken by a beach photographer, which I will be glad for you to do me the kindness of inspecting?"

He took a black-and-white print from an envelope. Dikran gazed at it impassively, but Julia saw that a muscle began to jump in his cheek. Filled with alarm, she moved around beside him and studied the picture. It showed Dikran on the beach in front of the Fleur de Lys Hotel; she recognized the thatched beach umbrellas and the garden behind. Dikran was wearing swimming trunks and carried a towel and a folded newspaper under his arm. He was talking to a man in a striped T shirt.

For a moment, Julia stared at the photograph as if she were paralyzed. Then she cried out, "But of *course* you didn't remember the man! Don't you see? There was only one day when you went on the beach in your swimming trunks, and that was the day you had your amnesia—when I was out shopping! Don't you remember? When I got back you had damp trunks on under your trousers! Of *course* he didn't remember the man," she repeated, turning to Captain Plastiras. "He was sick that day—he completely lost his memory. Dr. Adnan will be able to confirm that. And—" she added triumphantly, "you will be able to check the date from the headline on the newspaper that he is carrying. Won't you?"

"Yes, that is so," Captain Plastiras agreed. "In fact we have done that already." He said to Dikran, "Can you confirm that, Mr. Saint?"

Dikran looked at him haggardly. The muscle in his cheek was jumping even more. And his voice, when he answered, was full of exasperation. "How can I confirm anything?" he said. "I have no memory of that day."

Kerry Farrell, who had been an embarrassed spectator of this scene, now began to move away from it, looking suddenly troubled and uneasy.

"You don't want me, do you?" she said to Captain Plastiras. He shook his head. "Then, if you'll excuse me—I see M. Destrier going back into the hall. The rehearsal is going to start again."

She walked off to join Joop Kolenbrander.

{ 11 }

MAESTOSO

I woke up next morning feeling horribly sad. I suppose the real essence of Mother's revelation about Father had taken time to sink right down into my subconscious; it had finally been assimilated while I slept.

Now I understood that, ever since reading Mother's open-after-my-death letter, I had, without realizing it, been filled with a crazy hope that—despite her warning—Father was not really lost to me but that I was going to be able to recover him in some form or other—blind, crippled, mad, exiled, disgraced, the circumstances had not seemed important. I thought that, so long as he was alive, we would ultimately be able to re-establish our old relationship.

But during my sleep—which was brief and troubled by dreams—my psyche had evidently absorbed the fact that Father was lost indeed; I surfaced from a nightmare of missing trains and hunting for mislaid luggage to a mood of almost unbearable depression and bereavement. My father, as he had been, was gone for good. I must learn to adjust to this fact.

Mother was still asleep when I woke. She had been sleeping when I returned from my rather uncomfortable session with Mr. Saint and Lady Julia the night before, so I still did not know whether she had confided in Adnan about our relationship with Kerry Farrell. Nor did I know whether I hoped she had. Talking about it to Adnan would certainly have helped her; for her sake, I supposed I hoped she had done so, for I had no doubt of his good sense and practicality; but on the other hand I was not at all sure that I wanted him to know this bizarre fact about my background; our relationship was already complicated enough, it seemed to me, without adding such a burden to its toppling structure. I felt it might be the last straw; he would wish to wash his hands of the Meiklejohns, parents and child, and I would not blame him.

Helikon, to which I had come with such high hopes and happy memories, now seemed like a cage, and I longed to leave it. Without a shadow of doubt, Mother did too. I wondered if, while she was talking to Adnan, she had broached the matter of our moving to a hotel.

Moodily I got up and dressed. Mother still slept, so I went down to the dining room and had a mug of grape juice, longing for coffee. I didn't speak to anyone, wasn't in the vein for sociability. Adnan did not appear in the dining room; nor did Kerry Farrell. I couldn't think of her as Father, didn't feel like trying. *She* was quite all right, I thought, infected by some of Mother's resentment; she had her fine new life, with all its successes and friends; she never gave a thought, probably, to the orphaned family she had left. To hell with her! I didn't want to see, hear, or converse with her; all I wanted to do was get right away, as far as possible, preferably back to my flat, my friends, and the Theatre Royal, Crowbridge. Which would never be the same again.

When I went back to our room after breakfast, Mother was still sleeping—it must have been a real knockout drop that Adnan gave her, which was probably a good thing—so I went and checked on Lady Julia, who seemed in a queer state, nervous and preoccupied. I had felt, the night before, that she was truly terrified of her husband—and in fact I was terrified of him myself. I wondered if she had made some awful discovery about him. Or was it just his evident bad temper that frightened her? Plainly she was not a woman who was used to being bossed around by her men. She preferred to take the initiative. —I thought of the odd story told me, in a moment of confidence, by my friend Rickie, who had been at school with Lady Julia's son, Paul. At sixteen or so the two boys had been friends, and Rickie was invited to stay at the Gibbon house. And one night his hostess had come, in the most matter-of-fact way, to his bed.

"What was really queer," he said, "was next morning at breakfast. There she was, behaving as if nothing had happened —teasing me and Paul, telling us to hurry up and wash the dishes."

"Was that your first experience of sex?"

"Yes it was," he said, "as a matter of fact."

"So what did you feel about it all?"

"I felt," he said, "that I couldn't have a relationship with Paul *and* his mother, both; and I didn't want to lose Paul; so I invented an interview for an imaginary job and said I had to go that day. She laughed, she was quite good-natured about it, but I could see that she was annoyed. 'You'll never get on unless you learn to take the chances that you are given,' she told me when she was driving me to the station. But I felt I didn't want to get on if that was the only way it was to be done."

"I suppose she doesn't like people leaving before she's ready to let them go."

It seemed fairly plain now, from the mixture of dislike and irritation she displayed toward her husband, that she was ready to let *him* go; presumably she now realized what a hideous mistake she had made in getting married on the rebound from her divorce, and I imagined it wouldn't be long before she was in the market for another divorce.

Anyway, whatever she wanted this morning, it was not me, so, since she seemed to be reasonably recovered and able to

fend for herself, I went back to Mother, who at last had
waked up.

She, unlike Lady Julia, looked tired and pale and announced
her intention of staying in bed all day. I provided her with
breakfast and made her eat it, though she was reluctant.

Then, rather nervously, I asked her if she had confided in
Adnan the night before and whether she'd asked him about
our moving to a hotel. "I wouldn't suggest moving you
today," I added, "but I do see that it's not on the cards for you
to stay here at the same time as—as Father, and I'd think
Adnan would see that too—"

"Yes, I did talk to him," Mother said.

I had stuck all our combined pillows behind her and she was
reclining, propped against them, wearing the usual black turban and one of her plain white cotton nightdresses with long
sleeves. It suddenly struck me that, though white with fatigue
and hollow-eyed, she looked unusually serene, as if some knot
had been untied inside her.

"He's a good man, your Achmed," she said reflectively. "I
like him a lot. He's full of sound, solid sense, under that rather
worldly exterior."

I refrained from pointing out how far from *mine* he was but
concentrated on the rest of her remark. "Worldly? I wouldn't
have called him that, exactly. How do you mean?"

"Oh—all those frilly shirts and velvet waistcoats," she said
with indulgent scorn. She added, "However, I daresay he'll get
over that stage," as if he were about seventeen. I could see that
he was well into her good graces, and when she said, "In some
ways I think the Turks are very like the Scots," I was quite
thunderstruck and wondered by what arts he had contrived to
wind her around his little finger.

"So, what did he have to say?"

"Well, we agreed that it would be quite unreasonable to ask
James—to ask Kerry Farrell to cancel her performance now,
after such a lot of effort has been put into it, besides being the
old man's birthday treat—"

I was even more amazed that Adnan should seriously have considered such a step.

Mother went on, "When I suggested our going to a hotel, he seemed rather taken aback and said that was a lot of unnecessary trouble, as the performance will be over tomorrow and Ja—Kerry Farrell will be leaving again at once. He said if I didn't mind lying low for forty-eight hours—which I don't at all—he saw no reason why there should be any awkwardness or embarrassment."

"But what did *you* feel?" I asked, amazed at all this sweet reason. She certainly had changed from the previous night.

"Oh—we had a long talk," said Mother vaguely. She was never much good at reporting the nuances of conversation. At the end of a committee meeting, clear as a clock striking she could announce, "So-and-so was proposed, such-and-such was discussed, this-and-that was decided," but the meanderings of emotional current were beyond her power to chart. She said, "I expect he'll tell you about it sometime." She added, after a pause, "But he did say that—for my own peace of mind—I ought to talk to James, at least once."

"Gosh!" I said, but internally, to myself. Aloud, after a moment, I merely asked, "*Could* you?"

"I don't know. —I'm thinking about it. It would be hard. I told Achmed so."

When did the pair of them get onto Christian-name terms? I wondered.

"But he pointed out," Mother went on calmly, "that I was doing both James and myself an injustice by not seeing him." A tinge of pink appeared in her cheeks. She went on, "He said —he said I might even *enjoy* seeing James."

This seemed to me a highly doubtful proposition. I said with caution, "Are you sure? Don't do anything in a hurry. Remember, you're still only convalescent. And you had that horrible shock yesterday. It might be drastically upsetting—for both of you. I don't think you should make any move to see him before the performance."

"Oh, dear me no. Of course not. I haven't come to any con-

clusion yet about it. I'll go on thinking. But Achmed has made
me feel better about the whole thing, I must say."

Oh, bless him, I thought, with loving exasperation. My
thoughts warmed toward the maddening creature. How, I
wondered, could he be so kind, so intelligent and understanding in one way, and so hopelessly, infernally dumb and
infuriating in another?

"And he said," Mother continued, "that it was absolutely es-
sential *you* should make yourself known to James. He said all
your hang-ups—Father complex, Jocasta complex, feelings of
insecurity and deprivation and so on—couldn't begin to be
sorted out until you had faced the fact once and for all that
your lost father had turned into someone completely
different." She put on her reading glasses and peered curiously
at me over them. "*Have* you got all those different complexes?
I was quite surprised. You have always seemed unusually balanced and sensible to me, for a person of your age, I told
Achmed."

She looked so thin and anxious in her black turban—so
unlike my formidable Ma—that I felt a stab of compassion for
her and only said gently, "I expect I put on a bit of a false
front for you. What *is* a Jocasta complex, anyway?"

"Female form of an Oedipus complex."

"Oh, I see. —So old Achmed thinks I should rush to Kerry
Farrell and throw my arms round her, crying, 'Daddy, Daddy,
here's your little long-lost Priss!' does he?"

"Well, not before the performance, he thought."

"That's very considerate of Achmed!" I snapped, suddenly
out of patience with him again. "Fine for Father, but what
about me, having to go around for two whole days, fixing the
costumes and everything, with that load of dynamite inside
me?"

"You can do it if you have to, dear," Mother said, suddenly
giving me a firm, warm look of confidence and approval.
"That was another thing Achmed said—that when it came to
the point, you had a remarkably mature judgment and would
be able to decide for yourself on the right moment to speak to

your father. If you feel the situation is becoming too strained and artificial—then you'll have to speak out. Achmed said he felt sure you could be relied on to do it in a way that wouldn't be too upsetting for James."

"He did, did he? Well—I'll do some thinking, too." I looked at my watch. "Heavens! it's nearly twenty past eleven—I've already missed half the rehearsal. I'll get you a cup of broth and then I must dash."

"I don't want any of that disgusting bouillon. I've only just had breakfast."

"Rubbish! It's good for you."

"Oh, very well."

I ran down to the loggia and fetched it. When I returned—

"All this careful discussion and planning," Mother said, with her first full smile for two days, "but there's one possibility we haven't taken into account."

"What's that?" I asked, setting the steaming cup on her bedside table.

"Why, that James might simply recognize you. You're awfully alike."

So I ran back to the quadrangle with this new hazard to worry about.

By now the Helikon routine was getting back to normal. The police were less in evidence, people had stopped huddling and chattering and gone off to their dance or music practice or various treatments. In fact there was no one about in the quad, except, of course, God, and also Mr. Saint, who came out of the little telephone room by the loggia as I arrived, and stood brooding like a heron, with a suspended expression, as if he did not quite know what to do with himself.

As always with him, I had the instinctive feeling that he was better *occupied;* that if he were left to brood, Satan would find mischief still. So I said, "Why don't you come with me to the rehearsal and see if they get off to a better start than when we went last time?"

I didn't particularly want him with me—I had plenty to think about—but, as some Saki character observes, one must occasionally do things one dislikes. He gave me an odd look, glanced at his watch—then at the sky—and finally said, "Very well. But for ten minutes, no more."

So we went into the big hall together.

There were fewer spectators today. It was a time of day when most people were either in classes or having treatments; also, there had been an earlier session, which had probably satisfied such people as were simply out for sensation. There were only half a dozen watchers scattered among the pew-like seats. We stole softly down toward the front.

It was easy enough to do this without causing any disturbance: the King, the Queen, Polonius, and Ophelia were in the middle of their quartet and making quite a lot of noise. They were wearing my costumes, and the effect was just what I had intended, which cheered me somewhat.

As we settled ourselves, they sang down to a rousing conclusion and trooped off the dais. After a moment or two, Kerry Farrell came on. She was not in costume but wore black trousers and shirt, which seemed suitable enough for Hamlet. She looked extremely pale, but that might just be in contrast with all the black. I gazed at her, as old Annibal launched into a discussion with Joop about the previous scene, and thought, Yes, it's true, we are alike. The bones of that face are the same as the bones of mine, the eye sockets, jawbone, forehead are built in the same way as the structure of bone and muscle which contains my thoughts—how strange! How strange that is! That person up there has stolen the body of my father, whom I loved, and changed it into something different. The person there has gone to extreme trouble and expense—pain, shame, humiliation, the struggle of learning a whole new bodily language and set of skills—*simply to become what I already am.*

And what did I feel toward her? I really could not decide. Terror, partly—a wish to postpone our first meeting for as long as possible. But also longing—longing to cry, "Do you remember? Do you remember the games we used to play—the things we used to do? The pet names you had for me? Do you know who I *am?* I am Lady Goodheavens, Miss Fizz, the Timber-footed Wonder. I used to hold your hand all the way down the Banbury Road and along St. Giles's; you used to buy me sweets called Snowdrops and played me a special tune on the piano which you christened The Mad Marchioness's Funeral. And look at me now! I'm grown up! Listen while I tell you about all the things that have happened to me. . . ."

Watching her—although I still felt troubled, uncertain, bitterly sad, hostile, and confused—I began to have an inkling of the new kind of relationship which it might be possible to achieve with this person. All is not lost, I thought. All is *never* lost. Matter can neither be created nor destroyed. It falls apart into fragments, and out of those fragments new shapes are formed, new organisms are born.

The orchestral group started to play their introduction. It trickled to a gentle close, and Kerry Farrell, standing in the middle of the stage, opened her mouth and lifted her voice into the first clear, thoughtful note of the aria. "*Être ou ne pas être* . . ." And pitched forward heavily on to her face, and lay still.

There was a horrified gasp from someone standing at the side of the stage, the singer who played Laertes. King Claudius and Queen Gertrude rushed out and knelt by the prone black figure.

I heard old Annibal, who was sitting just ahead of us, whisper, "*Ah, mon Dieu! Non—non—NON!*"

Joop dropped his baton. He jumped forward, his Adam's apple working convulsively. Everyone else in the scanty audience was up and moving toward the stage. Only my neighbor and I remained sitting still. A premonition, some kind of inner, instantaneous knowledge, had told me, in the moment of Kerry Farrell's collapse, that I need not have worried or tried to plan what I was going to say. I would never have the chance to express the things I had just been thinking.

Joop rose from his knees. His face was ashen.

"Fetch Dr. Adnan," he said hoarsely.

Somebody ran out at desperate speed. But I knew their bustle and activities were useless. Not Adnan nor anyone in the world had power to breathe life back into that motionless body. This time, Father was gone for good.

My silent neighbor stood up and took my arm in a firm clasp.

"Come," he said. "We can give no help here."

I did not resist when he led me out. I was in a state of shock, I suppose. Round and round my thoughts went, in a stupid circle. Why did it have to happen? I don't understand. Was the strain too great for her? But she was not afraid of the part. I *knew* this would happen. Right from the start, in my bones, I knew it. But why? I don't understand. Was the strain too great?

"Come," said Mr. Saint.

I didn't know where he was taking me but I followed mechanically, since I certainly had no other plan, either for my immediate future or for the rest of my life. I was in a state of suspended animation.

We walked under the clock arch to the shaggy bit of ground near the lemon orchard where Adnan's car stood. It was there, just as I had left it, with the keys in the ignition.

Mr. Saint opened the passenger door for me and himself got into the driver's seat. It's kind of him, I thought numbly; he's taking me for a drive in order to distract my mind. But how does he know that this affects me so particularly?

At the gate of the drive we passed a policeman, who looked as if he might stop us, but when we turned left he changed his mind. We went up the steep hill that would bring us presently to Archangelos and then on to the archaeological site at the top of Mount Atakos. Mr. Saint was driving quite fast—faster, indeed, than I would normally have considered safe, but he seemed to be a reasonably good driver and I was not in a critical mood. Stupidly I found myself crying; the beautiful figs and olives, the dark cypresses and pale, sage-green shrubs between them flowed past me in a tear-blurred haze.

Then we went through the village; rather too fast, I thought again; past the *taverna*, with its vine-draped pergola, where Calliope and I had once sneaked out to have our first ouzo with a couple of boys; unknown to her parents, we had thought, but of course the news had got back like lightning and there had been a terrific row; "I look on you as my child," Kyrie Aghnides had said, "so I chastise you as my child." Which I had accepted at the time as fair enough, but now, looking back, I felt that all my long sojourn in Greece had been *perfectly unnecessary;* all the time I had spent there mourning for Father, he had been still alive. What a stupid piece of deceit! If ever I have any children, I vowed, they shall learn to swallow the truth in great gulps, whether pleasant or unpleasant.

Mr. Saint drove on up toward the top of Mount Atakos.

I looked at my watch. "I'd pull off onto the next lay-by if I were you," I said.

"Why?" he asked in the disagreeable tone that drivers fall into when advised to stop by their passengers.

"Because it's a Sunday, even hours; you are likely to meet the excursion bus coming down, and they come at a terrific lick."

"Oh, very well." Still surly, he drove on a quarter mile and pulled off onto a rock platform that had been chewed out of the hillside by lowering the level of the road, so that the next bend was twice as steep. The little Volks was red hot and panting like a pug from the climb we had done already. Below us extended a terrific spread of coastline; there lay Helikon at the foot of its glen, square and gray, with the clock tower above and the orchard and gardens beyond; over to the right, beyond a shoulder of mountain, a few of the roofs of Dendros town could just be seen, a bit of crusaders' castle and the green tip of a mosque; more rocky, cliffy coast to the left, and ahead the blue Aegean and the blue, mysterious coast of Turkey. For once the magnificent stretch of scenery failed to lift my heart; I wiped my eyes and observed it without enthusiasm.

"Why do you weep?" said my companion. "You cannot have been in any way devoted to that singer—you had not even met her."

"How do you know?" I asked childishly—as if it mattered.

"You said so yourself, last night."

"I might have met her this morning."

"But you had not. For we were talking at morning break time, my wife, and she, and I, and she asked who you were."

At this I wept afresh.

"Really, this is stupidity!" he said angrily. "I thought you were supposed to be unusually mature—unusually intelligent. My wife never ceased to sing your praises. So why carry on like a stage-struck child about someone of whom you know nothing?"

"I *do* know something about her—him." Stung by Mr. Saint's unjustified scorn, I turned to look at him resentfully. "He was my father!"

Just then, as I had foretold, the excursion bus came hell-for-leather down the hill, at a pace that scared the doves from the trees all along the road and left a cloud of scorching dust in the air behind it. I was glad I'd persuaded Mr. Saint to pull over.

The noise of its passing drowned his next remark, which seemed to be an oath; he had turned very pale and stared at me incredulously.

"Your *father?* This I do not believe."

"It's true! His name used to be James Graffin. My name is really Graffin, but my mother and I went back to her maiden name when they were divorced."

"Your mother . . . Christ's bones!" he muttered. "What an entanglement!"

Mechanically he started the car again and drove on up the mountain road, negotiating bend after bend with the minimum of attention, so that I sat sweating slightly, with eyes glued to the windshield; if he had brought me on this ride with the object of distracting my thoughts, he was beginning to succeed, but I was not certain now that *had* been his aim; I was starting to wonder what he really did have in mind, and a nibble of fear began to make itself felt under my grief and shock.

"Well, look!" he said suddenly, making a wild swerve

around another bend; I could feel the grit shoot from under our wheels as we skidded. "Look, I am sorry if he was your father, but, damn it, he was not *really* your father; you could not have seen him for many years, and what kind of a father is that? No good at all."

"It wasn't his fault! My mother wouldn't allow him to see us, because she thought it would be up—upsetting." I took a deep breath and blew my nose.

"Bones of god!" he muttered again. "What a crazy situation! If he had had any guts at all, he would have taken no notice of such a prohibition."

"I'd rather not discuss it, if you don't mind!"

To my utter astonishment, he then said, "Well, *I* will be a father to you." He snapped it out quite angrily, as if saddled with this tiresome obligation by circumstances that he saw no means of escaping.

I gaped at him as we missed death by a hair's breadth around another acute bend. Then I said, "Thank you for the offer, but I don't need a father any more."

"Of course you do! Every girl needs a father until she is married—to help her select a suitable partner."

I said resentfully, "I have no plans of that kind at present, and I suggest you leave me to my own resources and look after your own children."

"I have no children," he said shortly. "They sterilized me in Dachau."

Shocked by this flat statement, I was silent for a moment, then muttered, "I'm sorry. I wouldn't have said that if I'd known."

"It does not matter. It is long ago. I have been rich for many years now—I could have adopted children if I had wished."

"That wouldn't be the same as your own."

"No." He glanced sideways at me, and again we narrowly missed death.

"*Please* keep your eyes on the road. We're about eight hundred feet up, here, and if we went off we'd roll right down to sea level."

He ignored that and went on moodily, "I suppose you think I could not be so good as your own father. But I assure you I would be a great deal better. I would look after you—pay for any education you wished—take you about the world—"

It seemed too rebuffing to tell him that I didn't particularly want any more education and certainly had not the least wish to travel about the world in his rather surly company. Besides, what would Lady Julia have to say? But I was truly puzzled by this abrupt—and, it seemed, reluctant—piece of generosity, and couldn't resist asking, "Why? Why do you suddenly make me this offer?"

"Oh, why! Why must you always ask *why?* Is it not enough that I offer?" He added in a sharp, irritable voice, "It is because I already have all I want, and it is not enough. I have money for houses, travel, a beautiful, famous wife, cars, yachts, and so many treasures that I could not begin to describe them to you. But what is the use of it all if the health is not good and the heart is sad?"

He must have detected something that he interpreted as skepticism in my expression, for he suddenly stopped the car with a fearful screech of brakes, about ten inches from a four-hundred-foot drop, and pulled a little leather box from his pocket. It was about the size of the kind that holds contact lenses. "Look!" he said. Flipping up the lid, he exhibited its contents—a drab-looking stamp. "Do you know what that is? It is an 1848 Mauritius two-pence; one stamp was wrong in every sheet printed. It should be a one-penny stamp. At any dealer's, I could get twenty thousand pounds for it. *Twenty thousand pounds!*"

"Oh? I'm not very interested in stamps, I'm afraid."

"No? But I have plenty of things that *would* interest you," he said, putting the box away, furiously throwing in the gear and driving on. "Art treasures—paintings—curiosities of literature—for instance, I have a letter from Jane Austen to her sister about the man she loved who betrayed her—aha!" Triumphantly he caught my eye. "*That* you would like to see!"

"I should think I would! But that must be *priceless*—if it's genuine. Where in the world did you get hold of it?"

His face closed. He said, "I have my sources of supply. I do not reveal them."

"Are you going to publish the letter?"

"Never! I keep it to look at myself and enjoy the knowledge that I alone in the world can do so."

Privately I began now to wonder if he was a nut, which did not increase my confidence as we went on corkscrewing up those endless bends.

"Where do you keep your treasures?" I asked.

"In Switzerland. In a bank."

"Has Lady Julia seen them?"

"No. And she will not do so now," he said vindictively.

"Oh, why?"

"I leave her. She is a spoiled, selfish bitch. A man could not have a worse wife."

"Poor Lady Julia!" Though certainly I could not imagine a more ill-assorted couple; they were both well out of that marriage, I felt. I said, "Does she know your intentions?"

"I left her a note."

This struck me as odd; it seemed to indicate that he thought he had already left her—left Helikon. I said, with caution, "You didn't think this was the road into Dendros, did you?"

"*Hein?* No, we are going up the mountain."

"Oh, that's fine, then. So long as you knew that," I said rather absurdly. We described another fearsome U turn. I was glad that the bus had gone by. "Tell me about your other treasures," I suggested. They seemed a safer topic to occupy his mind than the failings of Lady Julia.

"Old masters I have many—Goya, Rembrandt, Titian, Tintoretto—"

"All in this bank?"

"All."

"You don't have any of them on display in your house?"

"Nup." He made a short, very emphatic negative noise. "Too dangerous."

"They might get stolen, you mean?"

To this he made no answer, and it struck me that possibly they already *were* stolen, which would account for his cagy behavior about them.

"Well," I said, "I hope they have good lighting in the bank."

I cheered up a little as I imagined it, the walls above the serious Swiss tellers covered with Rembrandts and Tintorettos.

"Do you have any Pieros?" I asked, remembering how well informed he had been about that painter.

"Yes, I have five."

"*Five?* But there are only *three* in the National Gallery!"

"Do you doubt me?" he asked coldly.

"Of course not, if you say so. What are their subjects?"

He did not answer, and I thought of the great paintings by Piero which had been stolen from the ducal palace in Urbino. Were only copies returned? Were the originals now reposing in a Swiss bank? I said, "I certainly would love to see those."

"If you do so, you will have to promise not ever in this world to reveal your knowledge about them."

I said—to cover the fearful chill on my heart caused by these words—"Oh, then, I think I'd rather not, thank you. I don't like keeping other people's secrets. It's too much responsibility."

"But you keep the secret that Kerry Farrell was your father?"

My thoughts, which had temporarily been distracted by this crazy conversation, turned back to what had happened; the sense of loss engulfed me once more. I put my hands over my face, pressing fingers to the high, narrow forehead which was not mine only, and cried out, "Oh, why did he have to die just *now*, of all times?"

"I am afraid that was my doing," said Mr. Saint matter-of-factly, as if he were talking about a missed train. "I had to kill him."

It took a moment for the meaning of what he had said to

sink in. Then I took my hands away from my face and stared
at him.

We had reached the top of the mountain at last; there was a
flat parking area, where the bus could turn around. He drove
into it and stopped the car.

There was a pause.

"You *killed* him?" I said. "You killed Kerry Farrell?"

"I regret so—yes."

"But why? *Why?*"

The hot sun beat ferociously down on the roof of the car.
Mr. Saint got out, and I followed him automatically. "It was
necessary," he said. "We were together once, in a room, in a
clinic where at one time I had to have my appearance
changed. It was a most unfortunate mischance. I had been
under an anesthetic and was not conscious at first. When I discovered that we had been placed together, I was angry about
it. But by that time he had left and I could not find what became of him. I thought perhaps we will not meet again so it
does not matter—though I am not pleased to think there is a
person in the world having this knowledge about me. But then
we do meet again and he does recognize me. It is a pity."

"So—you—just—killed him?" I said slowly.

He made an impatient gesture. "What is one death to me?
In Dachau every day one saw thousands go—do you think I
should distress myself over one? But I am sorry he was your
father. That is why I offer to make reparation."

"Thank you, but I don't want it."

I could not help looking at him curiously, though. Now I
began to suspect that he was not exactly a nut but—which was
more chilling—lived by standards completely alien to mine.

"What *are* you?" I asked. "A king of crime?"

"I have an organization," he said seriously. "And, at the moment, they are trying to seize my power. They believe that
since my sunstroke I lost control. But they will find that they
are wrong."

"I think I'm frightened of you."

"You are lucky," he said in an oddly paternal, indulgent

manner. "Nothing frightens me since Dachau. There, every day, they would make us form into squares. Then some from each square would be taken off. One used to think about it at night."

"How old were you?"

"I was seventeen. Younger than you."

"So, after that, because nothing frightened you, you were able to devote yourself to getting rich."

"That is so."

"And now you have everything you want, and it isn't enough?"

He said irritably, "I shall find new things to do."

My attention wandered. That, I supposed, was why he had first been attracted to Lady Julia. She was a new thing for him —rich herself, beautiful, talented, notable; he could annex her, as he had the Rembrandts and the Jane Austen letter, but she would not have to be gloated over in secret like them; he could flaunt her all about the world. But then the plan had gone wrong; she turned out to be a person, after all, not a letter or a painting; she became bored, perhaps homesick, despised him and didn't bother to conceal it; in a mixed-up way I felt sorry for him.

And then, suddenly, cold with consternation, I saw, or thought I did, where this conversation was leading, where his plan for me fitted into all this. He was leaving Lady Julia, and he intended taking me along, not because he wanted me, but to spite her, because she had praised me and taken an interest in me and preferred my company to his. It was a final slap in the face for her.

I said, "Didn't Lady Julia know what you were—about your organization? How do you dare to leave her?"

"She knows nothing—nothing," he said. "She is interested in nothing but her own affairs."

"But when you had your amnesia? How can you be sure that you didn't let anything out to her during that time?"

A shadow of doubt crossed his face. I could see that he *was* worried on this head and possibly regretted that he had not killed her too. Maybe he had intended to but circumstances had prevented him.

He really was a bit unbalanced, I conjectured; doubtless the sunstroke had not helped his somewhat megalomaniac personality.

"I shall go away," he said. "Take on a new name, a new life —then even if Julia knows anything about my organization— it does not matter."

"In that case, I don't see why you needed to kill my poor father."

Perhaps, I thought, he had done so out of a kind of meddling curiosity? To create a happening? I had a sudden, horrible suspicion that he might get some of his kicks out of murder as an art form.

Or had he just panicked?

"I suppose it was you who killed the man in the steam bath?"

"Ah, I had to kill that one," he explained. "It was a safety precaution."

"Oh? Why?"

"He was my employee. He was supposed to come to Dendros to deliver this stamp." He tapped the pocket where the box reposed. "After that he should have left immediately. But he remained and was becoming a nuisance. He must have encountered me when I was having my amnesia—then he followed to Helikon—"

Mike, I said to myself, you are mad to stay here listening to this terrifying rubbish. Whether what he's telling you is the truth or not, he is the very last person with whom any sensible girl would wish to stand parleying on a deserted archaeological site.

I looked around us. It really was deserted. The ancient city of Archimandros sat on the flat top of nine-hundred-foot Mount Atakos. It had been a large town once, but sometime about 1300 B.C. the inhabitants decided that they would be more comfortable down below, and they moved down to Dendros, leaving behind them a lot of tombs, a Phoenician temple, a temple to Athene, an early Christian basilica, a Turkish barracks (ruined), and an Orthodox monastery (remains of). Well, most of those buildings came later, but you get the gist.

In between the busloads of tourists there is not a soul about; the curator, who sits in his little box dealing out five-drachma tickets, comes up and down with the buses, no sense in wasting the time here in between, since precious few cars find their way up the terrifying climb, and if they do they are welcome to see the place for free.

There were no cars today apart from Achmed's Volks, and, looking over the edge, scanning such turns of the road below as were visible, I could see no vehicle making the ascent. I wondered whether our absence had been noted at Helikon. Possibly not, in the upset following Kerry Farrell's death.

"I'm getting quite hungry, Mr. Saint," I said, trying for what I hoped was the right blend of calm common sense and childish appeal. "Aren't you? It seems hours since breakfast, and all I had was grape juice anyway. Why don't we drive into Dendros for lunch? I'd love a change from vegetarian food."

"Into Dendros? Are you crazy?" he said. My heart sank. "You will get a meal by and by," he went on. "In Samsun. That is where my cousin lives."

"*Samsun?*"

It is mortifying how, in times of real crisis, one's mind blanks out; although there were plenty more important things to worry about, I could not stop myself feverishly ferreting around an imaginary atlas, scanning the shores of pale-blue seas and the sides of gray, furry mountain ranges. Samsun? Was it in Syria? the Lebanon? Thrace?

"Mr. Saint," I said rather hopelessly. "Don't think me ungrateful, but I'd really much rather just go back to Helikon. If I promise to forget all you've told me, couldn't we just go back—or I'll *walk* back if you want to stay here? I—I—I *enjoy* walking."

"No," he said. He had taken out a small gun, nicely chased with silver and a couple of rubies set in as well, but businesslike also, which was why I was feeling so hopeless. He made a gesture with it—a kind of shrug—and said, "Naturally I do not wish to use this so long as you do not make a fuss." (*Fuss*, I thought; don't I just wish Adnan were here!) "I think you are quite a nice girl," he went on. "I can see why my wife likes you." Bother Lady Julia! I thought ungratefully. Much good her favor has done me. "But if you make a fuss I shall be obliged to shoot you—in the knee, probably. It is very uncomfortable."

"Then, I won't make a fuss."

"Very well. So we wait."

"What for?"

"What for? Why, the helicopter, of course. I phoned for it just before the rehearsal. It should be here in"—he looked at his watch—"twenty minutes or so."

At that point I remembered with a hollow sensation that Samsun was in Turkey. I looked over the side of the mountain, thinking about Captain Plastiras. Calliope and I used to make fun of him, when he came to play those weekly chess games with old Demosthenes, and call him Plaster-Ass; now I felt quite apologetic about that, and only thought how very, very pleased I would be if I could catch a glimpse of his blue Mercedes chugging up one of the seventy bends of the mountain road.

And there it was. Chugging up one of the bends.

"Which direction will the helicopter be coming from?" I asked, feverishly hoping to distract Mr. Saint's attention from the mountainside.

I was still not sure, in point of fact, whether I believed in his helicopter. One two-penny Mauritius stamp (especially since I was so ignorant of philately that I could not tell the difference between the guinea stamp and a penny black) was not enough evidence to clinch my belief in his tales of Rembrandts, Jane Austen, and Swiss banks.

Maybe he just had a paranoid delusion about it all. If he'd had a rolled-up Piero with him it would have been different.

But then he said, "There is the helicopter coming now," and pointed northeast, toward the Turkish coast.

❦ { 12 } ❦

PRESTISSIMO

Julia went to Dr. Adnan's office. Nobody acknowledged her knock on the door, but she could hear voices inside, so she turned the handle and walked in. Adnan and Captain Plastiras were there with the little fat sociologist from Baton Rouge.

Julia would not have believed that Adnan could look so stricken. He was pale as death, his large, plum-dark eyes were dilated with anger and grief. The look he turned on Julia was far from friendly. "Lady Julia! We are having a private discussion in here. I wonder if you would be good enough to come back at some other time?"

But Julia, standing her ground, said, "Captain Plastiras. I am glad I found you. My husband has left me this note. I think you should see it." She passed over the sheet of paper.

While Plastiras read Dikran's note, she had time to study the papers on the desk between the two men, and saw that there were several photographs of her husband: the one with the man in the T shirt, one taken sitting in a deckchair in the garden of the Fleur de Lys Hotel, a couple walking with herself on Dendros harbor front, and others she did not know. "I suppose you're from Interpol?" Julia said to the little woman, visited by a sudden flash of illumination. Nobody answered, and she went on musingly, "I've been terribly stupid, haven't I? Anyone else would have realized that Dikran was a criminal long ago. I just shut my eyes to it. —What has he done?"

The three looked at one another. Then Plastiras said, "Many things. He has been responsible for giant art thefts—kidnapings—forgeries. Interpol have been on his track for some time. Then in this last week we have also received definite proofs of his connection with the Rittenhouse case."

"Oh, no!" Julia cried out in horror. "That awful case? The baby who died?"

"Yes, Mrs. Saint. Your husband made four million dollars out of that baby's death."

"I didn't know!" she whispered, and sat limply down in a chair, covering her face with her hands. "Thank god," she muttered, "at least I wasn't married to him then."

Captain Plastiras looked at her without much sympathy and picked up the desk telephone. While he was instructing someone to come immediately to the office, Adnan read Dikran's note and said softly to Julia, "What does Saint mean here? He says he is leaving and intends to take with him one of the only two things you apparently found valuable in Helikon. What do you think he means by that crack?"

Julia said in a toneless voice, "I was afraid he might have meant *you.* That was why I came to your office—to see if you were all right. I was afraid—after I let myself understand that he must have killed the man in the steam bath—I was afraid he might have done something to you."

"As he did to Miss Farrell," Adnan said drily.

"*He* did *that?*" She was appalled. "It was not a heart attack?"

Adnan shook his head. "She was poisoned; almost certainly in the drink she had just before the rehearsal. Why, we do not yet know."

"Oh, my god," she muttered. "Why didn't I guess sooner about Dikran?"

A young policeman came in.

Miranda Schappin said cosily, taking the note from Adnan, "Never mind blaming yourself, honey; we can all be dumb at times. Just tell us what you think your husband means by this thing he intends to take with him? Is it some piece of your property—jewelry?"

Julia said dully, "No, I should think it's more likely he means the girl—Mike. He—he was jealous of our friendship, of the fact that I enjoyed her company more than I did his."

"*What?*" Adnan was on his feet staring at Julia, his face dark and congested with rage. "Saint has taken *Mike* with him?"

The young policeman, who was being questioned by Plastiras, said, "Yes, *Kyrie*. The suspected person went out at eleven forty-five with a young lady in blue jeans and a yellow shirt. They were driving in Dr. Adnan's Volkswagen and proceeded in a westerly direction. They were kept under observation and it was noted that they took the road up to the top of Mount Atakos."

"And you didn't send somebody to follow them?" said Plastiras, in a passion.

"What need, *Kyrie*? There is no other road down from that mountain. They are bound to come back the same way."

"*Numbskull!*" shouted Plastiras, and bounded from his chair.

He ran down the stairs, shouting orders behind him as he went. Adnan followed close behind. Julia hesitated.

"I'd stay here, honey, you can't do any good," counseled Miranda Schappin. "Keep from under their feet."

"But—Dikran is my husband, after all," said Julia, and ran after the two men. She found them getting into the police captain's blue Mercedes, which was parked under the clock arch.

"I want to come with you," she said breathlessly.

Adnan gave her an angry look. "That is not necessary, and your presence would be nothing but a hindrance," he snapped.

But Plastiras said, "Oh, let her come if she wants. If Saint has the girl holed up somewhere—this woman is his wife, it's true, she might be able to talk to him. Get in quickly, then," he ordered Julia, and she scrambled into the back of the car, feeling unwanted and humble.

The Mercedes took off with a spurt of gravel, shot down to the coast road, and turned left; another police car soon appeared and followed.

While driving up toward Archangelos at what seemed to Julia a terrifyingly reckless speed, Plastiras half turned his head and questioned her. "When did you first suspect that your husband was other than he appeared to be?"

His question was inappropriately framed, Julia thought. Dikran had always appeared to be wild and strange; that was what had attracted her to him. But she said, "It was after his sunstroke, I suppose. That must have frightened him very much. He must suddenly have felt that he was losing his grip on—"

"On whatever he gripped," Plastiras said smoothly.

"Yes. I remember his saying something about the fact that a man in his position simply couldn't afford to have amnesia."

"Indeed not. For as soon as his subordinates realized this weakness, they would start to move in on him. And gossip travels fast here. The news that a wealthy visitor at the Fleur de Lys was afflicted by sunstroke would soon spread—through the waiters, the chambermaids, the bellboys."

The captain slowed, minimally, blasting on his horn, and then shot through Archangelos. Hens, donkeys, cats, dogs, and old ladies in black scattered to the sides of the road, which was, luckily, wide.

The blue Mercedes flashed between the little blue, pink, yellow, lavender, and lime-green houses; then they were out on the shrubby hillside once more.

"Also, you recognized the man in the striped T shirt, did you not?" said Plastiras. "I could see, although you said no when I showed you the photograph, that his face meant something to you."

"Yes," Julia confessed without attempting to apologize. "Before Dikran's sunstroke we saw that man one day in the big, commercial harbor. He was on the outer bar with another man—they had a big, radio-controlled toy boat which they were demonstrating. I supposed they were taking orders for some firm. They guided it round the harbor from where they stood, with a sort of control bar."

"Yes, I have seen them," Plastiras said. "They were cautioned about committing an offense because their gadget made such a loud noise, and they left next day; or one of them did."

Julia was vaguely surprised. The radio-control motor had indeed made a tremendous racket, like a power saw or a supercharged motorcycle—but she had yet to learn that the Greeks objected to loud noise.

"Miss Schappin was observing those men," the captain explained. "She had followed them here from Damascus."

"I see. Anyway, the boat came right across the harbor to us," Julia said, "and got caught in a tangle of driftwood on our side. Dikran set it free and turned it round, and the man waved to thank him. I remember—" she laughed a little hollowly, "I remember thinking at the time what a good method that would be for secret agents to pass on information."

"It was not information," said Plastiras quenchingly. "Merely a stolen two-penny stamp." He did not enlarge on this enigmatic statement and Julia did not ask what he meant. He was slowing down, and now pulled off the road onto one of the infrequent lay-bys.

"Why are you stopping?" asked Julia fretfully.

"To let *them* get by." Plastiras jerked his head toward the road behind. An armored car dashed past, and Plastiras swung the Mercedes out after it, remarking, "There are times when one needs the help of a specialist. Luckily we have a few of those in Dendros—just in case of an invasion by you-know-who." He dug Adnan amiably in the ribs with his elbow.

"What have they got that you haven't?" asked Julia, and he answered briefly, "An AA gun."

All this time, Adnan had sat containedly silent. But now he muttered, "Look . . ."

The dangling shape of a helicopter was proceeding slowly southward toward the line of surf along the coast; it seemed to hesitate in its deliberate, bumble-bee-like flight, then turned and moved purposefully inland toward the summit of Mount Atakos. The threatening stutter of its engines became louder and louder, almost drowning the screech of the armored car's gears on the bends above them.

"You don't mean," said Julia in horror, "you can't mean that's coming for *Dikran?* He can't do that, surely?"

Plastiras contrived to shrug, while throwing the Mercedes around, almost on its haunches, as they circled a particularly acute bend.

"You don't appear to have much awareness of your husband's potential, Mrs. Saint, if I may say so? He has many, many contacts in Asia Minor and the Arab countries."

"But he can't just take Mike and go off to one of those places? They could be extradited?"

"From Turkey? From Iran? From Kuwait?" Plastiras gave another tremendous shrug. "Perhaps! And perhaps not. How are we to know where he goes? He will not stay in that helicopter for long."

Adnan said, "You believe he will take Mike just to spite you, Lady Julia? He is not fond of her for herself?"

"I wouldn't have thought so," said Julia. "He has chatted with her once or twice, but never showed any particular interest in her; I've heard him being quite disagreeable about her. And he didn't think she was at all pretty. —Well, she isn't!"

"He does not, in general, go after young girls?"

"How should I know?" Julia snapped angrily. "We were on our *honeymoon*, after all. I haven't noticed him doing so." Suddenly the voice of old Annibal came into her mind: "I see 'ow your flirtation with Achmed upset your 'usband—and this so soon after you are married; this I find sad." She fell silent. But, she thought, Dikran is a criminal. If I had known *that* about him, I'd never have married him. He was deceiving me all along. A cool, internal voice remarked, These arguments make no difference to the fact that your own behavior was unkind, inconsiderate, stupid, and bitchy. When are you going to stop landing yourself in this kind of mess?

From above them they heard two loud smacks of sound.

"That's the AA gun," remarked Plastiras. "Stephanos must have got up to the top already."

The helicopter had been out of sight, around a corner of the mountain; now it appeared, dodging back affrontedly, like a woman in a crinoline nipping away from the onset of a barking dog.

"Good for Stephanos," muttered Adnan.

"They won't shoot it down?" said Julia in horror.

"No, no. Merely fire warning shots. Unfortunately," said Captain Plastiras, "there is plenty of room on the mountaintop. The helicopter could go round to the south side and land there."

"What's to stop Stephanos from going over there and chasing it off?"

"The fact that there is no road across the top. The road ends at the bus park. And beyond that are many trees—oaks and cypresses, old and large—besides a whole, complicated mass of crumbling ruins—no way through for vehicles."

He jammed his foot on the accelerator and almost pushed the Mercedes up the final slope to the flat, turnaround area.

In another moment he had brought the car to a stop, and they all tumbled out.

Adnan's Volkswagen was parked there, empty. Mr. Saint and the girl were not to be seen. The armored car was standing in the middle of the space, with two men at the AA gun; four more were along at the far end of the car park, scanning the thickly tree-grown area beyond. One of them ran to Plastiras. "They went that way, *Kyrie*, through the trees. Unfortunately, if we try to drive the car after them, we lose sight of the helicopter."

The helicopter was circling over the wood, quite a long way off. Evidently it had lost sight of its would-be passengers and was hunting for them.

"Vassili and Alexandros, go through the wood. Fire at the helicopter if you see it—not to hit, just to scare it off."

The men were carrying weapons that Julia supposed to be Tommy guns; she had never seen one close up before. "Don't fire at the man on the ground," Plastiras cautioned all the men. "He has a girl with him; you might hit her. Keep in radio communication."

They nodded and vanished into the trees.

All this show of mechanical efficiency ought to have reassured Julia, but in fact it terrified her. "Sombody's *sure* to get hurt," she found herself saying idiotically to Adnan.

He gave her a cold look. "If that girl is hurt because of your husband, I can only hope he gets his head blown off!"

"Achmed!" she said miserably—the two of them were standing in the car park feeling painfully useless, while another carload of police and men in army uniforms arrived and dashed expertly about.

"Well, what?" he snapped.

"I wish you'd stop being so nasty to me! It isn't *my* fault that Dikran's gone off with that wretched girl."

"No?"

Another outburst of gunfire came from somewhere in the wood.

"Or if it is, it's yours just as much! You were quite prepared to—to flirt with me and play tennis—and so on."

"Yes," he said measuredly. "Which now I very much regret! It was irresponsible. But I was sorry for you—you seemed so lonely and unhappy. And at least *I* was not on my honeymoon. Nor was I then aware of your husband's particular disposition. If I had known of his pathological jealousy—if I had known what would ensue—wild horses would not have dragged me by my eyelids any nearer to you than the length of this car park!"

"Oh!"

"I am sorry," he went on more temperately. "But *you* know there was nothing ever—at any time—at all serious about our relationship! Your husband need not have troubled himself."

She sighed. "All right—I know."

"My affections are quite engaged—I think you know that too."

Startled, she turned to him, and for the first time took in the full significance of his haggard, sweating, anxiety-racked face. "You are in love with that *girl*—with Mike?"

"Of course I am!" he said furiously. "I love her now for five years—may the devil fly away with her!"

As the words left his mouth, the distant figures of Saint and Mike broke out of the trees at the northern end of the car park. Saint was dragging the girl by the wrist. Her face was covered with blood. He turned and fired back into the trees, then forced Mike to race at top speed to the Volkswagen. He pushed her in, fired into the wood again, then flung himself in beside her; the engine started with a rattle of sound. The car spun around and shot toward the exit, passing close to where Adnan and Julia were standing.

Adnan shouted something at the top of his lungs, but the roar of the engine drowned it; Julia could not hear what he said. Mike, inside the car, was huddled out of sight; it was doubtful if she had heard him.

"What did you say?" asked Julia, but her question was lost in the rage of Plastiras, who was cursing his men for not immobilizing the Volkswagen.

"Come on!" he shouted to Adnan, and leaped back into the Mercedes. Adnan jumped in beside him and they were off, without waiting for Julia, who found herself suddenly abandoned on the mountaintop with the crew of the AA gun. They were watching the helicopter, which was retreating rapidly from the mountain.

Julia ran to the edge of the car park and looked down the mountainside. On one bend of the hill she saw the blue Mercedes, and on another, much farther down, the red Volkswagen, skating recklessly around bends, zipping at a murderous speed along the straight sections of road.

The helicopter, hanging off from the mountain, seemed to be observing its progress.

"Looking for another pickup spot," Julia thought in agony.

The men in the armored car, evidently realizing this or receiving new instructions by radio, started their engine and followed the Mercedes.

"They'll never catch Dikran," Julia thought. "There are plenty of flat places down below where he could drive out and the helicopter could pick him up."

But then, down toward the foot of the mountain, on a bend of the road just above Archangelos, she saw something that made the breath stick in her gullet as if it were a solid lump of impenetrable matter.

The excursion bus, driven at its usual, devil-may-care pace, was starting to climb the hill.

❧{13}❧

CODA

I came to with very confused sensations.

I could remember seeing Achmed shouting.

"The hand brake!" were the words his mouth formed, though I couldn't hear them. I could remember our hurtling descent of the mountainside, with the helicopter watchfully accompanying our progress. And then I could remember the sudden vision of the yellow excursion bus, dead ahead on collision course, coming toward us. And I could remember dragging on the hand brake, which had the effect of opening the right-hand door. After that, memory came to a stop. I supposed I must have fallen out.

I tried to move, and found that it was impossible. Every bit of me seemed to be immobilized—strapped, tied, plastered, splinted. Which was probably just as well, for the least attempt to shift, as I soon discovered, brought such a cacophonous chorus of pains from all over me that I swiftly desisted. Parts of my body that I didn't even know about began to shriek and groan and gibber like the sheeted dead in the streets of Rome.

I lay quietly and sweated with agony.

Then it struck me that I had not yet tried to open my eyes.

Eyelids, it turned out, would move without pain, so, nervously, I raised them, expecting to see a thorny, rocky mountainside and bits of shattered Volkswagen.

Instead, to my surprise, I found myself staring straight into the faces of my mother and Adnan.

"Hello, Ma," I croaked. My voice worked, too, after a fashion, I was pleased to find.

"Priss!" There were tears in her eyes.

"Sorry about all the fuss," I muttered.

"*Fuss*—! Just be quiet, will you?" Adnan said, scowling down at me.

"You're going to be better soon, lovey," Mother said. "Don't worry. Just take it easy."

"First you, then me," I said, meaning beds in hospitals.

Adnan looked at Mother and said, "She is a tough nut, your daughter."

"What's the matter with me?" I asked.

"Broken collarbone, broken rib, broken arm, broken leg, concussion, and a scratched face," Adnan said. "You are going to have to refrain from meddling in other people's business for a long, long time."

"Oh!" I was outraged, but he was smiling at me in quite a friendly way.

He said, "See you later!" and walked out quietly.

Mother said, "Go to sleep, my dearest child. Everything is all right."

"Okay." Then I had a thought and said, "What's today? I mean, is it still Sunday?"

"No, it's Monday."

"Poor old Annibal's birthday. Will you wish him a happy *anniversaire* from me?"

"Yes, I will," said Mother. She cleared her throat and said, "*Now* go to sleep."

"Just one thing—what about the opera—what's happening?"

"Monsieur is going to take the part of Hamlet himself."

"Gosh!" I said. Then someone gave me an injection, and on the thought of a ninety-year-old Hamlet I drifted off into oblivion.

When I woke next time, things felt a little better. A Greek nurse appeared and supplied me with a big swig of lemon juice. I was, I learned, in the hospital in Hippokratous Street, as my breakages were a bit more than could be coped with at Helikon. I felt rather lonesome at that news, but quite soon Mother appeared again and explained that she had installed herself in a *pension* next door to the hospital so that she could spend most of the day with me.

"Me looking after you for a change," she said cheerfully. And she settled in without delay, giving me drinks at regular intervals, dealing expertly with bedpans, making me help her do the *Times* crossword, and reading aloud the works of Mrs. Gaskell.

I listened in a dreamy doze to long, hazy stretches of *Wives and Daughters*, every now and then breaking in to ask a question. "What's happened to Lady Julia?"

"She had to give a deposition to the police, but then they allowed her to go back to England. She was missing her children. I like her very much," Mother said unexpectedly. "She's had a bad time, poor thing. But I'm sure that she's a devoted mother, and, fundamentally, a Thoroughly Nice Woman." Commendation from Mother could go no higher. "I shall keep in touch with her when I get back to England," Mother said, splicing two bits of wool together in her knitting.

I had a slightly bizarre vision of Mother, Gina Signorelli, and Lady Julia settling down *à trois* in some North Oxford house. After a pause, I said, "And Father?"

Mother said, "He was buried in the cemetery in Dendros. It's a very beautiful spot."

I nodded; or tried to. I knew it. There were tall, graceful

eucalyptus trees, and chinaberry trees, and a lot of Turkish tombstones with turbans on them.

Mother said, "I'm sure he'd like that. The sea's only twenty yards off. He loved the sea."

I had shut my eyes, but a tear squeezed out. "If I could only have talked to him—just *once*—"

"Yes, I know. I know," she said. "I feel exactly the same. But we didn't. We just have to accept it. And if we *had* talked just once," said Mother practically, "we'd now be wishing it was just twice. So there it is. —Achmed is going to have a tombstone put up with both his names and SINGER OF INTERNATIONAL RENOWN underneath."

"That's nice." Then I chuckled—which was a mistake, as my busted collarbone gave a shriek of rage. "Tell you what—"

"What?"

"They'll have a problem about his tombstone. It's turbans for males, plain for females. Which does he rate?"

"I'm sure he'd have wanted a plain one," said Mother austerely.

I couldn't ask her about Mr. Saint. For that, I waited until Adnan's next visit. He came in the evening, looking careworn and fatigued; he explained that there was an awful lot of bureaucratic paperwork to be got through in connection with the late dreadful goings on at Helikon.

So many things I wanted to ask him. A whole ocean of strange occurrences and unexplained happenings seemed to have rolled between us since the last time we had had a proper conversation. Actually, looking back, I could not remember *when* we had had a proper conversation. In the workroom when I was painting the cliffs of Elsinore? I hardly knew where to begin.

But he seemed to have no doubts on the matter. He took hold of a couple of my fingers, where they poked out from the cast, leaned over the bed, and very carefully and gently kissed me on the lips. "Oh, what a terrible time you give me, my treasure!" he said. "Once you are out of all that plaster and strapping, I do not know how I shall ever dare to let you out of my sight again!"

"Achmed! You mean—"

"I mean that for the last five years I have been loving you and waiting for you to grow from a naughty, impertinent, teasing child into an age of sense and come back to Helikon. Now you *do* come back, I begin to fear that you will *never* grow to an age of sense. So I have asked your mother if I may pay my addresses to you, and she has said yes."

"She did, did she?" I remembered Mother's pronounced views on equality and Women's Lib.

Adnan grinned. "Even if she had said no, I would have paid them just the same. How do you pay an address, though? I shall have to rely on you to instruct me." He sat down, still holding onto the finger.

I said, "But what about poor Lucy? You were going to love her forever?"

"She knows that I will always love her," he said comfortably. "There is room in my heart for both. Indeed, you are very alike, you wayward, teasing English creatures!"

"That's all right, then," I said. And I lay beautifully relaxed inside all my plasters and began to feel that soon I would be better. "Achmed—what happened to Mr. Saint?"

"Oh, well, I am afraid that when your car rolls over about forty times going down a mountain and you are inside it, there is not much left of you. He ended up in the little valley just above Helikon—smashed a lot of trees," Adnan said crossly. "Also, my car is a write-off."

"Poor Mr. Saint. —He wanted to adopt me, you know," I told Adnan. "And educate me and travel with me and show me a Jane Austen letter he had and lot of Pieros in a numbered account."

"I would not have allowed it," Achmed said firmly. "He was really a very bad man, you know. He had done some dreadful things."

"I think I'd rather not hear about them just now. . . . Are

you going to be one of those domineering husbands?" I asked suspiciously. ("We are going to be married, I assume?")

"Your assumption is correct. We are going to be married as soon as you can walk; unless you care to be married on a stretcher?"

"No, let's wait till I am vertical. Dr. Kalafilaikis says I'll be on crutches in ten days. —I wonder what will happen to all Mr. Saint's ill-gotten wealth? Does Lady Julia inherit that? Oh, my goodness," I said, remembering. "He had a two-penny Mauritius stamp on him that he said was worth twenty thousand pounds. I don't suppose anyone picked it up?"

"My treasure," said Achmed, "you might as well look for a pin in Pompeii after the volcano erupted on it. And the answer to your question before last is yes, and no; I shall domineer whenever I get the chance. Which will not be often."

"You know I intend to go on with my career?"

"Of course; that is understood."

"But how can we combine that with your being at Helikon?"

"To tell the truth," he said, "I was beginning to find Helikon a little quiet. (Until the last couple of weeks, that is to say.) I had been thinking of installing a suitable successor and returning to Western Europe in search of you, as you showed so little sign of coming here."

"I have my pride! You never showed that you wanted me to come. —Anyway, I did come in the end."

"Only because of your mother."

"Hah! It was the first excuse. Poor Mother!"

"It has done her a lot of good, being here," he said seriously. "Of course I will always love Helikon. But it must be admitted that the medical problems in Western Europe are more interesting."

"But I've been dreaming of coming back here for five years! We'll have to come here for all our holidays."

"It is the place, not me, you love, in other words?"

I bit his finger, which happened to be handily accessible. "*Oh*, how angry I was with you. Flirting so with Lady Julia!"

"And what about you—so cool, so distant—thorny and prickly as an acacia—calling me Dr. Adnan and behaving as if we had never met before?"

"You were worse. You were much, much worse! You must promise never to tease me again."

"You know that I have a roving eye."

"Well, kindly don't let it rove!"

"The eye may rove," he said, "the heart remains in one spot." He gave me a long, long, serious look. It made me so happy that I had to lie breathing deeply and quietly; otherwise, I felt, I might have exploded right out of my plaster casts.

Then a thought struck me. "Achmed! When we are married —will you expect me to turn vegetarian?"

Our eyes met, measuringly, and then at the same moment we both burst out laughing.

Which did no good at all to my busted rib and collarbone.